Dark Encounters

OF THE CLOSE KIND

THE CHILDREN OF THE GODS
BOOK SEVENTY-FOUR

I. T. LUCAS

Copyright © 2023 by I. T. Lucas

All rights reserved.

No part of this book may be reproduced in any form or by any electronic or mechanical means, including information storage and retrieval systems, without written permission from the author, except for the use of brief quotations in a book review.

Published by Evening Star Press

EveningStarPress.com

ISBN-13: 978-1-957139-86-9

Gabi

"I'm sorry, Ms. Emerson." The gate attendant assumed a fake apologetic smile. "The flight has been canceled due to technical issues."

They had been having those issues for the past two hours, and every time Gabi had approached the desk, the attendant's answer had been that the problem was being worked on and that boarding should start shortly.

She had been afraid to stray away from the gate to use the bathroom or grab a cup of coffee, but when she'd finally dared a dash to the nearest coffee shop, the announcement about her flight had finally come—not that boarding was starting but that the flight had been canceled and the passengers should head to the customer service desk to make other arrangements.

It had been such a bad idea to book a flight straight from the conference to Los Angeles. She should have gone home, rested for a few days, and then hazarded another flight.

Except, Gabi knew that she wouldn't have done that. She would have chickened out.

"I just heard the announcement about my flight being canceled, and that's why I'm here. Can you please check if a seat is available on another flight to Los Angeles today?"

The woman affected another one of her fake smiles, but this one also had a condescending slant to it. "We don't handle flight bookings at the gate. You should go to the customer service desk."

There was a separate desk for that?

Gabi stifled a biting retort that would have felt awesome passing her lips but would have probably resulted in airport security escorting her away.

Her temper and her big mouth had gotten her in trouble before.

Still, she couldn't just let it go. "You could have told us that the flight might be canceled two hours ago, when you first announced that there would be a delay. Now, I'm probably not going to find a seat on another flight leaving today."

"My apologies, but I can only convey the information I receive, and until fifteen minutes ago, I was told that they were working on the problem. The customer service desk can help you book another flight, and if none work for you today, they will provide vouchers for hotel accommodations and meals."

Realizing that she wouldn't get any help from the woman, Gabi forced down a cuss word and took a long breath instead. "Can you point me toward the customer service desk?"

The gate attendant looked relieved at the prospect of finally being rid of her. "It's located in Terminal D, next to gate 98. Good luck, Ms. Emerson. And I apologize again for the inconvenience."

Practiced, empty words.

"Thanks," Gabi murmured as she grabbed the carry-on handle and rolled it in the direction the attendant had indicated.

Terminal D was at least a twenty-minute walk, and Gabi, for some unfathomable reason, was still wearing the high heels she'd put on for the last event of the conference this morning. She should have gotten a pair of flats from her carry-on while getting coffee, but she'd been in a rush, and she hadn't expected to have to march across the airport. She couldn't stop and do it now either, because with every minute she delayed, there was less chance of her getting a seat on a flight leaving today.

Perhaps the malfunction was a sign that she shouldn't go to Los Angeles.

Good God, she hated flying.

It made no difference to her that her brother was a pilot who owned a couple of jets and, until recently, had flown them for a living, and it didn't help that she knew that flying was statistically safer than driving. Gabi still preferred ground transportation.

If people were meant to fly, they would have been born with wings.

She should just give up on the idea of visiting her brothers, rent a car, and drive back home to Cleveland. It was only a five-hour drive from Toronto, and she could listen to an audiobook to pass the time.

No, she couldn't do that.

She wouldn't have a decent night's sleep until she found out what was going on with her brothers and her honorary adopted niece, and it wasn't as if she could drive all the way to Los Angeles to check on them.

Something was very fishy about the stories they had been telling her lately.

Her niece was a prodigy who had earned her PhD in bioinformatics at nineteen, but instead of accepting the teaching job that she'd been offered at Stanford, Kaia had abandoned her dreams, gotten engaged to some dude she'd met while working on a top-secret project and moved in with him.

The girl might be a genius, but she had zero life experience, and the last thing she should do was move in with a guy who was more than a decade older than her.

What Gabi found even more suspicious than Kaia's sudden engagement was that Karen and Gilbert had not only approved of her questionable life choices but had also moved to Los Angeles to be close to her, uprooting their family and leaving behind their beautiful house in the Bay Area. On top of that, Eric had fallen in love with a woman who worked for Kaia's fiancé, and he had joined the rest of the family in Los Angeles, giving up his executive jets chartering business.

At first, Gabi had been curious, then worried, and now she was panicking.

It wasn't like her brothers to act so impulsively, and Gilbert was the last guy on the planet who would have been okay with his honorary adopted daughter giving up her dreams for a guy.

Well, that was a slight exaggeration. There were probably more protective fathers and stepfathers out there, but despite the fact that Gilbert and Karen had never bothered to get married, and he had never officially adopted Karen's two daughters from her previous marriage, he was definitely up there with the worst of them.

Or was it the best of them?

Gabi should know. ·

Gilbert had always been more of a father than a brother to her, and when she couldn't get him on the phone for three days straight, she'd even called Kaia and Cheryl and tried to get them to spill the beans, but they had been as evasive as their mother, telling her the same story about a wonderful new business opportunity that Kaia's fiancé had offered Gilbert and Eric, and how it was keeping them both insanely busy.

Gabi wasn't buying it, so she'd booked the flight to L.A. right after the Nutrition, Fitness, and Health Management conference in Toronto was over. If she could have gotten out of attending it, she would have, but her ticket had been paid for months in advance, and attending the conference was important for her business.

Staying on top of the latest trends and learning about all the new research and discoveries was what her clients expected from her.

When Gilbert had finally called her, echoing the same crappy excuse Karen had given her about him being swamped with work, it had reinforced her decision to pay them a visit without advance notice.

Did they think that she was dumb?

Gabi felt tears misting her eyes.

What if Gilbert had a terminal illness, and that was why everyone had moved to Los Angeles, and Kaia had given up on her dreams?

What if that was where he was being treated?

But why keep her out of the loop? And couldn't Gilbert have come to Cleveland instead of Los Angeles? After all, the Cleveland Clinic was there, mere minutes away from her home.

Except, Gilbert wouldn't have come to her hometown even if Cleveland was the better option.

Her brothers treated her like a delicate piece of china that would break from the slightest touch, but she was their sister, and if Gilbert didn't have long to live, she needed to be by his side.

Did they think she wouldn't be able to handle it? That she would fall apart and cry her eyes out instead of being helpful and supportive?

Gabi could be brave if she needed to be.

God, she prayed it wasn't what she was thinking, and that Gilbert had just had a hair transplant or some other cosmetic procedure, and that was why he hadn't called her back and had asked Karen and the girls to cover for him.

Yeah, that was probably it.

Gabi had already lost her parents. She couldn't lose anyone else.

She wouldn't survive it.

Taking a fortifying breath, she wiped away the tears welling in her eyes, blew her nose on a tissue, and joined the long line of airline customers waiting to be helped at the service desk.

Kian

"Hello, Victor." Kian shook Turner's hand. "Thanks for coming."

The guy smiled. "I never say no to free food."

Next to him, Bridget chuckled. "Now look what you have done. You have given Kian the secret code." She lifted on her toes and kissed Kian's cheek. "If you want Victor's help, all you have to do is offer him a steak."

Kian doubted Turner would have enjoyed any steak Okidu had prepared. His butler sneered at anything produced on a grill, and if he cooked steak at all, it was in a pan or oven.

Turner, on the other hand, prided himself on being the best steak griller in the village, but his title was contested by Roni, who claimed that it belonged to him.

"I'm sorry to disappoint you, but Okidu is not serving steak for lunch."

Turner stopped and pretended to turn around. "Oh, well, I guess I have to go home and fire up the grill."

That was a rare display of humor for the guy, and Kian wondered whether Turner had been working on his people skills. It was also possible that he meant it literally.

"Don't be silly." Syssi gave Turner a brief hug. "Okidu made beef stroganoff. Wait until you taste it. You'll be licking your fingertips."

"I'm sure I will, but how would you know? Did you taste it?"

Yep. Turner was still as literal as usual.

Syssi shook her head. "I didn't have to. If the smells alone weren't mouth-watering enough to inform even a vegetarian like me, then Kalugal's frequent tasting and moaning were."

They needed to brainstorm the issue of the strange new signals that had popped up and immediately winked out twice so far, but Syssi hadn't wanted Kian to go to the office building on a Sunday, so she had invited everyone who could contribute to the brainstorming to lunch at their home.

Eighteen hours had passed since the last occurrence, so Kian's stress levels had decreased significantly, and he felt less urgency to send a team to investigate.

In fact, if not for Syssi's gut feeling about the importance of the occurrence, he might have been tempted to ignore the brief emergence of signals that had been supposedly emitted by alien trackers across the globe, but his wife's gut feelings were usually much more than a hunch, and ignoring them would be a mistake.

Ironically, what worried him the most about those new signals was that they were different from the ones emitted by the trackers that had been implanted in the Kra-ell settlers, meaning that they were not coming from the other assassins that Igor had told them about or the incredibly dangerous royal twins. Thankfully, it seemed that neither the assassins nor the twins had awakened from stasis. But the unknown source of the new signals was more concerning than a threat he'd already known about.

Okidu, who had deciphered the signals to identify their location, had said that they felt like an older model of those trackers, which probably meant that they belonged to earlier visitors to Earth.

Given that the settler ship had left Anumati seven thousand years ago, those trackers had to be even older than that. And since the signals were coming from Chengdu, the capital of China's Sichuan province and home to Lugu Lake and its Mosuo population, the assumption was that they had belonged to the scouting team that had been sent ahead of the settler ship to verify that Earth was suitable for the Kra-ell.

The problem with that theory was that there was no way any members of the original scouting team were still alive. The Kra-ell were long-lived compared to humans, but they were not immortal, and those males should have died out millennia ago. Furthermore, the Kra-ell cremated their dead, so there were no bodies for anyone to dig out either, and no one could have gotten the trackers out of the remains.

Could it be that the human descendants of those original Kra-ell males had kept the trackers, and they were now trying to activate them for some reason?

But if William, a genius who knew a thing or two about alien technology, couldn't break the trackers apart without destroying them, how could some humans in China manage that?

On top of that, the devices only worked when inside a living organism, so even if the descendants of the Kra-ell had kept them throughout the generations, they would have to know that live hosts were needed.

The only other possible option was that the scouts had managed to prolong their lives somehow, perhaps by staying in their stasis pods for hundreds of years at a time, and they were now starting to wake up, but something wasn't working right.

In the dining room, Kian pulled out a chair next to William. "I have a theory about the scouts and want to run it by you."

"Shoot."

"Do you think that the Kra-ell scouts could have used the stasis pods to stay alive longer? We know those pods could sustain life for thousands of years, so that's not a far-fetched scenario."

William exchanged knowing looks with his mate before returning his gaze to Kian. "Kaia and I talked about that last night. If I were in the scouts' shoes, that was what I would have done, and that also explains the discrepancy in what we assumed about them. For them to influence the Mosuo society, they must have been around during the time the Mosuo settled around Lugu Lake, and if the scouts arrived more than seven thousand years ago, they must have found a way to survive or left descendants who took it upon themselves to continue the tradition of their forefathers, and they were the ones who influenced the Mosuo."

"I had a vision about a cremating ceremony for one of the scouts," Jacki said. "And the subterranean chamber in which the ceremony was held was no older than fifteen hundred years." She turned to Kalugal. "Am I right?"

"Give or take a few hundred years. It's sometimes difficult to ascertain whether the most ancient occupants we can date used preexisting caverns or dug them out themselves."

"Anyway," Jacki continued. "If they could use the stasis pods to prolong their lives, why did some still die? They could have stayed in the pod for centuries at a time, woken up for a few days or weeks to check what was going on and whether the settler ship had arrived, and then gone back into stasis. They could have survived to this day."

"I really need to get to that pod," Kalugal said. "It's extremely difficult, and my team is basically digging by hand an inch at a time. I don't want anyone dying there because the scouts booby-trapped the site."

"Perhaps there is no pod there." Kian got to his feet and walked over to sit next to Syssi. "You just assume that a pod is causing the alien transmissions, but it might be something else."

"Right. Maybe it's an alien aircraft." Kalugal grinned. "That would be an even more exciting discovery than a pod."

"Not if the pod has live people in it." Annani floated into the room and waited for Kian to pull out a chair for her before sitting down. "I am much more interested in those lives than in the technology that brought them here."

Gabi

The customer service attendant looked like she'd been through the wringer, but she still managed a genuine apologetic expression for Gabi. "The only remaining direct flight to Los Angeles today is fully booked." She went back to her screen and kept typing. "Let me see if I can find you another way to get there."

Great. As if she needed two more takeoffs and landings.

"I hate flying," Gabi admitted. "I might not survive a flight with a stopover."

She should just give up.

No, she couldn't. She had to see Gilbert with her own eyes and hear him tell her he was okay.

"If you had gotten here fifteen minutes ago, I still had a couple of seats," the attendant murmured as she clicked on her keyboard. "Why did you wait so long?"

"I would have gotten here two hours earlier if the gate attendant at my original flight had told the truth about the flight being canceled and not delayed."

While waiting in line, Gabi had heard the other customers talking about how it was common practice. The airlines did it on purpose, so not everyone would storm the service desk at the same time, which explained why everyone else had gotten there ahead of her and she was the last one in line.

The woman's knowing smile confirmed the rumor. "I can put you on the first flight leaving for Los Angeles tomorrow morning and give you vouchers for a hotel and two meals."

"I don't want to stay overnight in the airport. I'm just going to rent a car and drive home to Cleveland."

She could go home, get some rest, and book a direct flight from there for the next day.

The attendant frowned at her screen. "It must be your lucky day, after all. I just had a cancellation in first class. I'm grabbing the seat for you." She typed furiously fast.

"Hold on." Gabi lifted her hand. "Do I have to pay for the upgrade?"

She rarely flew, so she didn't have any accumulated miles or preferred status or any of the other perks that airlines give to frequent travelers.

"It's a free special-circumstances upgrade." The woman lifted her head and gave her a conspiratorial smile. "I wrote down that it is an emergency. Your best friend is getting married tonight." She winked.

That was such an unexpected kindness that Gabi just gaped for a long moment. "Thank you," she finally croaked. "You're a miracle worker."

"Sometimes I am." The attendant handed Gabi the boarding pass. "Since you are flying first class, you also have access to the executive lounge. It's right across from here." She pointed at the opaque sliding doors across the aisle with the words Alliance Club engraved on them. "Enjoy."

"Thank you." Gabi snatched the pass. "You're the best airline employee I've ever encountered. If they send me a survey to fill in, I'm going to sing your praises."

"Thanks." The woman put up the closed sign on her desk. "Have a safe flight."

Gabi swallowed. The words safety and flight didn't belong together, not in her mind anyway, but since it was her lucky day, and she was flying first class and visiting the executive lounge for the first time, perhaps it was a sign that she was supposed to go to Los Angeles after all.

Rolling her carry-on, she sauntered over to the sliding doors and walked in as if she owned the place. The three-and-a-half-hour wait for the next flight didn't look so bad now when she could spend them having complimentary drinks at the bar.

The attendant took her boarding pass, scanned it, and handed it back, "Welcome to the club, Ms. Emerson."

"Thank you." Gabi rolled her carry-on straight to the bar and ordered a gin and tonic.

Since all the seats at the bar were taken, she took her drink to one of the round dining tables next to the buffet.

Come to think of it, she was a little peckish.

It had been a long time since she'd had breakfast, and she craved a salty snack along with her gin and tonic.

Hopefully, none of the conference attendees were in the club, or at least none of those who knew her, so she could indulge in peace.

A licensed nutritionist shouldn't consume alcohol and munch on pretzels in the middle of the day.

What kind of an example would she be setting?

Ugh, to hell with that.

She was a long way from home, and if anyone recognized her, she would pretend to be her own doppelgänger.

Putting the drink down, Gabi looked in the direction of the buffet, but her eyes didn't make it all the way to the food. They got snagged on three ridiculously good-looking men crowding one small table.

Had there been a model convention in Toronto she hadn't heard about?

Each of the guys could star in an ad for luxury cologne, cigars, whiskeys, watches, sports cars, or—

One of them must have felt her looking at him and turned toward her, taking her breath away.

The guy was unreal, with chiseled cheekbones that could cut granite and skin so smooth that it looked like his face was gold-plated. His eyes were dark, nearly black, but there was warmth in them as he looked at her.

He smiled, lifted his beer glass, and mouthed cheers.

Gabi swallowed. She couldn't take her eyes off him no matter how hard she tried, and she couldn't smile back or force her mouth to say cheers back to him either.

Damn, that was embarrassing.

It took a pinch to her inner arm to get her to stop staring, give him a slight nod of acknowledgment, and turn away.

Abandoning the idea of getting a snack because it meant passing by his table, Gabi sat down with her back to him, pulled out her phone, and pretended to read on it while sipping on her drink.

The book might have been written in Chinese for all she managed to read, and her stupid heart was racing as if she was a teenager with the hots for the most popular guy in the school cafeteria.

"Been there, done that, and I'm never doing that again," she murmured under her breath.

Gabi had married her prom king.

She'd snagged the hottest guy in school, married him after college, and divorced him five years later.

The problem with hot guys was that they were in high demand, and most didn't know how to say no, including her ex.

That had been eleven years ago, and she was still single, not because she lacked male attention but because she was a walking contradiction.

After divorcing Dylan, she'd vowed that if she got married again, it would be to a sweet nerd who attracted absolutely no female attention and would be hers and hers alone.

The problem with that was that she wasn't attracted to nice, nerdy men. She was drawn to the hot, bad boys who were bound to break her heart again.

Kian

As Okidu collected the empty plates, Turner leaned back and looked at Jacki. "The guy you saw in your vision didn't necessarily die of old age. He might have been killed in battle. The Kra-ell are not as fast healing as we are, and they can die from injuries that we can heal."

"True." Jacki nibbled on her lower lip. "But I thought about it, and there could be another explanation. They might have devised the idea of using the life pods only after several hundred years had passed and the settlers hadn't arrived. So, they were already old when they started using the pods."

"I don't think so." Kalugal draped his arm over the back of Jacki's chair. "The settler ship was supposed to take three hundred years to get to Earth, and in the meantime, the scouts had nothing to do. I bet they came up with the idea of using the pods early on, and I think they took turns in them. If it was me and my men, I would have assigned at least two to stay awake at any time in case something unexpected happened while the rest slept. When they realized that the ship wasn't coming, they might have decided that there was no point in waiting, and all got into the pods, probably in the hopes that someone would collect them at some point."

"What about communications with Anumati?" Syssi asked. "The scouts contacted the queen to tell her that Earth was habitable, so we know that they had the ability to communicate with home. But the question is how? Was there a god ship orbiting above the planet? Did they use the same satellites the exiled gods used before communications were severed? What were they told to do when it became clear that the ship wasn't coming?"

"Probably to go into the pods," Jacki said. "The queen would not have given up hope that her children were alive, and she would have told the scouts to sleep so they would be around when the twins finally arrived."

Kian had to admit that Jacki's assumption made sense. If Fates forbid his children were lost in space, he wouldn't have given up hope either and would have wanted the scouts to stay and wait for them.

The problem was that they were speculating, and by now they had so many ideas and possible scenarios that he had trouble keeping it all organized in his head.

"We should write down the sequence of events and all the good questions that are being raised. There are too many variables to keep track of."

Turner leaned down to pull his trusty yellow pad out of his satchel. "Let's do it now. What's our starting point?"

"Ahn and the Kra-ell queen have an affair," Syssi suggested. "The rebellion before that is less concerning to us. We need to determine the sequence of events from when the queen got pregnant with the twins."

"I agree." Turner wrote it down. "Next, the rebellion ends with a peace treaty, and Ahn and his cohorts are exiled to Earth. The queen is pregnant with his children, but we assume he doesn't know that. Does she know he's the father?"

Syssi pursed her lips. "The Kra-ell males know right away when a female is pregnant. The queen's consorts would have known it hadn't been one of them. How did she keep them from revealing her secret?"

"The vows," Kian said. "I'm sure the queen's consorts were bound by so many oaths of loyalty to her that they couldn't betray her even if they suspected that the father was a god, a big no-no in their society. Also, we know that the queen was a strong compeller. She might have compelled their silence."

"That wouldn't have been enough for her," Bridget said. "The Eternal King was the strongest compeller on the planet, and he could have overridden her compulsion and forced the truth out of her consorts. That's why the queen would never have trusted her consorts or anyone else with crucial information about her children. She probably lied to them, saying the father was a lowly Kra-ell male who she didn't want anyone to know about. Or even better, she could have commanded one of her consorts to claim that the children were his."

"And then had him killed," Turner said. "So, he couldn't be forced to reveal the truth."

Annani laughed, the sound breaking the somber mood that Turner's words had brought about. "We do not know what actually happened, and we are getting carried away with *Game of Thrones* types of scenarios. It is very entertaining, but we should stick to what we know or can make an educated guess about."

Syssi nodded. "I agree. The next item on the timeline is the decommission of the Odus, but since the exiled gods knew about that, we can assume that it happened before they were sent to Earth or shortly after."

"Probably before." Turner wrote it down. "That's why I always leave several empty lines between each item. Otherwise, things get messy."

Kian stifled a chuckle. "We wouldn't want that." He continued, "The peace treaty also included a Kra-ell settlement on Earth, but that's where it gets muddy. If Ahn knew about the terms of the treaty, he would have said something about expecting the Kra-ell's arrival, but he and the others said nothing about it. They never even mentioned the Kra-ell. Why is that?"

His mother shrugged. "They also never said that they were exiled. They did not even tell us they were from somewhere else in the universe. Khiann's father told Khiann and me in confidence about an ugly war a long time ago, but he talked in general terms and never mentioned the Kra-ell either." She looked at Toven. "What about you? Did Ekin or Mortdh tell you anything or at least hint at it?"

"Ekin did not like to talk about politics, and he never talked about the home planet. Mortdh, on the other hand, threw a lot of hints around, but I did not take him seriously. Even our own father said that Mortdh was a lunatic and that I should not listen to his rants. Now I'm starting to think that maybe my brother was not as crazy as everyone thought. He was power-hungry and lacked scruples, but that did not make him insane. Those two character traits describe ninety-nine percent of the world's leaders."

Annani shifted in her chair. "Insanity comes in different forms. Mortdh was smart, but he was crazy. Navuh told Areana things that no one else knew about his father, and it confirmed what everyone suspected about Mortdh. He was prone to fits of rage, he was a megalomaniac, he was violent, and he believed in patriarchy and the subjugation of females." She sighed. "He also believed that he was doing good things for the population under his rule and that they had nothing to complain about."

"Was he right?" Jacki asked.

"They were not hungry, and no one dared attack his region, but they were all his to do with as he pleased. He treated everyone as mindless slaves, as cattle—the immortals in his army, the immortal and dormant females in his harem, and the humans serving him."

"That was common back then," Jacki said. "Not that it was right, but that was how those in power treated everyone else in the ancient world." She snorted. "Heck, they still do. They are just more circumspect about it now."

She should know. Kalugal had built an empire by manipulating people's herd mentality to his advantage.

With everything that had been going on, Kian hadn't had time to look into Kalugal's social media company. Hopefully, his cousin wasn't doing anything overly nefarious.

As Okidu walked in with a tray loaded with desserts, Annani's mood brightened. "Let us take a break and enjoy these lovely sweets with tea."

"That's a wonderful idea." Syssi pushed to her feet. "Does anyone want a cappuccino?"

Gabi

Thankfully, the three hot guys hadn't stayed long in the club, or Gabi would have been starving by now.

Like a coward, she'd waited until they were gone to walk up to the buffet and load her plate with whatever junk food was offered. Well, most people would not call pasta with meatballs junk, but to a nutritionist, it was.

No one wanted advice about diet and fitness from an overweight or out-of-shape nutritionist. Heck, she would have no clients.

Nevertheless, it was free, and she was allowed to indulge once in a while. Just not too often. With a sigh, she put her fork down and pushed the plate away. It hadn't even been tasty.

What a waste of calories.

If she was sinning, she at least wanted to enjoy it.

Gabi softly chuckled as the impossibly gorgeous face of one of the three hunks popped into her mind's eye, the one she'd aptly nicknamed 'the devil.' The man was sin personified, and she wouldn't mind a tumble with either of his two buddies either.

No, that wasn't true.

They were just as gorgeous as her devil, but in a different way, and although they were nice to look at, she couldn't see herself naked with either of them.

Mr. Devil, however, was a different story. She could see herself doing a lot of naughty things with him.

Gabi sighed.

After the way she'd ignored his covert glances and his smiles when she'd caught him looking, it was pathetic of her to imagine herself doing anything with him. If she had given him the slightest indication that she was interested, he might have come over to her table and perhaps offered to buy her a drink.

He didn't seem like the shy type, but men these days were cautious about approaching women, and he was smart to stay away unless invited.

Not that she would have made a big deal of it if he had come over to talk to her uninvited, but she wouldn't have done anything more than talk, and if he wanted more, she would have politely declined.

Mr. Devil was too good-looking and too young for her.

Gabi knew that she looked incredible for a thirty-eight-year-old woman. She worked damn hard for it, and most people thought she was a decade younger, but she had experience and perspective that Mr. Devil most likely didn't have.

She shouldn't make assumptions based solely on his age and looks. Maybe he was a small business owner like her? With the muscles he was packing, he could be a personal trainer. But had he ever been an overweight kid who the other kids made fun of?

Not likely.

Had he ever been cheated on by his girlfriend?

What woman in her right mind would replace that face and that body with another? Or what man, for that matter? Not that Gabi thought Mr. Devil swung that way. The looks he had given her had not been the platonic kind.

Whatever.

She should get going. The boarding for her flight had started several minutes ago, and although she had a first-class seat and could board without standing in line, she shouldn't delay too much.

With her luck, something would happen on the way to the gate, and she would miss her flight.

Gabi cleaned her table of the mess she'd made, pushed to her feet, and gripped the handle of her carry-on.

"Miss!" Someone called from behind her. "Miss!"

When she turned around, a man was pointing to the chair she had just vacated. "You forgot your purse."

"Thank you." She rushed back to retrieve it. "My passport and my boarding pass are in there." And her money and credit cards.

"You are welcome. Have a safe flight."

"You too." She smiled at him. "Thank you again. You are a lifesaver."

If the friendly man hadn't noticed the purse and called her, Gabi would have gotten all the way to the gate before realizing she'd left it behind. She would have been forced to run back to get it and would have missed her flight.

Was it lucky that the guy had noticed, though?

Or unlucky?

Was she supposed to be on that flight or not?

She was well aware that it wasn't smart to base her life decisions on what she thought was lucky or unlucky, and she shouldn't look for signs at every turn, but when someone was living in a state of constant fear, they clung to anything that could be a directional pointer in the chaos of life.

With panic seizing her lungs, Gabi forced her feet to keep moving. She was afraid of too many damn things, but her family needed her, and she needed to conquer these fears, at least for this one flight.

Hopefully, Gilbert and the rest of her family were fine, and she was panicking for nothing.

On the way back, though, she might rent a car and drive all the way home.

Annani

Ready to continue working on the timeline, Annani lifted her empty teacup, signaling to Okidu that she needed a refill.

"I hope Allegra is having fun at Amanda's," Syssi said. "I didn't want any distractions while we were brainstorming the signal issue, and Amanda volunteered to babysit, but it's not easy to take care of two babies at the same time."

As Okidu rushed over with the carafe and filled everyone's cups, starting with Annani's, she smiled at him. "Thank you, Okidu."

"It is my pleasure, Clan Mother."

He said that with so much conviction that there was no doubt in Annani's mind that he meant it, but she also had no doubt that it was part of his programming to enjoy serving his masters. Evidently, the gods had a way of programming even emotions, and she wondered whether that was part of their genetic manipulation. Could they make one person inherently happier than another? Or sadder?

She had read somewhere or heard from someone that people had a set point of happiness and that they always returned to that point no matter what happened in their lives, either good or bad.

It could have been wonderful if everyone was naturally happy, and if the gods were truly benevolent, they would have engineered people to be more cheerful. But maybe they had tried that, and it did not work.

Perhaps sadness was needed so that happiness could be appreciated.

Annani was the happiest when she was around her children and grandchildren, especially the little ones. There was no greater pleasure than holding a baby to her chest and kissing their little cheeks.

"Amanda has Onidu and Dalhu to help her," Jacki said. "I am sure Allegra is happy to spend some time with her aunt and uncle. What surprises me is that Amanda didn't want to join our discussion."

Kian huffed. "That's because she has nothing to say on the subject. We should have invited Jade." He cast his wife a look. "Somehow, it didn't occur to either of us."

Syssi's eyes widened. "Should I call her? We can wait for her to get here."

Kian shook his head. "She will be offended that we invited her as an afterthought. If we need to ask her anything, I'll text her."

"Good idea." Turner pulled out his yellow pad again. "Let me remind everyone where we were before the break. The last item on my timeline is Ahn's exile, and before that, the Odus's decommission." He cast a quick look at Okidu, but Kian's butler remained impassive. "Kian wondered why Ahn and the other gods had never mentioned the Kra-ell, and the Clan Mother hypothesized that they didn't want their descendants to know that they had been exiled from their home planet. The gods pretended they had always been on Earth—a divergent species." He looked at Annani. "Am I right so far?"

She nodded. "Yes. And since they wanted us to believe they were earthlings, they could not mention another species of intelligent humanoids."

Jacki looked like she was bristling to say something but did not want to interrupt.

Annani smiled at the young woman. "Go ahead, Jacki."

"Thank you. It has just occurred to me that the gods might have been spreading propaganda against the Kra-ell by telling stories about demons and vampires. I checked online, and both creatures were mentioned in the Sumerian myths. Isn't it suspicious that demons and vampires are often described as having forked tongues, fangs, and glowing red eyes? The resemblance to the Kra-ell is too much to be a coincidence."

"That does not make sense," Annani protested. "Ahn and the other gods were exiled because they supported the Kra-ell's emancipation. They would not have spread malicious stories about their friends."

Jacki's face fell. "Maybe some among them became disillusioned or bitter because of the price they'd been forced to pay."

"Or some of the so-called rebels might have been planted by the Eternal King," Kian said. "Although I don't know what he could have hoped to achieve by spreading those rumors. Did he want the humans to turn against the Kra-ell and eliminate them? Why did he care? He didn't want his children and the other gods to thrive on Earth. He wanted them all dead. The gods and the Kra-ell, and he wanted to blame their annihilation on the humans so their deaths couldn't be traced back to him."

Turner lifted his pencil. "That's your answer. He planned for Igor and the assassins to eliminate the gods and the twins and then for the humans to eliminate the Kra-ell."

"That's ironic," Bridget said. "Did he believe that the weak, easily-manipulated humans could get rid of a powerful compeller like Igor and many super-strong Kra-ell? There is strength in numbers, but still."

Syssi sighed. "The king had plans within plans, and all of them were meant to shield him from blame while accomplishing what he wanted. He only had to make it look like the humans eliminated the Kra-ell while sending others to do the job and then getting rid of them." She lifted her gaze to Kian. "Maybe the signals we picked up belong to another team of scouts or assassins that the king sent to deal with his problem. Maybe he still sends people to Earth occasionally to check whether the Kra-ell ship has arrived. A century or even a millennium is nothing for him and the other gods. The last team he sent might have paid Earth a visit hundreds of years ago and reported that there were no gods or Kra-ell to be found. This might be a new team that has just arrived."

Kian shook his head. "That's not likely given that the signals are coming from trackers that are an older technology than the ones implanted in the settlers. Also, it is too much of a coincidence that they started transmitting on the day we put Igor in stasis. I still think he had some kind of telepathic communication with Anumati. When they realized that Igor had found a descendant of Ahn, they might have activated a sleeper cell that had been in stasis on Earth all along."

Annani wanted to tell Kian that she had checked Igor's mind thoroughly and had not found a telepathic connection, but what if she had just not delved deep enough to find it?

Igor had been unaware of transmitting, but it could have happened subconsciously, and could have been buried too deep for her to discover.

Annani knew better than to let arrogance make her complacent.

Turning to her son, she nodded in acquiescence. "I wish I could tell you that you are getting carried away on the wings of imagination, but the truth is that what you said sounds logical to me. Igor might have been transmitting subconsciously, which was why I could not detect it. And a sleeper cell sounds like something the Eternal King would have done. A plot within a plot, a contingency within another contingency."

Kian

Kian didn't know whether he should feel satisfied or worried that his mother had finally admitted that his suspicion about Igor transmitting information telepathically was valid. Not that he knew for a fact that Igor had done that, but he appreciated knowing that his speculation was no longer being dismissed.

Turner tapped his pen on his writing pad. "Our current working theory is that a sleeper team is waking up, and their trackers are malfunctioning. It's either the scouting team or one the gods subsequently sent to finish Igor's job."

"Gods would not have trackers," Bridget said. "Their bodies would have rejected them. The signals have to come from Kra-ell, which most likely means that they belong to the last surviving scouting team members. Since they are coming online and winking out, I assume they are coming out of stasis, but something is not working right, and they are slipping back in. That's the most logical explanation I can think of."

"I agree." Turner nodded at his mate and then looked at Kian. "What do you want to do about it? For obvious reasons, I advise against sending a local human team to investigate."

"Naturally." Kian leaned back in his chair. "We can't let humans discover a stasis pod. Especially not the Chinese."

Kalugal chuckled. "They would immediately reverse engineer it and make one for their Chairman so he could live forever."

Turner didn't even smile. "My recommendation is to send a team of Guardians with Kra-ell reinforcements. If Jade is willing, and if you trust her, she should lead the team."

Did he trust her?

Kian nodded. "That's a good suggestion, but I don't know whether Jade can leave her people at a critical time like this. Some of them are unhappy about the trial results, and they might stir things up in her absence."

"Can't her second-in-command hold the fort?" Syssi asked. "Kagra seems like a capable female."

"I doubt she's ready to take over full command." Kian lifted the delicate teacup and sipped the fragrant jasmine tea. "Kagra is full of swagger, but she's young and inexperienced. She can, however, join the team, not as its leader but as a second-in-command. I'll feel better with a Guardian in charge, but since none speak Chinese, Vrog could be a great asset to them because he speaks the language, knows the local customs, and can pass for a human. I will speak with him about joining the team and perhaps leading the Kra-ell portion."

"Good choice," Kalugal said. "Which Guardian do you want to put in charge of the team?"

"Yamanu is the obvious choice." Syssi turned to Kian. "Right? If there is a pod and shrouding is needed, he's the perfect Guardian for the job."

"You also need a doctor," Bridget said. "Merlin has experience treating Kra-ell, so he should go. The Kra-ell waking up from stasis might be in critical condition and in need of hospitalization. Yamanu's thralling and shrouding ability might come in handy in getting them into a hospital."

"I wish I could go." Syssi sighed. "I've never gone on any exciting missions."

Kian shuddered, just thinking about her in a dangerous situation. "You have a baby." He used the one argument that wouldn't make him sound like a chauvinist. "You can't leave Allegra, and you can't take her into a danger zone. She's still human."

"About that." Syssi turned to Annani. "Perhaps she should start spending time with you?"

Kian nearly choked on his tea. "It's too early. Usually, the girls turn at two years old. Right, Mother?"

Annani nodded. "The earliest was eighteen months. But I would be delighted to spend time with my granddaughter, and she will transition when she is ready."

They both knew it didn't work like that, and he was tired of hiding it from Syssi. Toven knew, and perhaps Mia did too, but Kian didn't want Syssi to be burdened with the knowledge. It had to remain a secret, and it was better that she didn't know. He hated keeping things from her, but to tell her would be selfish. He would unburden himself from the guilt but burden her with the knowledge.

"You know what has occurred to me?" Jacki said. "If those scouts were alive for much longer than we previously believed, and they took turns, with some staying awake and some going into stasis, then one of them must have fathered Mey and Jin. Perhaps the sisters should join the team going to China."

Bridget shook her head. "If Mey and Jin were fathered by a pureblood, they would have been born Kra-ell hybrids. But since they were Dormants and needed activation, we have to assume that their mother was a dormant immortal, and their father was either a hybrid Kra-ell or even a human with Kra-ell recessive genes like the children of the hybrid Kra-ell males."

"Right." Jacki pushed a lock of blond hair behind her ear. "It was a brain fart." She winced. "My apologies, Clan Mother. I shouldn't use such language in your presence."

"You are forgiven," Annani said magnanimously.

Turner cleared his throat. "We have a working assumption on what we expect to find and who we are going to send to find it. When do you want the team to leave?"

"Tomorrow is the earliest," Kian said. "I need to talk to Yamanu, Jade, Kagra, Merlin, and Vrog. If everyone is on board with the plan, we can make a flight plan and get the team to China on our jet."

"I'll make the flight arrangements," Bridget said.

"Is there anything else we need to discuss?" Turner asked.

"I think that's it." Kalugal turned to Kian. "I just hope we find them before it's too late. They can shed more light on what happened on Earth or what was supposed to happen."

Kian nodded. "I just hope our assumptions are correct and the signals came from the scouts and not some other unknown threat."

Gabi

G abi had never flown first class before, not because she couldn't afford it, but because she wouldn't spend money on something she hated no matter how comfortable and luxurious it was, and she had the same philosophy about food.

Why waste her allotment of daily calories on something that didn't taste great?

Well, the truth was that she didn't make as much money as she pretended to her brothers, and she couldn't afford first class if she flew often or overseas, but she did it so rarely that she could have indulged once in a blue moon if it was important to her.

Naturally, it wasn't.

"This way, Ms. Emerson." The flight attendant motioned for her to go around to the other row. "Your seat is in the middle."

Looking at her boarding pass, Gabi rechecked the seat number. It was row number three, seat D. The first class had lie-flat seats, two in the middle and one on each side by the window. She would have preferred to have a window seat so she wouldn't have to chat with the passenger seated next to her, but since she wasn't paying for this, she shouldn't complain.

Besides, having someone sitting next to her would force her to keep the panic at bay and pretend that she was okay, and pretending courage was sometimes the best way to overcome fear. Also, if she was busy chatting, she might not notice the takeoff, which for her was the scariest part of the flight. For some reason, it scared her even more than the landing, perhaps because it was the start of the torment and not the end of it.

"Let me help you with that." The older gentleman in the seat behind her got up and reached for her carry-on.

"Thank you." She gave him a smile and let him lift her luggage to the overhead bin even though she could have easily done so herself.

To decline the help would have been rude.

An hour of strength training three times a week ensured that Gabi had strong muscles and bones, and she even splurged on a personal trainer to instruct her on proper form and monitor her progress. Her trainer made the session bearable with her quirky humor and merciless teasing, and that alone was worth the price she was charging her, but the other benefit was the new clients Becky sent her way.

The seat beside hers was vacant, but Gabi knew it wouldn't stay that way. The flight was fully booked, so it was only a matter of time before she had company.

The attendant leaned toward her with a tray. "May I offer you champagne, orange juice, or water?"

"Champagne, please." Gabi smiled. "I need liquid courage."

The attendant smiled back. "I'll get you another one before takeoff."

"Thanks." Gabi cradled the flute in her palms, took a long sip, and closed her eyes.

Maybe the comfort and pampering would make flying less stressful. She could put on her headphones and watch a movie or listen to a book narration to take her mind off the fact that she was several thousand feet in the air. Getting a seat in the middle aisle and away from the window was also a stroke of good luck.

"What a happy coincidence," a deliciously male voice said on the other side of the aisle. "We meet again."

Thinking that he was talking to someone else, Gabi didn't bother to open her eyes, but then she felt the seat move and turned to see who was sitting next to her.

No way!

It was none other than Mr. Devil from the lounge, and he was smiling at her with those lips that were made for kissing.

How could it be?

He and his friends had left the lounge hours ago. She'd been certain that their departure meant their flight had been boarding.

"Hi," she croaked while eyeing the divider between the seats.

She hadn't pulled it across, and now it was too late. She couldn't just slam it in his face.

He rose on his knees, leaned over the wide center console, and offered her his hand. "Since we are going to be neighbors on this flight, we should get acquainted. I'm Uriel."

"The light of God." She put her hand in his, and as she'd expected, the contact was electrifying.

Smiling, he held on to her hand for longer than was necessary. "Is that your name? The light of God?"

She pulled her hand out of his gentle grip. "No, that's your name. My name is Gabi, short for Gabriella, which means heroine of God. We have that in common. Also, my last name is Emerson, which means brave, so basically, I'm a brave heroine of God, which is the least befitting name for me."

Her ex's last name would have been a better fit, but she hadn't taken it even when they'd been married. Perhaps it was a premonition that things between them were not going to last.

"Why is that?" Uriel asked.

"Why is what?"

"Why is the name not befitting?"

She snorted. "Because I'm terrified of flying, among many other things, so having a name that means brave is a joke."

"Fear is not the antonym of bravery. You are on a plane despite being afraid of flying, which means you are brave."

He had a point. He also hadn't told her his last name even though she'd revealed hers.

Oh well, maybe he was a famous movie star who wanted to fly incognito.

"Are your friends here with you?"

"They are in the first row." He pointed. "But I'm the lucky one. I get to sit next to you." His smile was so brilliant that it was blinding.

She tilted her head, the champagne finally doing its thing and loosening the tight muscles in her shoulders. "Do you believe in luck, Uriel?"

"Definitely." He leaned even closer, his dark, longish hair falling forward and framing his chiseled face. "I'm a big believer in fate."

Jade

J ade arched a brow. "You want me to go back to China?"

Kian shrugged. "You can send Kagra instead. But I'm sure you can understand why I need Kra-ell on the team."

When Kian had called for a meeting on a Sunday afternoon in the village square, Jade had assumed that he wanted to discuss the school Vrog was organizing. The last thing she could have imagined was a new complication in the form of signals from old trackers.

That sort of talk shouldn't be done out in the open where anyone could hear them, but it was Kian's business where and when he wanted to conduct his meetings, and apparently, he didn't want to be in his office on the weekend.

That reminded her that she needed to ask him for a space for Kra-ell headquarters. She couldn't continue having people show up at Phinas's home whenever they needed to talk to her. The space didn't have to be big or fancy, and she would even settle for a classroom in the underground structure. She hated being below ground, but beggars and choosers and all that.

She would take whatever he had.

"I'll gladly go," Vrog said. "Chengdu is a long way from my school, but it's still closer from there than from here. After we finish the investigation, I can book a flight to Beijing and visit." He rubbed his chin between his thumb and forefinger. "As part of the purchase contract, the new owners stipulated a certain number of hours I needed to dedicate to the school for the first two years. I've been doing that remotely via video meetings with the new management and Dr. Wang, but I really should visit in person. I'm curious to see how things are running under the new ownership."

"Can I go too?" Aliya asked Kian. "I mean to Chengdu. Vrog wants me to come with him to visit the school, but if I can't join the team, I can fly directly to Beijing and meet him there."

"You are welcome to join the team." Kian gave her an appraising look. "You don't blend in as easily as Vrog among humans. I wonder how the scouts' hybrid children went unnoticed in the human population. Or perhaps they were noticed, but back then, it was easier to keep things contained, especially when possessing the ability to thrall."

Aliya waved a hand over her face. "I don't blend in easily, but I managed to live among the Mosuo. If my mother hadn't died and I hadn't been so distraught after her death, I might have been able to hide my differences better. I would have just been the strange girl with eyes that were too big and who was too strong and too flat-chested."

Leaning over, Vrog wrapped his arm around her shoulders. "You are beautiful and perfect as you are."

She smiled. "You're sweet, and I might be perfect to you, but I definitely wasn't to the Mosuo boys."

"Their loss is my gain," Vrog said.

Kian turned to Jade. "So, what is it going to be? Are you going, or are you sending Kagra?"

"Why do you need either of us? I can assign a couple of the young pureblooded males to your team."

"I want someone with authority who can speak for your people. If the signals are coming from the scouts, and if they are in the process of emerging from their stasis pods, they will want to know what's going on, and they won't accept the word of a couple of young foot soldiers."

Jade sighed. "Kagra is young too, so even though she would be my representative, they might not accept someone who was born on Earth. Perhaps assigning one of the older females to the team is a better choice."

Kian hesitated for a moment. "Is there a way you can make the female your official spokesperson? Something that the scouts would recognize?"

Jade groaned. "The only thing I have is the dark triangle on my tongue to show my meager royal blood. The scouts would respond to that. But I don't want to go. I have a people to lead, and I can't leave them, especially not now that the tensions are high and threats have been issued."

The truth was that she didn't want to go because she wanted to stay with Phinas and Drova and enjoy the unit they had created. They were all still learning how to be a family, and it would be a mistake to press the pause button on that.

"I understand," Kian said. "Is there anyone else with royal blood among the settler females?"

"Yeah, with a very faint triangle and a combative attitude. Sheniya, who I personally don't like, but she will have to do." She drummed her fingers on the table. "On second thought, that could actually work to my advantage. Since Sheniya and Rishana are inseparable, they can both go, and I will get rid of two troublemakers."

They were instigators, and without them, the rest of her people would be much less antagonistic to the former prisoners, allowing them to acclimate to their new community faster.

Given his grimace, Kian was as unhappy about including Rishana and Sheniya in his team as Jade was happy about getting rid of them.

"Do you think they will want to go? I don't want them if they have to be forced. Yamanu doesn't need to babysit a pair of cantankerous females."

"Of course." Jade smiled. "I'll throw in Pavel as well. He's a charming guy, and he can be the peacekeeper. He's done a very good job of advocating for his father, and he might be able to talk some sense into them and change their minds about the former prisoners. Some additional compulsion from Toven would be helpful as well. He can compel them to be cooperative and do whatever Yamanu tells them. Naturally, I will command them to listen to him too, but they don't fully accept my authority either."

"Indeed." Kian gave her an assessing look. "But I think your motive for sending Pavel on the mission has more to do with keeping him away from Drova than changing Sheniya and Rishana's minds."

She snorted. "Haven't you heard? Pavel is with Lusha now, but I wonder how long that will last. She's human, and he's a pureblood. Need I say more?"

Drova didn't seem upset about Pavel's interest in the attorney, so perhaps they were just friends.

"When are we supposed to leave?" Vrog asked. "And for how long?"

"Tomorrow," Kian said. "And I hope it will take no more than a couple of days in addition to travel time. We have the exact coordinates of the signals' origins, so there is no need to search, but if the pods are buried underground and booby-trapped like Kalugal's archeological excavation site in Lugu Lake, then digging them out might present a problem."

Jade shook her head. "I'll assign four young purebloods to your team. They can dig out whatever you need with shovels, and since they are nearly as strong as your Odus and don't need any heavy equipment to dig, it will be much safer all around. You can even send them later to help with Kalugal's site. "

"I like your idea." Kian regarded Vrog. "I'll put you in charge of the Kra-ell, including the two females. You know the language, you are the best diplomat of the bunch, and you know how to deal with the local authorities in China."

The color leached out of the guy's face. "I'm a hybrid. They will never listen to me."

He was correct, of course, but forcing the two females to answer to a hybrid would be one more way of putting Rishana and Sheniya in their place.

"They will do what I tell them," Jade said. "This is a new era for us, and blood purity will no longer determine one's status. It's going to be based purely on merit." She gave Vrog a smile. "Given your accomplishments in my absence, you've earned your place as my third alongside Kagra."

His eyes widened. "Thank you. It's a great honor, but I'm not interested in a leadership position. I'm not a politician."

"You don't need to be. You are a great administrator and educator, and you will be in charge of finances and education. Kagra can manage the more military and disciplinary aspects of our community."

That had been Valstar's job in Igor's compound, but she wasn't about to restore his former status. First, he had to earn redemption and prove himself to her and the rest of their combined community.

Vrog dipped his head. "In this case, I accept the nomination."

"Good." She pushed to her feet and turned to Kian. "I'll talk to Kagra and text you the list of names of the pure-bloods we choose for the mission."

Gabi

By the time the captain asked the flight attendants to prepare for takeoff, Gabi had finished another two glasses of champagne, and her head was spinning, but she was still panicking despite the alcohol. The only thing it had managed to do was to make her speech a little slurred and the looks she was giving Uriel a little less guarded.

"Here, hold my hand." Uriel extended his arm over the center divider.

She hesitated only for a split second before taking his offer. Holding his hand would not make her any less fearful, but touching him would surely distract her.

Already, the warmth was spreading throughout her body, and it was the kind that was not calming in any way. She was feeling Uriel's innocent touch in the most un-innocent way possible.

Did he know the effect he had on her?

Uriel was surprisingly pleasant and unassuming for someone who looked like a god. Usually, people who were blessed with beauty either by birth or by scalpel were full of themselves and expected others to admire them.

Uriel was respectful and polite to a fault, and his flirting was so gentle that she wasn't sure he was actually flirting with her.

Maybe he was just being nice.

Mr. Devil had turned out to be a very nice guy who was just devilishly handsome.

"How come you and your friends are so good-looking?" she blurted out. "Did you all just come from Korea and have a layover in Toronto?"

He glanced at his arm, frowned, and then looked back at her with confusion in his eyes. "What made you think that we came from Korea?"

Had he had surgery on his arm?

Gabi hadn't heard about bicep implants, but who knew? If women had breast implants because guys liked buxom ladies, men could have bicep implants because women liked buff guys.

She laughed. "Everyone is raving about the plastic surgery in Korea. Supposedly, it is so popular that they have great surgeons with a lots of experience, and it's much less expensive to have it done there than in the States. They also have the best cosmetic products. My cosmetologist only carries stuff from Korea."

For a long moment, he stared at her with his dark, intense eyes. "Did you have plastic surgery on your face?"

That was a rude question, but she'd started it, so she'd earned it. "No. Did you?"

"I did not. I was just born with the right genes." He smiled his brilliant smile. "My father was a weatherman, and my mother was a supermodel."

For a moment she took him seriously, but the way his lips were quirking at the corners betrayed him.

"That's a line from a movie. At least the first part about your father being a weatherman is. That's what Brad Pitt said to Sandra Bullock in *The Lost City* when she asked him why he was so handsome."

As he laughed, the masculine sound went straight to her feminine center, making her tingly and needy.

Damn.

"I watched that movie on the way to Toronto," he admitted. "It was very funny."

"So, you did come from Korea."

"My friends and I toured the area."

"What were you doing there?"

He leaned over and whispered, "We were looking for a lost treasure."

His closeness was making her literally swoon like some heroine from a historical romance novel, but her mind was still working just fine. "I'm serious." She gave him a mock hard stare. "Don't quote that movie again."

"I wasn't." He returned to leaning against the back of his seat. "Why would I do that?"

Uriel had an annoying habit of answering her questions with his own.

"If you don't want to tell me what you were doing in Korea or can't, just say so."

He could at least make up a better story than looking for a lost treasure, especially after just quoting a line from a movie on the same subject.

Leaning over, she regarded his handsome face.

Uriel could have some Asian genes in him. Maybe one of his parents was half-Asian, and he'd been visiting family? But then his friends looked nothing like him, and she doubted they had gone with him to visit his relatives.

"We deal in antiques," he said. "Finding lost treasures in flea markets and secondhand shops is what we do."

Why did Gabi have a feeling that Uriel was once again basing his answers on something he'd seen on television?

She'd watched *Flea Market Flip*, and some of the contestants were hot, so that might have given Uriel the idea. He and his friends were probably actors, and all three had gotten enhancements in Korea. Those cheekbones couldn't be real.

"Right. And I'm the Queen of England." Gabi leaned away. "But whatever." She waved a dismissive hand. "Keep your secrets."

He frowned. "The queen died. England has a king now."

"It's an expression."

"I know. But maybe it should be modified now that there is a king."

Gabi's brain was hazy from too much champagne, but she was starting to notice more and more anomalies about Uriel.

His English was perfect, maybe even too perfect, because his accent was all American and not regional, but there was a hint of something else in it.

Children of immigrants who spoke a different language at home sometimes had a slight accent even though they had been born and raised as Americans, and Uriel had such an accent, but Gabi couldn't identify the language of origin.

"Where are your parents from?"

He chuckled. "They are not from Korea."

"But they are immigrants, right?"

"Why would you think that?"

Again with a question instead of an answer. "You have a slight accent. I assume that you spoke another language as a child."

"I did. You guessed correctly."

Uriel still hadn't told her where his parents were from, but she was tired of trying to get him to tell her things about himself.

He had told her about being a flea market flipper, though, so maybe he would answer questions about that. Not that she thought that was really what he did for a living.

"Did you find what you were looking for on your trip?"

"We did."

"So, are you rich now?"

"It wasn't that kind of treasure." He pulled out the remote and turned on the screen with the flight information showing. "Look, Gabi. We are at cruising altitude, and you haven't panicked."

"You distracted me." She pretended an accusatory tone. "Thank you."

"It was my pleasure." He released his seatbelt and got to his feet. "I'm going to talk to my friends. Will you be okay here without me for a few minutes?"

That was such a sweet thing for a stranger to say.

"I managed thirty-eight years without you. I think I can manage a few moments longer."

Better get her age out in the open before he asked for her phone number, they went on a date, and then he discovered that she was at least a decade older than he was.

Uriel didn't seem to care one bit about her age, though, and he also didn't seem to know how to respond to what she'd just said and smiled instead. "I'll be back in a few minutes."

The flight attendant came down the aisle with her notepad. "What would you like for dinner, Ms. Emerson? We have chicken with potatoes or pasta with vegetables."

"The chicken, please."

"Of course. And what would you like to drink?"

"Water, please."

"Naturally. If you would like a cocktail after dinner, you can browse the selection on the flight menu."

"Thank you. I will."

Gabi turned on the screen and started browsing. There was a large selection of movies, and she also discovered that satellite internet was complimentary in first class and that she could text if she wanted to.

Perhaps she should text Gilbert and let him know that she was coming?

After all, he couldn't tell her not to come when she was in the air, right?

She pulled out her phone and typed.

Hi, Gilbert. Believe it or not, I'm sitting in the first-class cabin of a Dream Liner on my way to Los Angeles. My ETA is five fifteen in the afternoon your time. I didn't book a hotel, and I hope I can stay with you and Karen or Eric and Darlene, but if it's inconvenient, I'll get a room in a hotel. I want to see all of you as soon as possible, though, preferably at your new place, and I hope you're not going to stonewall me again. I need to know what's happening with you, Eric, and Kaia.

His answer came a couple of minutes later.

I'm in the middle of something right now. I'll text you as soon as I can.

Gilbert

G ilbert threw the phone on the couch and
groaned. "Gabi is on her way, and we are not
ready for her."

His sister must be really freaking out to be on a transcon-
tinental flight, and it was his fault. He hadn't come up
with a convincing enough story for why they had all
moved to Los Angeles, and she was worried.

Karen put down her book. "What do you mean she is on
her way? When is she coming?"

He lifted his phone and checked the time. "She lands in
four and a half hours. How the hell are we going to be
ready for her by then? We can't just bring her to the
village."

"Why not? We can ask Kalugal to compel her after she's
here."

"No, we can't. It's against clan rules to compel people
without their consent. We need to meet her in a neutral

place, explain that we can't tell her anything without her agreeing to be hypnotized to keep it a secret, and only when she agrees can we tell her what's going on."

"Right." Karen reached for her phone. "I'm calling Darlene. I'll ask her to talk with Orion. I hope he's willing to help."

Gilbert nodded. "I'll call Eric."

About half an hour later, the family was gathered in their living room, including Orion and Alena, Kaia and William, Eric and Darlene, Cheryl, and the little ones.

Gilbert had wanted Cheryl to take them to the playground, but she'd refused. She wanted to be part of the conversation about her Aunt Gabi, and that was sweet, so he hadn't argued with her about staying.

Eric handed Gilbert a beer, and he took it even though he wasn't sure he should drink alcohol so soon after his transition. He was still weak, but he was getting stronger by the day. Regrettably, there was no change in his hair or wrinkles situation yet, but maybe it was for the best. Gabi wouldn't be shocked when she saw him.

"We need to give Kian a heads up that we might be bringing Gabi to the village," Eric said.

"Might?" Cheryl arched a brow. "Do you expect her to say no to the hypnotism, aka compulsion?"

He shrugged. "I never know with Gabi. She's afraid of so many things, but then she's so brave too. She might be terrified of letting someone take over her free will, even if it's for something as innocuous as ensuring that she keeps a secret."

"I'll come with you and convince her," Cheryl said. "She will believe me more readily than the two of you."

Gilbert frowned at the girl. "We are her brothers. Why would she believe a teenager over us?"

Cheryl rolled her eyes. "Because she knows you, and she knows me. You and Eric keep things from her because you think of her as your baby sister who can't handle anything. I'm a straight shooter."

"She is right," Karen said. "Gabi doesn't believe you two. She always double-checks with me, and I'm a terrible liar. That's probably why she's on a plane despite how much she hates flying. She thinks something is wrong with you, and we are not telling her."

"Yeah." Gilbert ran a hand over his thinning hair. "She's probably freaking out."

Ever since they had lost their parents, Gabi had been anxious about losing him and Eric. She'd begged Eric not to join the Air Force, and when he did that anyway, she hadn't spoken to him for a whole year.

"You can leave the kids with me," Kaia offered.

Gilbert shook his head. "We should all go, including the little ones, so Gabi doesn't think something is wrong with one of them. You know how she is. When she sees that I'm fine and not dying, she will immediately assume that someone else in the family is."

Karen didn't look happy about that. "I don't want the kids to witness Gabi losing it or making you lose it. They should stay here, but Kaia should come with us."

"My mom could babysit," Darlene said. "And I can ask Cassandra to help her out."

"I'll help as well." Alena rubbed her rounded tummy. "I have plenty of practice caring for children, but more importantly, I love doing it."

"Thank you." Gilbert dipped his head. "If Gabi wants to see them, she can agree to the compulsion and come with us to the village."

"Do you need me to come too?" William asked.

"If you can." Gilbert gave him an apologetic smile. "I know how busy you are, but part of my sister's anxiety is over Kaia's decision to get engaged so young and move in with an older guy."

"She can also meet William in the village," Eric said. "As always, Gabi's theatrics are making everyone jump through hoops to accommodate her."

His brother wasn't wrong, but Gabi deserved some coddling. Life hadn't been kind to her. She'd lost her parents at fourteen, had gained nearly a hundred pounds trying to eat her grief away, and then had worked her butt off to get rid of the excess. Her trouble with regulating her eating habits had led her to study nutrition and fitness, and for a while, it seemed like her life finally had been going well. She'd had her own practice that was steadily growing and gaining clientele and a marriage that had seemed stable.

Then she'd discovered that her bastard of a husband had had multiple affairs behind her back, had gotten divorced, and had gained back all the weight that she'd lost as a teenager. Her practice had gone down the drain along with her weight gain, and for nearly a year, she'd lived in Gilbert's house and grieved the death of her marriage and her professional career.

It had taken a lot of effort and courage to pull herself back up and start over in a new place. She'd chosen Cleveland because it was far from her ex-husband and her brothers, and no one had known her there.

Her practice was thriving again, but her personal life hadn't improved. She dated many guys but never stuck with anyone for more than two weeks. To her, everyone looked like a cheater who was bound to break her heart.

Sighing, Gilbert looked at his younger brother. "Gabi has her faults, but she has a heart of gold, and she loves us as much as we love her. I don't mind jumping through hoops for her. If you do, you can walk away and leave her to me. She won't hold it against you."

Gabi

From the moment the pilot had asked the flight attendants to prepare the cabin for landing, Gabi had been clutching Uriel's hand in a death grip, and she didn't let go until the plane was on the ground and taxiing.

The poor guy had probably lost circulation in his hand, but he hadn't complained, and he'd even tried to amuse her with a string of bad jokes that Gabi would have laughed at if she hadn't been fighting nausea.

After such a display of mental instability, there was no chance he would want to see her again or ask for her phone number. She'd told him her full name so he could find her on social media, but would he bother?

Was that the reason he hadn't given her his last name?

Nah, Uriel definitely had been flirting with her throughout the flight, and she doubted he had done it only to help a fellow passenger and keep her from panicking.

Should she initiate and ask for his number?

He could make up a girlfriend or give her a fake phone number if he didn't want to see her again.

Gabi had been guilty of such tactics herself, so she wouldn't hold it against him, but it would be humiliating, nonetheless.

How to do that, though?

She had no practice initiating things, not because she was shy but because she'd never had to do that. When she was a depressed, overweight teenager, she hadn't dared to even look at the hot boys, let alone flirt with them, and once she'd gotten in shape, all she'd had to do was give a guy an encouraging smile, and he would do the rest. After discovering Dylan's infidelity, she'd gone down the rabbit hole again and had gained a ton of weight back. She hadn't been interested in dating anyone back then, but once she'd pulled herself together, she again had plenty of offers.

Regrettably, people judged one another based on looks, and when she looked good, the fish were plentiful.

In fact, usually her problem was keeping men from asking her out when she didn't want them to. She hated saying no and seeing the disappointment in their eyes, but she wasn't willing to go out with a guy just because she felt bad about declining. It required some finesse, but she usually managed to do it in a way that didn't hurt their feelings too much.

On more than one occasion, she'd pretended to be in a long-term relationship to stave off advances without offending the guy, but things were more complicated when she didn't want to go out again with someone she had already seen once or twice. That was one of the reasons Gabi didn't date much.

Who had the patience for all that drama?

If only a magic wand could conjure Mr. Perfect out of thin air and end the search so she would never have to go out on first dates again.

Uriel was the closest to the perfect guy Gabi had ever met. He was gorgeous, funny, not full of himself, and kind, but then every woman who met him would think the same thing and do everything in her power to get him, and that was less than perfect.

Ugh. If only he was a nerd. Some adult acne and thick glasses would have been nice.

A Clark Kent to the world and Superman to her.

Gabi sighed. A girl could dream.

As if acne and glasses could have diminished his appeal.

How was Uriel even single?

He hadn't mentioned a significant other, but he might have chosen not to mention her. Dylan surely hadn't told the women he'd been cheating with that he was married.

To this day, Gabi couldn't understand what made him cheat on her.

She had been a good wife, the sex had been above average and plentiful, and they had been comfortable with each other. Had he done it for the simple reason that he could? That the opportunity presented itself?

His excuse had been that she'd never really loved him and that he'd felt lonely even when he'd been with her, but that was a load of crap. He'd been her first boyfriend, her first lover, and she'd thought herself the luckiest girl in school for snagging the hot basketball star all the girls had drooled over.

She'd even enrolled in the same college he got into so she could be close to him, when she could have gone to a better one.

"We've arrived at the gate," the flight attendant announced over the speakers. "Please check the pockets of the seat in front of you to ensure you haven't forgotten anything. Once you deplane, you won't be allowed back to retrieve your item. If you find that you've left something behind, please ask an airline representative for assistance."

Gabi checked the pocket even though she was certain her phone and tablet were in her purse, and she verified that she had the purse with her before getting up.

As she reached for her carry-on, the older gentleman who had offered to help her at the beginning of the flight pulled it down for her.

"Thank you." Gabi smiled. "I appreciate your help."

"It's my pleasure."

Holding the handle, she glanced at Uriel, who was standing in the other aisle and talking with his friend, who was behind him. They were both so strikingly handsome that everyone was looking at them, including the gentleman who had helped her before.

The third member of their party was behind her, and since he was a head taller than the woman standing between them, Gabi was treated once again to the full beauty of his face.

She wondered which show they were playing in.

She would definitely watch it.

There was no way those three were flea market treasure hunters. Maybe they were method actors starring in a movie that had flea market treasure hunting as its theme, and the three had to stay in character throughout the production.

Uriel had told her a few anecdotes about his bargain hunting, but they had sounded like a combination of something he had seen on television and some real-life experiences. He had evaded every question she asked him about his family or where he lived, answering with another question, an evasive comment, or a change of subject.

On the other hand, she had told him about Gilbert and Kaia, her young niece's engagement to an older guy, and every other suspicion she had about what her brothers might be hiding.

It was the alcohol's fault. She'd had too much of it, partly because she was anxious about being thousands of feet above the earth and partly because of Uriel's presence, which had been curiously comforting and nerve-racking at the same time.

She wouldn't have made it throughout the five-hour flight without him constantly distracting her, and she would have gladly continued spending time with him and having him distract her some more.

Surprisingly, she found him waiting for her just outside the door. "I forgot to ask. Did your brother answer your text?"

"Yes." She grimaced. "My brothers are meeting me in a hotel, and Gilbert said everything was fine and that I should stop imagining terminal diseases and other catastrophes. He promised to explain everything when we meet."

"Did you believe him?"

"I don't know." Gabi let out a breath. "Gilbert likes exaggerating and telling tall tales, but he's not a liar. Then again, he's very protective of me, so if he or Eric have a major health issue, they are not going to tell me about it unless I wring it out of them. I guess I'll find out soon enough whether my suspicions were right."

"In which hotel are you meeting your brothers?"

Hope surged in her chest. Was he going to ask to see her again?

"It's downtown. I have the information on my phone. Why?"

"My friends and I are also staying downtown, so maybe we can meet for breakfast tomorrow?"

Gabi's heart did a happy flip.

One of his friends cleared his throat. "We are leaving very early for that appointment we came here for. We won't have time for breakfast."

"Yes." Uriel pushed his long dark hair back. "We have some meetings scheduled for tomorrow and some more that we hope to schedule for the rest of the day, so I don't know when I will be free. Can I call you once we both get settled?"

"Sure." She pulled out her phone. "What's your number? I'll call you so you'll also have mine."

After he gave her his number and she called him, he entered her information and then looked into her eyes. "Until we meet again, Gabriella Emerson, the courageous defender of god."

Gilbert

"Learning about your world was so much simpler for us," Gilbert said as they entered the hotel's top-floor restaurant. "We were already in Safe Haven, visiting Kaia, and there were two compellers on site."

"Shhh." Onegus put his hand on Gilbert's shoulder. "You need to watch what you say here." He pointed with his chin at the hostess.

After they had informed Kian about Gabi's arrival, he'd insisted on Onegus accompanying them to the meeting to ensure everything was handled correctly.

What had he thought, that Orion would compel Gabi without getting her consent first and that they would approve?

Well, to be honest, Gilbert would have considered that if Gabi proved to be as stubborn and as contrary as ever. Her not turning immortal was not an option.

"I love running script ideas by you." He clapped Onegus on the back. "You always think I'm talking about real stuff."

Karen chuckled. "We are all very talented screenwriters. I wonder what Gabi will think about our latest movie idea."

Orion looked amused, but he didn't say anything. Alena had stayed behind to help Geraldine and Cassandra babysit the kids, and he obviously didn't like going anywhere without her.

Gilbert could empathize.

Now that he was immortal, everything felt much more acute, and it wasn't just his hearing and eyesight that had gotten sharper. His feelings for Karen and the kids had intensified tenfold. He'd thought that he was an overprotective partner and father before, but it was nothing compared to what he was experiencing now. That included love so intense for his mate that he couldn't imagine continuing to go on business trips without her.

"McBain party of ten," Onegus told the hostess. "We reserved the private room."

"Of course, sir." She collected ten menus and walked around her station. "Please, follow me."

If the hostess had counted heads, she would have realized that there were only nine of them and one was missing, but she hadn't.

Gilbert fell in step with the woman. "My sister will be here shortly, and she'll be looking for the Emerson party. Can you make a note of it?"

Gabi had taken an Uber over an hour ago, but traffic was heavy this time of day, so it was anyone's guess when she would get there. Onegus had made the reservation for six in the evening, and they were a few minutes early.

"Naturally," the hostess smiled. "Mr. McBain had already asked me to note that the party would include the Emersons when he made the reservation."

"That's right," Kaia said. "The Emersons and the McBains."

Gilbert wondered how many clan members were using the same fake last name. Kian wanted him and Eric to get fake documents as well, but since they still had business interests outside of the clan, it was more challenging for them to just disappear as the Emersons and emerge as McBains. Besides, he wasn't rushing to give up his family name.

"I hope the kids are okay," Karen said. "That's the first time they have had Geraldine, Cassandra, and Alena babysit them."

Idina had looked delighted to spend time with three fancy ladies, as she had called them, and the boys were fascinated with Cassandra after she'd shown them a mini explosion.

Gilbert had no doubt that his kids were having a good time, he just hoped it wouldn't be too big of a blast, given what Cassandra could do.

Orion chuckled. "Don't worry. My sister is forgetful, but she never forgot to take care of Cassandra when she was little."

As the hostess opened the door to the private room they had reserved, Darlene let out a breath. "This brings back memories. Not too long ago, it was my turn to read the new script. I had Roni to help me absorb it all, and Gabi has you." She put her arm around Cheryl's shoulders. "It's nice of you to do this for your aunt."

"Gabi is not really my aunt." She cast Gilbert a reproachful look. "Not yet, anyway. She will be my step-aunt when he finally marries my mother."

"Don't look at me." Gilbert tilted his head in Karen's direction. "It's your mother who is putting on the brakes. I'm ready to have the ceremony tomorrow."

Karen shook her head. "You know what I'm waiting for."

Yeah, he did. She wanted them both to be immortal when they finally tied the knot, and he couldn't wait for her to turn immortal, but he wasn't looking forward to what was required to achieve that.

The hostess waited until everyone was seated before distributing the menus. "Your waiter will be with you shortly. In the meantime, can I get you a bottle of wine?"

"That's a splendid idea," Gilbert said. "What do you have?"

"We have a large selection." The hostess lifted the wine menu and offered it to him.

As he chose three of the most expensive bottles, Karen regarded him with an amused smirk. "Are you hoping to get Gabi to relax with a good wine?"

"That's my plan."

"Can I have some?" Cheryl asked after the hostess closed the door behind her. "I know I'm not supposed to have wine in restaurants, but we are in a private room."

The girls had been allowed to have a small amount of wine with dinner since they were twelve, but only at home.

"I'll let you drink from mine." Kaia patted her sister's arm. "My ID says that I'm twenty-two."

"You don't look it," Darlene said.

Kaia shrugged. "The ID is as legit as the clan's forger can make it. Besides, having an older man by my side helps." She leaned her head on William's shoulder. "So, who is going to tell Gabi about us all being immortal?"

Cheryl grimaced. "I think it's going to be most believable coming from me. She knows that I'm too cynical to get brainwashed into believing something that's not true."

"I can show her illusions," Orion suggested.

"Don't show Gabi anything scary," Eric said. "Go for something like a rainbow unicorn or a tiny fairy with wings, and don't spring it on her. Tell her what you are about to do before you do it. She gets scared easily, and if she gets agitated, there will be no way to reason with her until she calms down."

Gilbert hated how it made Gabi sound, but Eric was right. Their sister needed to be approached carefully and with kid gloves.

Orion nodded. "Thanks for the warning. I'll keep that in mind."

Gabi

As the Uber driver stopped in front of what looked like an office building and not a hotel, Gabi checked the address to make sure she was at the right place.

The number on the building matched the one Gilbert had texted her, and the name of the street matched as well.

"The restaurant is on the top floor," the Uber driver said as he opened the door for her. "It's called the Seventy-Second because it's the number of the floor it is on. I've heard that it has a great view."

"I'm sure it does. How about the food?"

The guy made a face that indicated it wasn't the best.

She laughed. "You can't have everything, right? A beautiful view and a good meal? That's asking for too much."

"Yeah. It's like what they say about translations. If it's beautiful, it's not faithful, and if it's faithful, it's not beautiful."

The saying actually compared a translation to a woman, but in her experience, it was no less true about men. Dylan was handsome, and he had been unfaithful.

"Regrettably, that's true." Gabi got out, checked that she had her purse on her, and took the carry-on he'd pulled out of the trunk. "Thank you. Have a great evening."

"You too. Enjoy your meal. I'm sure it's going to be great." He got in his car and drove away.

There was no one on the sidewalk on either side of the street, and as she walked toward the front door, she was relieved to see a reception desk with an actual person behind it.

The guy saw her and buzzed the door open.

It certainly didn't feel like any hotel she'd stayed in before.

"Good evening," she said as she stopped in front of the desk. "I don't know if I am at the right place. Is this the —"

"It is." He smiled. "The hotel occupies the top ten floors, and its lobby and reception are on the sixtieth floor. The elevator marked hotel lobby will take you directly there."

That explained it, but they could have placed a sign so guests wouldn't get anxious about being at the wrong place.

Not that she was sure she was going to be a guest. Gilbert hadn't given her an answer about where she was staying tonight, and she hadn't wanted to push. Perhaps there was a reason they didn't want her to stay with them.

"Actually, I'm meeting my family in the restaurant first."

"Not a problem." He clicked on his keyboard. "What's the last name on the reservation?"

"Emerson."

"Excellent. Your party is already there. Take the elevator that has the Seventy-Second logo on it. It will take you straight to the restaurant without stopping at any of the other floors."

"Thanks." She gave him a polite smile. "Have a great evening."

"You too."

Gabi wasn't looking forward to riding the elevator alone. It was one more phobia on a long list of them, but it wasn't as bad as flying. She wouldn't be comfortable, but she wouldn't panic either.

Yeah, well.

Live and learn.

There were always new experiences to scare the crap out of her, and the guy at the reception counter hadn't warned her that the elevator would take off like a rocket.

Holding on to the rail, Gabi closed her eyes tightly and counted, hoping she wouldn't get ejected into space. On the count of twelve, the elevator slowed down, and on the count of fourteen, it stopped so smoothly that it was almost as shocking as the speed of going up.

As the doors slid open, Gabi exhaled, stepped out on shaky legs, and approached the hostess. "Hello. I'm with the Emerson party. Can you point me in their direction?"

The hostess smiled a well-practiced, professional smile. "Good evening, Ms. Emerson. I will be more than happy to escort you to the private room your party has reserved."

A private room?

Had she forgotten someone's birthday? Anniversary?

Gilbert was a big spender who enjoyed grand gestures, but even he wouldn't have splurged on a private dinner in a fancy place like this for no special reason.

Then again, reserving a private room might not cost more than dining in the main one.

Walking behind the hostess, Gabi looked through the restaurant's windows at the cityscape. Thankfully, fear of heights was not on her list of phobias, so she could enjoy the view without choking from fear.

As the hostess opened the door to the private room, Gabi's eyes misted with tears to see her family's smiling faces, and as her brothers rose to their feet, she left the carry-on by the door and ran into Gilbert's open arms.

"I was so worried." She hugged him fiercely and then stepped back and slugged his arm. "That's for being an evasive bastard and keeping secrets from me."

He just kept grinning as if her punch was no more than a pat when it had been hard enough to leave a bruise.

"I missed you too," he said.

"Come here." Eric pulled her into his arms. "Are you okay? I mean, after the long flight."

"I'm fine." She pushed out of his arms and gave him an appraising look. "When I couldn't get ahold of Gilbert, and everyone was giving me lame excuses why he couldn't call me back, I suspected that he had a hair transplant or plastic surgery, and that's why he was hiding in Los Angeles, but I was wrong. It was you. What possessed you to do that?"

Eric smiled. "Do I look good?"

"You look fantastic, but you are too young to do stuff like that."

"And I'm not?" Gilbert asked.

She huffed out a breath. "You are much vainer than Eric, and you've been talking about a hair transplant for years."

"That's true." He ran a hand over his balding head. "I might still have to do that. I hoped I wouldn't."

"Hi, Gabi," Kaia said. "Let me introduce my fiancé, William."

By his looks alone, the guy was perfect for Kaia. He was handsome, tall, and with gorgeous, smart eyes, and he seemed like a sweet nerd. No wonder Kaia had snagged him quickly before anyone else had a chance to discover such a rare diamond.

"Hi, sweetie." Gabi hugged her adopted niece and then offered her hand to William. "It's a pleasure to meet you. I wondered about Kaia's rush to get engaged, but now I understand why she did it."

William looked confused, which further endeared him to her. "Thank you. I'm glad to finally meet the famous Gabriella Emerson."

She tilted her head. "Famous? How?"

His cheeks reddened. "Your brothers talk about you a lot."

"They do, do they?" She cast them both hard looks. "What have you two been saying about me?"

Gilbert

"Only good things." Gilbert made room for Cheryl to get to her favorite almost step-aunt.

"Oh dear, you've grown at least two inches taller since the last time I saw you." Gabi kissed Cheryl on both cheeks. "And your hair got longer. You are so pretty!"

"Thanks." Cheryl took the compliments in stride. "You look good, too, Gabi. I've missed you." She kissed her and gave her another hug. "It's been too long since I last saw you."

Gabi hadn't visited since right after the twins were born, and that time, Eric had had to fly her in because she'd been too terrified to get on a commercial jetliner.

Gilbert hadn't wanted to tell her that commercial airliners were safer than private jets because then she would have been obsessing about Eric flying them. She'd either learned that on her own or had made some progress with her phobias.

He wondered if she'd started seeing a therapist.

Next came Darlene, who didn't wait for Eric to introduce her and pulled Gabi into her arms for a fierce hug. "If you haven't guessed already, I'm Darlene, Eric's fiancée."

"Hi." Gabi laughed. "You are stronger than you look."

Darlene let go of her. "Sorry about that. I've been working out, and I underestimate how strong I've gotten."

Gabi was still smiling. "You must show me your routine. I lift weights thrice a week with a personal trainer and don't have half your upper body strength."

"It's also genetic," Darlene murmured as she stepped away to let others welcome Gabi.

The last ones were Onegus and Orion.

Gabi's eyes widened as she took a gander at them. "What's going on in this town? Is there a hunk conference in Los Angeles?"

Onegus chuckled or coughed. Since the chief was covering his mouth with his fist, Gilbert couldn't tell which one it was.

Orion laughed. "Thank you, I think."

Hopefully, Gabi hadn't gotten the wrong impression, thinking he had brought two single men to the family dinner as potential dates.

"No, I'm serious," Gabi said. "Three gorgeous guys were flying in first class with me, and one of them was even seated right next to me. He said that they were flea market bargain hunters and flippers, but I suspect that they were actors who were playing characters who flipped flea market finds, and they were staying in character. The guy sitting next to me was super polite, like someone from the forties, so maybe the movie was about that era. An Indiana Jones style action thing. Now that I think of it, that makes perfect sense. If I were a casting director, I would have cast all three as action heroes."

Poor Gabi tended to talk fast when nervous, and they hadn't even told her anything yet.

Onegus and Orion exchanged loaded looks, but then Onegus shook his head. "They wouldn't have been flying first class. Navuh is not that generous. Also, they are typically not as good-looking and definitely not as polite as Gabriella described the one sitting next to her."

"The ones Navuh claims as his sons might be flying first class," Orion said. "You told me that they are closer to the source because of who their mothers are, so they are good-looking, and because he claims them as his they are also well-educated, which in turn could make them better mannered than the rank and file."

Onegus shook his head. "There wouldn't be three of them on the same flight. Navuh believes in the method of divide and conquer."

"Who is Navuh?" Gabi asked. "And what's the deal with his sons, who he claims are his but aren't?"

"We'd better sit down first." Karen hugged Gabi briefly and then led her to a chair. "So, how have you been, Gabi? Anyone interesting you've been dating lately?"

Gabi shook her head. "The only interesting guy I've met in a long while was the handsome dude sitting next to me during the flight from Toronto." She looked at Onegus. "The one who may or may not be one of Navuh's sons, whoever Navuh is. The name sounds biblical. Is that the nickname of some cartel boss?"

Gabi had always been sharp, and Onegus shouldn't have spoken so freely about Navuh before Orion ensured her silence. Then again, if she refused, he could thrall the memory from her mind.

"Good guess," Orion said. "The name is biblical, and the guy is the boss of a nefarious organization, but the name was given to him at birth."

When he didn't continue, Gabi arched a brow. "And? Now that you got me curious, you have to tell me more. By the way, we haven't been introduced yet."

"My name is Orion. I'm Darlene's cousin."

He was her uncle, but cousin would be more appropriate for now, given how young he looked.

"I'm Onegus," the chief said. "I'm mated to Darlene's sister, who apologizes for not joining us. She's helping Darlene's mother babysit Karen and Gilbert's kids."

Gabi's relieved expression confirmed Gilbert's suspicion that she'd thought the two men were there as potential dating material.

"That's so nice of her." She cast a quick glance at Darlene. "Eric and Gilbert are terrible at keeping me in the know. They didn't tell me anything about your family. I didn't even know that you have a sister."

"Her name is Cassandra, and she's much younger than me." Darlene pulled out her phone, probably intending to show Gabi Cassandra's picture, but Onegus put a hand on her shoulder. "Let's save family photos for later."

Understanding dawning, she nodded. Darlene no longer looked like Cassandra's older sister, and Geraldine definitely didn't look like the mother of two adult women.

As the door opened, two waiters came in with the wine Gilbert had ordered and baskets of assorted slices of bread.

"I didn't even look at the menu yet." Gabi started leafing through the pages. "There is so much to choose from." She turned to Gilbert. "Have any of you eaten here before? I need recommendations."

Gilbert shook his head. "Onegus and Darlene recommended the place. It's the first time here for the rest of us."

"Everything here is excellent." Darlene reached for the bread. "But this is my Achilles heel. I can't say no to a freshly baked baguette smothered with butter." She grimaced. "As a nutritionist, you probably think that's terrible."

Gabi laughed. "I love a baguette with butter as much as anyone, but I allow myself to indulge only on special occasions." She snatched a piece. "Today qualifies as such. I've flown over the entire continent today. I deserve a treat."

Gabi

s one waiter poured the wine and the other took the orders, Gabi looked at Eric again and was stunned at his transformation. He wasn't that much older than her, and he'd been in good shape before, but he looked a decade younger now.

Was it love that made his skin glow with health and his hair look thicker, or was it the cosmetic procedures for which Los Angeles was known? Not that it was difficult to get Botox and fillers in Cleveland, but it wasn't as prevalent.

Heck, maybe she should book an appointment at a clinic while she was in Los Angeles.

So far, she'd managed to keep her youthful looks with careful adherence to a nutritional plan and a rigorous fitness schedule, but soon it wouldn't be enough. The feathering of barely-there wrinkles around her eyes didn't bother her, but she had dark circles under her eyes that she masked with concealer and foundation, and it would be nice to look good without anything on her face.

"What's your secret, Eric?" she asked as soon as the waiters left with their orders. "Love or cosmetic procedures?"

Smiling, he draped his arm over the back of Darlene's chair. "It's definitely love."

"Gabriella," Orion said. "I want to ask you something."

"Yes?" She looked at him.

Really looked at him.

If she hadn't met Uriel, she would have thought him the most gorgeous man she'd ever seen.

It was hard to look away.

"What did you want to ask me?"

"Remember the nefarious organization Onegus and I mentioned?"

"I do."

"Do you remember the name of its boss?"

Gabi frowned. She remembered thinking that the name sounded biblical and that she'd asked whether it was a cartel boss's nickname, but she couldn't remember what it was.

What the hell?

She was too young to have memory issues.

"I'm sorry." She looked at her wine glass. "I must have drunk too much today. Usually, I restrict my alcohol consumption to one glass of wine a week, but today was a stressful day, and I overindulged. It must have affected my memory."

For some reason, Orion seemed very happy with her answer. "It didn't. I made you forget the name. It was a test to see whether you were susceptible to hypnosis."

She frowned. "You didn't do anything. You didn't swing a watch in front of my eyes or tell me to count back from ten or any of those things. How could you have hypnotized me without me knowing you were doing that?"

It was scary to think it was possible to hypnotize people without their knowledge or consent, but she was sure Orion was just pulling her leg.

"I have my subtle ways, and I apologize for not asking your permission first, but I had to know that you can be hypnotized before we can tell you more about Eric's marvelous transformation."

That got her curious.

Stress was a major cause of premature aging, which she tried to combat with exercise, but perhaps hypnosis was the secret?

"Was it relaxation that did it?" she asked.

"No." Looking frustrated, Orion pushed his long bangs back. "I don't really know how to approach this without sounding creepy."

"Let me explain," Cheryl said. "Eric, Gilbert, and Kaia have the secret to immortality. You can have it too, but it's a big secret, and the only way they are going to tell you about it is if you allow Orion to hypnotize you so you can't tell anyone on the outside about it."

"What?" Gabi gaped at her niece.

That sounded insane, but Cheryl was as sane as a person can get, and she was also cynical and questioned everything. She wouldn't have said what she just had if she didn't believe it was true.

Perhaps she was referring to some new method of prolonging life.

Except, Cheryl hadn't included herself among those who had the longevity secret, and that bothered Gabi.

"Why don't you have it?"

Cheryl chuckled. "I have it. I just can't implement it yet because sex is involved, and I'm too young."

That was completely bonkers.

Sex was good and healthy, but it wasn't the secret to longevity. What had all of them gotten into? Had they been brainwashed by some guru to part with all their money in exchange for some bogus claims about long life that involved sex?

Was it some crazy sex cult?

It was fortunate that she'd overcome her fear when she had and came to see them.

She had to save them.

Turning to Gilbert, Gabi glared at him. "Have you all joined some crazy cult and gotten even poor Cheryl brainwashed?" She turned her gaze to William. "It must have started with you. You brainwashed Kaia first and then the rest of her family." She shook her head. "Un-freaking-believable. You look like such a sweet nerd, I would have never suspected you of such powers."

Hell, maybe it wasn't his power but Orion's?

After all, he was the hypnotist who didn't need to swing watches or do anything overt to get someone's mind enslaved to his will. That was one hell of a talent to have.

"You got it all wrong," Kaia said. "No one brainwashed anyone. Orion can show you proof."

Gabi lifted her hands in the air. "No, thank you. I don't want him to use his mind tricks on me."

"It's not mind tricks." Eric leaned over to Darlene and did the last thing Gabi had expected. He lifted her off her chair as if she weighed nothing, pulled her onto his lap, and kissed her like his underage niece and other members of his family weren't watching.

"What the heck, Eric? If you are so desperate for your fiancée, get a room. There are kids watching."

"I'm not a kid," Cheryl grumbled. "In some countries, girls my age are already mothers."

"We are not in those countries," Gabi spat. "If this is not some alternate reality I somehow stumbled into, we are still in the United States of America."

Finally, Eric let go of Darlene's mouth, turned toward her, and smiled with a pair of small fangs that were, nevertheless, definitely not the canines he'd had moments ago.

"This is not real." Gabi felt faint. "The plane must have crashed, I must be dead, and I'm in hell."

Eric

As Gabi's eyes rolled back in her head, Gilbert leaped from his chair to catch her before she fell.

"Way to go, Eric," Kaia said sarcastically. "You've literally scared her half to death."

"What else was I supposed to do? You know Gabi. She's contrary on a good day and impossible to talk to on a bad one. She wouldn't have believed anything other than the hard facts, and it's difficult to argue with the sharp points of my fangs. I had to convince her to let Orion compel her."

Karen chuckled. "Your baby fangs are not much to show, but you managed to scare her with them anyway."

"It's not going to work," Cheryl said. "Gabi is too scared to let Orion manipulate her mind, but since she's obviously susceptible to thralling, you can tell her everything without compelling her first, and if she still doesn't want

Orion to get into her head, Onegus can thrall the memories away, or suppress them, or whatever it is that thralling does. I'm still not sure what the difference is between thralling and compulsion."

"A person is aware of compulsion," Onegus explained. "They are not aware of thralling. It feels like their own thoughts and decisions."

Eric waited until Onegus was done explaining. "Is that okay with you if we tell Gabi first?"

The chief nodded. "That's how we traditionally did that before we had compellers, but that was when the Dormant was already in a relationship with a clan member and was willing to stay in the village until she or he transitioned or failed to do so. So far, we've been lucky that all the suspected Dormants eventually transitioned. Once we had compellers join the clan, things got much easier." He looked at Darlene. "Like in your case. There was no doubt that you were a Dormant, but you were hesitant about leaving your husband."

"I was so stupid." She looked at Gabi, and her eyes softened. "No, I take it back. It wasn't stupidity. It was fear. I was scared like Gabi is now, just for different reasons."

"What happened?" Gabi murmured in Gilbert's arms.

"You got overexcited and passed out." He took the glass of water Karen handed him and brought it to Gabi's lips. "Here, take a sip, and no more alcohol for you today."

She took a couple of sips, sat up, and realizing that she was sitting in Gilbert's lap, pushed to her feet. "Get out of my chair. I'm not a little kid anymore."

He rolled his eyes. "Could have fooled me with that tantrum."

"He had fangs in his mouth!" She pointed at Eric without looking at him. "I thought that they were real. Which one of you morons came up with such an idiotic stunt?"

"It was me." Eric lifted his hand. "But it was not a stunt. I'm immortal now, and I have fangs."

By now, his fangs were back to normal size, so he had nothing to show her. He also couldn't produce illusions like other immortals because, supposedly, that could be learned only at a young age, but he was going to prove them all wrong and master the skill.

Plopping down on the chair, Gabi groaned. "Do me a favor and stop with all this nonsense. My nerves are already frayed after having flown for over five hours. I need a couple of days to relax."

"It's not nonsense," Kaia said. "And regrettably, we can't wait a couple of days. It has to be done today. There is nothing magical or supernatural about immortality or Eric's fangs. It's genetics, and I can explain how it works. But you need to stop arguing and start listening."

That finally pierced through Gabi's stubborn shields. "Okay, Ms. Genius Prodigy. Enlighten your dumb step-aunt."

"You're not dumb, Gabi," Gilbert grumbled. "You're just as stubborn as a mule and closed-minded."

"I'm not closed-minded," she bristled. "Any normal person would have reacted the same way I did. Perhaps minus the fainting, but I blame that on excess alcohol."

"I'll make it short and simple," Kaia said. "And if you have questions, keep them until I'm done. But before I start, I want you to know that if you don't let Orion compel you to keep everything that I tell you a secret, all that knowledge will be erased from your memory the same way the name of the nefarious leader was. If this information falls into the wrong hands, our lives will be in danger." She waved a hand at everyone sitting around the table. "As you can imagine, there is nothing people won't do to get their hands on the secret to immortality."

Gabi swallowed. "I will never do anything to endanger my family. If this is for real, I'd rather die than reveal your secret."

Eric chuckled. "It would be easier and less traumatic to just let Orion compel you to keep the secret so you can't reveal it even if you try, but that can wait until after Kaia is done explaining. Although I suggest we wait with that as well because I can see a bunch of waiters heading this way with loaded trays." He waved a hand at the glass doors.

Gabi

As Gabi waited impatiently for the waiters to be done distributing the appetizers and the main dishes, she was glad that Gilbert had asked for everything to be delivered at once so they wouldn't be disturbed again.

When it was finally done, she didn't even look at what was on her plate.

Who could think of food at a time like this?

Kaia, on the other hand, cut off a big piece of the roasted chicken she'd ordered and put it in her mouth.

"Am I supposed to wait until after everyone is done eating?" Gabi asked.

Kaia lifted a finger and chewed faster. When she was done, she wiped her mouth with a napkin and took a sip from her Coke. "I'm sorry, but this smelled so good I couldn't wait. So here is the story in a nutshell. The myths about the gods were not really myths. They were history. The gods were aliens who had been exiled from their home planet for their part in a rebellion. There weren't enough of them to provide genetic variety, so they took human mates. The children born from those unions were immortal, with some of the powers of their ancestors but not all. When the immortals took human partners, though, their children were born seemingly human, but the girls carried the dormant godly genes and transferred them to their offspring because they are transferred only through the mother. The gods and immortals discovered that it was possible to activate those dormant genes, and when the gods were still around, it was done when those carriers reached puberty. After most gods and immortals perished, what was left of their population got dispersed, and many of the Dormants born after the destruction didn't even know that they were carriers. Our mother and her children happen to be such carriers, and the fantastic coincidence is that your family has those genes as well, a gift from your mother and before that her mother and so on. Gilbert, Eric and I went through the process and transitioned already. Cheryl and the younger kids have to wait a little longer before they can attempt it."

With that, Kaia smiled, cut off another piece of the chicken, and put it in her mouth.

Apparently, she was done, so Gabi was allowed to ask questions.

It all sounded like science fiction, not science, but she knew better than to doubt Kaia.

"What about Eric's fangs? Do you have fangs, too? And what about Karen?" She looked at her brother's partner. "Did you turn immortal?"

"Not yet." Karen winced. "Gilbert is a baby immortal, and he's still growing his fangs. So is Eric, which is why his fangs are still so small. They are going to get much larger before they are operational."

Those were small baby fangs?

She turned to Onegus and Orion. "You are not baby immortals, right? Can you show me how long those fangs can become?"

Onegus shook his head. "Some of us can do it at will, but most of us need aggression or arousal for our venom glands to activate and our fangs to drop. I can probably do that if I concentrate, but I prefer not to if you don't mind."

Orion chuckled softly. "For most of us, it's a struggle not to let them elongate at inappropriate moments. Regulating aggression is one of the first skills a newly turned male immortal must learn."

"Yeah," Kaia said. "I forgot to mention that females don't have elongating fangs or venom glands, so you don't have to worry about that."

"Awesome." Gabi gestured as if erasing an item from a list.

If any of this was real, which it seemed to be unless she was dreaming, the last thing she needed was a pair of fangs that made an appearance every time she got angry or horny. She would have been flashing fangs nonstop.

Except, she knew better than to hope there would be no other weird side effect to gaining immortality.

"What do I need to worry about?" she asked. "How are those genes activated?"

"I told you," Cheryl said. "Sex. You need to find a male immortal to bond with, and when he bites you during sex, his venom will induce your transition, and it usually takes more than one time to do that."

Having her sixteen-year-old niece explain the immortal birds and bees to her was extremely awkward. It should have been done by Karen, Darlene, or even Kaia. Not Cheryl.

"What do you mean by bonding?" She looked pointedly at Darlene. "Is it another term for sex?"

"No, it's precisely what you think it is. You need to fall in love and create a bond. Supposedly, it makes the induction process easier. But in my case, I was bitten by a friend who did Eric and me a favor, so I obviously wasn't bonded with him. I was bonded with Eric, but his fangs and venom weren't operational yet. They still aren't."

Confused, Gabi shook her head. "So, you were a Dormant when you met Eric? Not an immortal?"

"Correct." Darlene nodded. "I was a confirmed Dormant because my mother and sister were immortal, but I couldn't find an immortal male I was drawn to. Then Eric showed up when he flew the family in to visit Kaia, where she was working on a secret project with William, and when I saw him, I knew he was the one for me." She smiled at Eric. "Well, I knew I wanted him, but I had no idea he was a Dormant like me. I thought that I was just attracted to a very handsome human."

Eric lifted Darlene's hand to his lips and brushed them over her knuckles. "I felt the connection right away. I couldn't keep away from Darlene, and I reorganized my schedule so I could see her again."

"It was the Fates' work," Karen said. "You were destined to be together."

Gabi knew Karen well, and she wasn't the type who believed in divine intervention or any other supernatural force. After losing her first husband when Kaia and Cheryl were practically babies, Karen had become an atheist, and Gabi could understand why.

"I'm surprised to hear you say that. You didn't use to believe in anything."

Karen let out a breath. "I still struggle with that, but I can't deny the facts. There aren't many immortals left, or Dormants, although I suspect there are many more Dormants than immortals. Still, Gilbert and me finding each other was too much of a coincidence. The same is true for William and Kaia and many other immortal/Dormant or two Dormant couples. The clan believes in the three Fates, and it's easier for me to accept three capricious female entities as the supernatural power in charge of pairings than a benevolent creator who doesn't seem benevolent at all."

Karen

Karen had lost too many people she loved—
good people who deserved a long, happy life—
to still believe in divinity, and although she
shouldn't base her beliefs solely on her life experience,
there was so much ugliness in the world that it almost
seemed as if the devil was in charge and not the supposedly good creator. But since she didn't believe in the devil
either, she chose to believe in chaos.

Nothing was predetermined, and things just happened
for no good reason.

Except for immortal pairings that were orchestrated by
the Fates.

The irony of her conflicting beliefs wasn't lost on her,
but Karen was both experienced and humble enough to
realize that neither she nor the greatest human minds had
all the answers. What had been held as the absolute truth
yesterday was proven just as absolutely false today, and
the same would happen to the accepted truths of today.

In fact, the cycling of scientific dogmas was becoming much faster because the power of computation was increasing exponentially, and the dawn of the artificial intelligence age would accelerate that process by an order of magnitude.

"So let me understand," Gabi said. "I am the descendant of gods, and I can turn immortal if I have sex with an immortal male, preferably one I can bond with, but that's not absolutely necessary. Falling in love is optional, but hooking up is not."

"Correct," Karen said. "You are the youngest sibling of the three, and you're in excellent physical shape, so you don't have to rush to find an inducer. You can take your time and check out the selection."

Darlene chuckled. "The selection is impressive, but those pesky Fates won't let you lust after just anyone. I was surrounded by hot males, but none of them stirred anything in me. I thought I was damaged goods after being married to a jerk for so long, but then I met Eric, and the rest is history. Regrettably, I'm much older than you, so I didn't have the luxury of waiting until Eric was done growing his fangs and venom so he could induce me, and we had a friend provide the biting services."

Karen cleared her throat. "This isn't the place or time to get into the particulars." She quickly glanced at her daughters and then turned her gaze to Gabi. "What you need to decide now is whether you want to forget everything we've just told you and go back to being oblivious, or agree to Orion compelling you to keep everything a secret."

"Can't I just promise not to tell anyone? As I said, I will never do anything to endanger my family."

"You might do it unintentionally," Onegus said. "Or, Fates forbid, you fall into the hands of someone who wants to torture the information out of you. Wouldn't you feel better knowing that no one can force you to reveal the secret that keeps your family safe?"

Gabi's eyes widened. "Is that just hypothetical, or is it a real possibility?"

"It's hypothetical." Karen rushed to answer before Onegus could scare Gabi even more. "But too much is at stake to take unnecessary risks, and that's why these rules are in place. It's either forgetting everything you were told or compulsion."

"There is a third choice," Onegus said. "You can come with us to our village, stay for a bit, and then decide what you want to do. You won't be allowed to leave the village without choosing either thralling or compulsion, but you will be able to see for yourself that everything we told you is true."

Karen hadn't known that was an option, and given Gilbert's surprised expression, he hadn't known either. Their entire family had been compelled to secrecy before ever setting foot in the village, so it hadn't occurred to them.

"How long is a little bit?" Gabi asked.

"Two weeks, more or less. The longer the duration and the number of memories accumulated, the harder it becomes to thrall them away, and if forced, it could cause damage to your mind. Two weeks is the Goldilocks zone."

"That actually makes sense." Gabi turned to Gilbert. "I would love to see your village. Can I stay with you and Karen?"

"Our house is really small, and you'll have to sleep on the living room couch. Darlene and Eric have a spare bedroom, so you'll be more comfortable with them."

Onegus lifted his hand. "One more thing. You have to leave your phone behind. I will put it in a locker downstairs, and you can get it back when you are ready to go home." He smiled. "Either compelled to keep a secret or minus your memories of immortals and everything else you have learned and will continue to learn during your stay in the village."

Gabi

"**W**hy do I need to leave my phone behind?"

Gabi couldn't leave her phone. What if Uriel called her?

What if she wanted to call him?

Onegus smiled indulgently. "We don't want anyone to be able to track you to our village by your phone."

"Who is going to track me? I'm a nobody."

"We can give her a clan phone," Gilbert said. "William even brought one with him. She can forward her calls to the new number."

Onegus shook his head. "I can't allow Gabi to talk to anyone outside the village unless she's under Orion's compulsion."

Crap. Unless she agreed to let the immortal compel her, she couldn't talk with Uriel, and if he called her, got her voicemail, and didn't hear from her within a reasonable timeframe, he would assume she was ghosting him.

But wait, hadn't she decided that he was too good-looking and too young for her?

Maybe it was for the best if the decision was taken out of her hands?

"You look conflicted," Darlene said. "Are your clients expecting you to always be reachable? Or is it personal?"

"Both." Gabi reached for the glass of wine and then changed her mind. "My clients always text me with questions about food substitutions, cheat days, and the like. I usually respond within an hour or so. My friends are used to me taking a little longer to get back to them, so that's not a problem."

Except for Uriel, who was neither a client nor a friend.

What was he?

A potential hookup?

Yeah. That was the extent of what she should expect from him, and now that she had come to that realization, she knew that she had to have him either tonight or the next or never.

If what her family had told her was true, and she had no reason to think it wasn't, even though it sounded like a delusional fantasy, then she would have to go to their village and choose an immortal male to induce her into immortality.

If she wanted a tumble in bed with Uriel, this might be her last chance.

God. How could they expect her to make life-changing decisions on the spot like that?

Besides, she couldn't stay in their village for more than a few days. She had a flight booked back to Cleveland on Wednesday, and she had a full day of appointments with clients on Thursday. Was she expected to drop everything she'd worked so hard for and concentrate on finding a guy?

It sounded like something that belonged in the fifties.

"Let me ask you a question." She looked at Onegus, who seemed to be the authority figure in the group. "If I move to your village, what am I supposed to do for a living? Do immortals require a nutritionist or a lifestyle coach?"

William cleared his throat. "I used to be significantly overweight, but I was the exception. It's rare for immortals to have problems regulating their appetites. Our bodies are very efficient machines, and it takes a lot of abuse to get them out of equilibrium."

"That's what I thought. What the heck am I going to do after I turn immortal? Can I go back to Cleveland after I become one?"

Given the looks everyone was giving her, that was a no.

"You can open a new clinic in Los Angeles," Karen said. "Some of the village residents commute to the city every day."

That was good to know, but the thought of starting from scratch was still disheartening. She had a business she'd worked hard on building, a group of friends she would miss, and a two-story condominium that she'd furnished and decorated exactly how she wanted it.

Gabi needed time to process everything, and she needed to have at least one night with Uriel, or she would forever regret missing the opportunity.

There wasn't much she could do about the changes looming on the horizon, but she could do something about tonight.

Even if he ended up declining her offer, she would at least know that she'd given it a try.

One night.

That was all she wanted.

Well, maybe two.

Three at the most.

Gabi shook her head. She'd just decided that Uriel would be a one-time hookup, and by definition, that meant that she would give him only one night.

"If you don't mind, I would like to stay in the hotel tonight and think everything over." She looked at Orion. "I guess what I'm saying is that I agree to your offer to compel me to keep everything I learned today a secret."

Gilbert frowned at her. "Why? Is it because I said we don't have room? It wasn't an excuse. We really don't. I would love to have you stay with us."

"You can have my cabana," Cheryl said. "I'll sleep in Idina's room."

Gabi smiled at her niece. "Thank you for your generous offer. It's very sweet of you. But it's not about the sleeping accommodations. I just need one night by myself to process everything I've learned today and everything in my future. It's a lot to take in."

"That's understandable," Onegus said. "I can get you a room in this hotel." He pulled out his phone and started texting.

Gabi turned to Orion. "So, how are you going to do it?"

"It's very simple. Look into my eyes and focus on the sound of my voice."

"Hold on." Kaia stopped him. "Compulsion doesn't erase memories; someone with thralling ability can pluck them from Gabi's mind. Those three hunks on the plane worry me. What if they are Doomers?"

What the hell were Doomers?

Onegus stopped texting and leveled his gaze on Gabi. "Did you exchange phone numbers with any of them?"

She swallowed. "I did."

"Don't call him." He turned to Orion. "Make sure that she doesn't. I don't want to take any chances."

Damn. That was the whole reason for her staying in the hotel.

"Come on, he was just a good-looking guy. A human. You can't compel me not to have contact with whomever I choose just because I made a stupid comment about how handsome he was."

Orion regarded her with his shrewd eyes. "I can compel you to forget what you were told until one of your brothers picks you up from the hotel tomorrow afternoon. That way, your guy won't be able to peek into your mind even if he is one of us."

"That's fine. Well, maybe—"

What if Uriel couldn't make it tonight?

Damn. Why was she so obsessed about hooking up with him?

So, he was hot, so what?

It wasn't just about the hookup. She felt as if the old Gabi was about to disappear, and she had to treat herself before it happened. Except, she hadn't decided yet whether she was going to leave everything behind and join her family as an immortal.

Ugh, who was she kidding?

As if that was a choice. Of course, she would do that, but maybe not right away. She had to go back to Cleveland, transfer her clients to a colleague, sell her condo or rent it out, and tell her friends a very convincing story about why she was moving away and couldn't give them her new address.

"What do you mean by maybe?" Orion asked.

"I might not be ready tomorrow either."

"Gabi," Gilbert said in the same tone he'd used when she'd done something he'd disapproved of when she was a teenager. "You came here because you were concerned about your family, you wanted to know what's going on and see where we live, and now you are willing to put everything on ice because of a guy? What kind of an example are you setting for your nieces?"

"A very good one," Cheryl grumbled. "Gabi is an independent woman who doesn't let her older brothers dictate who she has fun with and when."

Gabi shook her head. "I've just learned that I'm not fully human, that I will have to leave behind my friends and everything I've worked for and move across the country to live in a hidden immortal village. I will also have to find an immortal lover to hook up with and hope my godly genes get activated. Forgive me for wanting to get a breather and cling to normalcy for a little longer than eighteen hours."

Orion

Orion felt for Gabriella. Gilbert loved his sister and wanted the best for her, but he was also a prick to her, allowing his frustration to get the better of him and taking it out in the form of scolding that wasn't helpful.

Compared to Orion's own sister, Gabi had taken the news about her alien genetics remarkably well.

He still remembered the first time he'd told Geraldine that she was the daughter of a god and, therefore, immortal. Suffice it to say that she hadn't been nearly as calm and accepting as Gabi.

Then again, the circumstances had been different. He'd been a stranger who had shown up out of the blue, and he hadn't had an entire family of immortals to back up his claim. Geraldine, or Sabina as she'd been named by her adoptive parents, simply couldn't believe him.

Nevertheless, it wasn't his place to correct Gilbert. The guy had been the de facto parent for his younger siblings for a long time, and they had their own family dynamic.

Gabi turned a pair of pleading blue eyes at him. "Is there a way you can leave my memories of today intact so I can think about them and plan for the future, but so no one else can see them if they peek into my mind?"

Gilbert snorted. "As always, you want to have your cake and eat it too. You can't have both. If you want to think about what you've learned and discuss plans for the future with your family, you should come with us to the village. If that guy is so interested in you, he can meet you when you return to Cleveland to settle your affairs there."

Gabriella cast him an incredulous look. "How is that going to be any different? I will still have memories that Uriel can supposedly see if he's one of you, which I doubt. Seriously, what are the chances of me sitting on a plane next to an immortal? How many of those guys are there?"

"Counting our enemies, many thousands," Onegus said. "Although I don't know what three of them would be doing in Toronto. Were there reports of attractive young women disappearing in the area?"

Gabriella blanched. "Why? What do they do to those women?"

"They finance their operation by dabbling in trafficking." Onegus shook his head. "But that's a topic for a whole different conversation. For now, I just want to rule out some variables."

She shrugged. "I was in Toronto for a three-day conference on nutrition and fitness, and I didn't watch the news. Besides, Toronto was just a layover for Uriel and his friends. They'd come from Korea, where they probably had their faces perfected. It's a popular destination for people looking to have plastic surgery on a budget."

Gilbert pursed his lips. "People flying first class are not concerned with saving a few bucks on surgery. The difference in cost between first class and coach would eat up whatever they saved on the procedures."

"They could have gotten a free upgrade like I did."

"What kind of luggage did they have?" Cheryl asked. "You can tell a lot by that. All the rich guys have Tumi backpacks."

"Not only Tumi," Karen said, "there is also that other brand." She waved a hand at Gilbert. "You know. You ordered one and then returned it. What was the name?"

"Briggs & Riley. But they are not that expensive. There are more luxurious brands out there." He looked at Gabriella. "Did you notice what kind of luggage your hunk had? Or were you too busy ogling his body?"

The small smile lifting her lips confirmed Gilbert's assertion, but she didn't seem at all embarrassed or upset about it, which Orion applauded her for. She had every right to admire a male's physique.

"He had a backpack, but I wasn't paying attention to the kind it was. He had a simple white T-shirt on and a pair of jeans. I didn't notice the brand of the jeans either."

"Of course not." Cheryl smirked. "Who cares about the clothes? It's what's under them that's interesting."

Gilbert groaned. "Why can't little girls stay little forever?"

"Wait until Idina is Cheryl's age," Kaia said. "You will miss how tame we were as teenagers."

Gilbert grimaced. "I have no doubt."

As entertaining as it was to watch the family dynamics, Orion wanted to be done so he could go home to Alena.

"I have a solution that will satisfy everyone. I can compel you not to think about what you've learned when you are around other people. You'll only be able to think about it when you are alone."

Gabriella's smile was brilliant enough to illuminate the room. "Perfect."

Gilbert, on the other hand, didn't look happy with Orion's solution. "What if he can get into her head from afar?"

"Thankfully, it's not possible," Onegus said. "A very strong thraller can plant suggestions and illusions in people's minds from a distance, and a strong empath can feel what others are feeling in a wide area. But neither can pinpoint which thoughts are emanating from whom unless they are right next to that person. "

"What about Vivian and Ella?" Karen asked. "They can communicate telepathically from wherever regardless of distance."

"That's a very different paranormal talent," Onegus said. "And it is also extremely rare. I doubt any of the Doomers have this kind of telepathic ability. At most, some of them might be weak telepaths who won't be able to pinpoint which thought is coming from whom."

Gabi groaned. "You're giving me a headache. Do all immortals have paranormal abilities?"

"Not all," Kaia said. "I'm still trying to figure out mine."

William looked at her with adoring eyes. "Your talent is solving scientific puzzles."

"Maybe." Kaia let out a breath. "I'm still transitioning, so maybe something cooler than that will emerge."

Gabriella turned to Onegus. "Will I also develop a paranormal talent once I'm immortal?"

He shook his head. "If you don't have any special talents now, you probably won't get any after. Usually, existing talents intensify after the transition." He smiled. "My mate can blow things up with her mind. She could do that before her transition but had difficulty controlling it, and her explosions were small. After the transition, she started practicing, and now she has full control over her power and can blow up a car."

Eyes wide, Gabriella turned to Darlene. "Can you blow things up like your sister?"

"Regrettably, I can't. Cassandra is a badass, and she has a badass talent."

"What is your talent?" Gabi asked.

Orion lifted his hand. "If you don't mind, I would like to commence with the compulsion, and I need a few quiet moments with no distractions to do so. I don't want to leave any wiggle room in my phrasing."

Jade

Kagra strode into Phinas's home as if it was her own. "You're going to love me for this." She pulled out one of the dining table chairs, turned it around, and straddled it. "Ask me why."

Phinas arched a brow. "I'm almost afraid to, especially when you use the word love in the sentence, but why?"

She waved a hand dismissively. "It's just an expression." Mischief danced in her eyes as she winked at Jade. "I know that you love me no matter what. I'm just so lovable." She batted her eyelashes.

"Can you get to the point?" Jade pulled out a chair next to her second-in-command. "We have a lot to talk about."

"I've got us an office, and it's not in the underground. It has a nice big window that overlooks the ravine."

The office building overlooked the village square, as did the building that housed the clinic and Bridget's research facilities, so she wasn't talking about a room there.

"Where is this lovely office?" Phinas asked.

"In Ingrid's design center. Kian gave her an entire house to use as her base of operations, and it has a living room and two bedrooms. She only uses the living room as her showroom and one of the bedrooms as an office. She has no problem with you using the other bedroom as the Kra-ell headquarters. You can use the sliding door to the backyard to come and go without going through the center, and if you need to have meetings with several people, you can do that in the backyard."

That sounded like a great solution, but in Jade's experience, nothing was ever given out for free. "What's the catch?"

Kagra shrugged. "Ingrid said that she needs help with deliveries from time to time, and the Guardians are not always available. She will collect the favor by asking us to help carry things."

"I'd rather pay rent," Jade grumbled.

It wasn't because she was averse to using her people as pack mules but because she had the money, and she didn't like to feel like a beggar.

Phinas pushed to his feet. "You can't pay rent because the house does not belong to Ingrid, and she doesn't pay rent either." He stopped next to the bar cabinet. "Can I offer you ladies something to drink?"

"Sure," Kagra said. "I'll take a vodka with cranberry juice."

"Coming up." He glanced at Jade. "I assume that you want one too?"

"Since you are already making a cocktail for Kagra, sure."

Taking Ingrid up on her offer would at least give Phinas his house back. Jade tried to hold as many of her meetings as possible in the café, but not everything could or should be discussed in public, and her place of residence was the only other option. During the week, Phinas spent time at Kalugal's office building in the city, so she could see people while he wasn't home, but some always showed up after hours, and it wasn't fair to him.

As for Drova, she was rarely home, and when she was, it wouldn't be a bad idea for her to witness what was involved in leading a community. One day she might become a leader herself, and the experience she could gain by watching Jade would be invaluable.

The problem was that she had trouble getting through to the girl, and most of her suggestions were met with such opposition that she kept them to a minimum. Drova was still struggling with her father's fate, and she needed time but, at some point, Jade would have to stop coddling her and start enforcing more rigid rules.

"When can I start using that other room in Ingrid's design center?" she asked.

"Right now, it is furnished as a bedroom." Kagra pulled out her phone. "I took a picture if you want to take a look." She handed the phone to Jade.

It was identical to Drova's room, with a sliding glass door leading to the backyard.

"It will do." She handed Kagra back her phone.

"Ingrid said that as soon as you give her the okay, she'll order proper office furniture to replace what is there now. She suggested that you drop by during business hours and look through some catalogs so you can choose what you like."

Jade didn't really care. A dining room table could serve as a conference table, and she could also use it as her desk.

"I'll go to see the place tomorrow."

Kagra grimaced. "So, I assume you decided not to go to China after all, and you want me to go instead."

"I can't leave the village right now, and frankly, I'm not happy about you going either. I wanted Vrog to lead the Kra-ell portion of the team. Kian even seemed like he was okay with that, but then he called me and said that he wanted either you or me to co-lead the team with Yamanu because Vrog wouldn't be able to handle Rishana and Sheniya. Even with Toven's compulsion and my direct orders to follow Vrog's lead, they would find ways to make his life miserable."

Kagra sighed. "If Yamanu were single, I would jump on the opportunity to co-lead with him, but he's happily mated, and immortals are obsessively loyal to their mates. I think you should go. I can hold the fort in your absence."

That was probably true, but Jade didn't want to go.

"It'll be good practice for you. Did you speak with the males on the list?"

Kagra nodded. "They are all eager to go, including Pavel. They regard it as an honor to be chosen and trusted to leave the village, and an opportunity for an adventure."

"I bet." Jade took the glass Phinas handed her. "I wish at least one person on the team was a compeller. I don't trust Sheniya and Rishana."

Kagra looked offended. "Don't you trust me to keep them in check? They won't dare do anything with me in charge."

Jade wasn't sure about that at all.

Kagra was a great fighter and in much better shape than the two older females. But she was too young and cheerful to be taken seriously by them. She also had a temper, which she sometimes failed to control.

In short, she suffered from the maladies of youth and temperament, but the mission was a perfect test to see how she handled leading a team.

"I'm sure you'll do your best, but you are young and Earthborn, which might diminish your authority in their minds. It will be a good test, though."

Kagra took a sip from the drink and put it down. "Don't worry. I can handle them, and if they underestimate me, they will learn never to repeat that mistake."

Gabi

The hotel room was much more luxurious than Gabi had expected. She wondered how much it would cost her. Onegus had made the reservations, but she had no doubt that she would have to pay upon checkout.

Just one more thing to fuel her anxiety.

Perhaps she should just call the front desk and ask?

The truth was that her business was not as profitable as she'd made her brothers believe it was, and she had to be very calculated with how she spent her money.

Oh well, soon none of that would matter because she would again have to give it all up and live with Eric and Darlene until she got a new clinic running in Los Angeles.

Renting office space in the city would be much more expensive than what she was paying in Cleveland, but she could probably charge more for her services. Except, she would have to build up a client base from scratch, which would take time. Perhaps she could keep helping her Cleveland clients remotely? They might not object if she lowered her fees, but would they keep recommending her to their family and friends?

In the meantime, she could probably get by on the money she would collect for renting out her condo. She'd bought it twelve years ago and had taken out a fifteen-year mortgage, so in three years it would be free and clear, and since it had tripled in value, she could charge much more for rent than what she was still paying on the mortgage and all the other expenses associated with homeownership.

Gabi was very well aware that those thoughts about mortgage, rent, and other mundane things were nothing more than a delaying tactic. Sitting on the couch in her hotel room and clutching her phone, she hoped Uriel would call her first so she wouldn't have to call him and risk rejection.

Perhaps she could wait a little longer and, in the meantime, ponder the bigger issues of immortality and the pending changes in her life. After all, she wouldn't be able to do that with Uriel around.

Orion's compulsion worked so well that it was disturbing.

When Gabi had collected her room key from the front desk, she couldn't remember anything she had talked about with her family, and she'd thought that she wanted to stay in the hotel so she could meet with Uriel. That was true, but there was so much more to it that she remembered as soon as she entered the elevator and the doors closed behind her.

It was the weirdest feeling. It was like trying to remember a word or a name or something important that she needed to do and struggling with it for hours, and then it suddenly popped into her mind when she was least expecting it.

Perhaps she should write it down somewhere so it wouldn't be as jarring the next time?

She could make a note in the application she used for monitoring her clients. She checked it frequently, especially when she was anxious, so when she felt like she was forgetting something, she would open the application and check her notes.

"Quit stalling," she murmured. "Call him and get it over with."

What was the worst that could happen? Uriel would come up with some polite excuse for why he couldn't see her, she would be hurt, and she'd get over it.

Case closed.

Would she still remember everything she'd been told about immortals while talking on the phone with him? Or would she forget the moment he answered?

Perhaps she should start with a text.

If he rejected her via text, it would feel less personal. It would also be a good test to see whether her memories were affected by texting.

"You are such a damn coward," Gabi murmured as she opened the text application.

Hi, Uriel, it's Gabi. I'm spending the night in a hotel after all, and I'm wondering whether we could meet for drinks. The hotel I am staying in is in downtown Los Angeles. It's called the 72nd like the restaurant on top of the building. If you want to come over, I'll text you the address. I can also take an Uber and meet you in a bar or come to your hotel.

She read over the text twice, corrected a couple of typos, and then hesitated with her finger hovering over the send button.

"I'm not a coward." She tapped the screen and sent the text.

Her heart was racing like crazy until the three dots appeared, indicating that he was typing an answer, and when they kept blinking for long moments, it went into hyperdrive, threatening to burst out of her ribcage and commit suicide by jumping off the window of her room on the sixty-ninth floor.

Good thing that the windows couldn't be opened and there was no balcony.

Uriel's reply was taking so long that he was either typing a very long text, someone was interrupting him, or he was writing and erasing and writing it again.

Finally, when the words appeared on her screen, she felt faint with relief.

I can be there in an hour. Do you want to meet in the lobby?

Gabi let out a breath. It wasn't a polite letdown, and he was willing to come to her.

Feeling emboldened, she typed, *you can come up to my room, and we can order room service. I'm on the sixty-ninth floor, room 6914. I'll check the exact address and send it to you in a moment.*

This time the three dots blinked for only a few seconds. *No need to send me the address. I know where your hotel is. I'll bring a bottle of wine.*

Smiling, Gabi typed back, *I can't wait to see you again.*

The three dots danced for a couple of seconds. *I'm eager to see you again too.*

Vrog

"It's so nice in the café in the evenings." Aliya stretched her long legs in front of her. "Especially since it is closed, and I don't have to serve customers." She cast Vrog a sidelong smile. "Don't get me wrong. I love working in the café, and I love the village, but I'm excited about visiting China. I haven't been back since I left."

Vrog reached for her hand. "It will be like a honeymoon for us."

Aliya was allowed to leave the village now, but they hadn't done it often. She worked long hours at the café, and in the evenings, she worked on supplementing her education. That didn't leave much time for leisure, and he was glad she was finally willing to take a vacation.

He was also glad that Kian had convinced Jade to send Kagra as the Kra-ell team leader, and Vrog's job description had been reduced to an advisor.

Wendy sighed. "Yeah, except you are not married, and neither are Vlad and I. We don't even know if the wedding cruise is still happening. Did anyone hear any updates about that?"

Vrog shook his head. "Maybe now that the trial is over and things are back to normal, Kian will announce when the cruise will take place."

Vlad chuckled. "Things are never back to normal for long. I bet that those signals you are going to investigate are another crisis that's brewing." He leaned toward Wendy and planted a kiss on her cheek. "We should just elope. How does a Vegas wedding sound to you?"

Vrog didn't know whether his son was jesting, but given Wendy's laugh, she seemed to think it was a joke. "I have a gorgeous wedding dress that's fit for a grand wedding. I'm not wasting it on a ceremony in a stinky chapel in Vegas."

"Why is the chapel stinky?" Aliya asked.

"It's just an expression to describe something that's not up to par," Wendy explained. "On another subject, this trip to China means that Wonder and I will have to hire one of the hybrids to take your place while you are gone." She affected a pout. "We've gotten spoiled having you around, and now we can't manage without you."

"About that." Aliya straightened in her chair. "The timing is actually good. I wanted to talk to you about cutting down my shifts. I want to speed up my online studies so I can finally get my high school equivalency diploma and apply to colleges."

"Did you decide what you want to study?" Vlad asked.

She smiled shyly. "Until recently, I thought about becoming a teacher, but after seeing Lusha handling the trial, I want to study law. I'll start with an English major, maybe with a minor in education, and then go to law school."

Vrog still hoped she would change her mind about that, but she was enamored with the idea of becoming a lawyer.

"I don't know if that's a good idea," Wendy said. "Does the village need another attorney? You should ask Kian whether he needs legal services for the clan's many businesses. If he doesn't, you will have to find a job in the human world, and with your looks, it's not really practical."

Vrog could kiss the girl for saying all the things he'd been trying to tell Aliya without offending her. Wendy had just said them without trying to sugarcoat a thing.

Shrugging, Aliya lifted her coffee cup and took a sip. "Maybe I will study international law and write books about it. Or maybe I will write courtroom drama stories. I don't have to become an actual lawyer."

"Then why bother?" Vlad asked. "It doesn't make sense to invest the time and effort. You can easily learn everything you need from reading books on the subject."

"Well, I'll start with the English major and decide what to do with it later. I can always teach English in the village school."

Vrog stifled a relieved breath.

That was precisely what he wished Aliya would choose, but he didn't want to appear to be dictating her future to her.

"How is the school coming along?" Wendy asked. "Any progress?"

"It's progressing well, given the limitations." Vrog leaned back in his chair. "The older kids are set up with laptops and self-learning programs, but they need a lot of help from me to get going. They are less proficient with computers than other kids their age, and many struggle with the language. Jade initially agreed to teach the little ones, but she doesn't have time, so I will have to find someone else to do that."

Wendy's eyes brightened. "I can teach a preschool class. I can do arts and crafts with the little ones."

Vrog smiled apologetically. "That would be lovely if you spoke Kra-ell. Regrettably, none of the little ones speak English, and I need a Kra-ell to teach them."

"Oh." Wendy's face fell. "Well, I'm sure you will find a volunteer. It's not like there is much for the Kra-ell to do in the village."

"It will have to wait for when I get back." Vrog glanced at Vlad. "I had an idea I wanted to run by you. What do you think about teaching the older kids and some of the young adults graphic design as an after-school class? They weren't exposed to any art in Igor's compound, and they could benefit from an introduction."

What Vrog really had in mind was getting Vlad more involved with the Kra-ell community.

So far, his son was like an outsider looking in. Even after the impromptu band performance Jackson had organized with his old band members and his new stepbrothers, Vlad was still too reserved to pursue friendships with the young Kra-ell, hybrids or purebloods. Teaching a class would give him an opportunity to get to know them better and for them to get to know him.

"I can spare an hour a week if you think they would be interested. I can also teach guitar playing. I think music will be even more appealing to them than art."

"That's a wonderful idea," Wendy said. "I wish I had an artistic skill I could teach, but even though I'm studying to become an art therapist, I can't do more than basic arts and crafts that are only good for little kids."

"Not necessarily," Vrog said as an idea started coalescing in his mind. "The Kra-ell carry a lot of emotional issues that they have no tools to express or deal with. I think that even the adults could benefit from a therapeutic arts and crafts class."

"I'm not licensed yet." Wendy chewed on her lower lip. "But since outside human world rules don't apply in the village, I can lead a class and see if I can help guide a discussion." She looked at Vrog. "What do you think?"

"I think it will not be easy to convince the Kra-ell that arts and crafts are a suitable way to pass the time, but I will find a way to market it. Perhaps we can call it conversational English practice. They all want to get proficient, and you can correct them when they make a mistake."

"That's an awesome idea." Wendy rubbed her hands together. "I'll have a curriculum ready when you get back."

Gabi

G abi searched her carry-on for something sexy to wear, but she hadn't packed anything that fit the bill. Traveling with only a carry-on as her luggage, she could only pack the bare necessities, which were six light dresses that didn't wrinkle, didn't take up much space, and were more professional in appearance than sexy.

She had one pair of pumps, which she was now wearing, flip-flops that served as slippers at the end of the day, one black cardigan that matched all six dresses, a nightshirt, two simple bras, and ten pairs of underwear that took nearly no space at all.

The fact that she hated flying didn't mean she didn't travel or didn't know how to pack light. People could use other modes of transportation, like trains and buses, cruise ships, and her old trusty car.

The problem was that she hadn't planned on hooking up with anyone during the conference or her family visit, and now she had none of her single-girl weapons with her. No sexy lingerie and no tight-fitting skirts or leggings. All she had to work with was a hairbrush and some makeup.

After showering, she put on the sexiest of her six dresses, a black off-the-shoulder stretchy number that flared around her hips and reached below her knees. There was no time to do anything elaborate with her long hair, so she didn't even wash it to save on blow-drying time. Instead, she teased it to give it some volume and tied the ends in a loose braid. She then applied a little makeup, just a concealer under her eyes, some eyeliner, and a touch of gloss.

She didn't want to look as if she was trying too hard.

After all, they weren't meeting in the hotel bar, so she had no excuse to put on the glossy red lipstick that would have made her entire face pop with color and provide a contrast to the simple black dress.

Oh, fine. Red lipstick it is.

A girl needed her armor, and if all she had was red lipstick, then that was what she would use.

After applying the bright cherry color, she smacked her lips and batted her eyelashes at her reflection. "Sweet and sexy. An irresistible combination."

Or so she hoped.

When the knock on the door sounded a little earlier than she'd expected, Gabi walked over and looked through the peephole to make sure it was indeed Uriel.

Looking even more gorgeous than she'd remembered, he was smiling as if he knew she was looking at him, and as she opened the door, his smile got even wider.

"Hello, Gabi." He leaned and kissed her cheek as if they were longtime acquaintances.

Her heart was beating like a marching band possessed by demons, but her brain still functioned well enough to find it odd that no one had called her from the reception desk to ask whether it was okay for Uriel to come to her room.

"Hi." She smiled back. "Did you have trouble getting up here?"

"Not at all." He put a large paper bag on the coffee table. "The reception guy was busy checking in a family of six, so when I told him I had a delivery for Gabriella Emerson in room 6914, he just let me through."

She chuckled. "He should have called and asked if I was expecting a delivery. Anyone can claim to be a delivery person and do unmentionable things to the hotel guests, who could then sue the hotel."

He frowned. "You said that you were a nutritionist. Are you also an attorney?"

Was he serious, or was he teasing her?

He looked serious.

"I'm not a lawyer, but that's common knowledge. People sue over things like a cup of coffee being too hot. Do you think they wouldn't sue for something like that?"

"I guess you are right."

Realizing he was still standing because she hadn't invited him to sit, she pointed to the couch. "Let's sit down so you can show me what you've got in that bag."

As he sat right next to her, so close that their thighs were nearly touching, his scent permeated her senses, and her eyes threatened to roll back in her head. Forcing them to stay focused, she leaned closer to sniff him better. "What's the name of the cologne you're wearing? It's amazing."

He looked embarrassed. "I don't know. My friends and I went shopping in a department store earlier, and a lady sprayed it all over me. I don't know what it's called."

Was it her imagination, or was Uriel kind of nerdy for the hottest guy she'd ever met?

He wasn't full of himself, and he wasn't boastful about anything. He was like the boy next door, just on steroids and with lots of plastic surgery.

"What were you and your friends looking for at the department store?"

She didn't really care about his shopping excursion, but it was a good conversation starter.

"Oh, this and that. Clothing mostly. I got a new wallet." He pulled it from his pocket, but regrettably he didn't open it to show her what was inside.

She didn't care about the credit cards he carried or how much cash he had in there, but she would have liked to know his last name, and so far, he'd managed to wiggle out of telling her every time she'd asked.

Onegus

"Thank you so much for babysitting." Karen held one of her sleeping boys over her shoulder. "Did they give you any trouble?"

Geraldine smiled. "None at all. They were three little angels. Anytime you need someone to babysit for you, I'm here."

Looking a little doubtful, Karen glanced at Cassandra and then Alena, but both nodded their agreement.

"Idina is such a smart girl," Alena said. "It's hard to believe that she's only three and a half years old."

Karen's expression was filled with pride. "I think kids grow up faster these days. They are exposed to so much more information than we were as kids."

Onegus didn't want to point out that she shouldn't include the immortals in her collective we. The world was different for each of them growing up.

"We need to go, Mom," Kaia said. "Idina is tired."

The girl was in William's arms, making grumbling noises about wanting to sleep.

"Yes. We should go." Gilbert adjusted the other sleeping boy on his shoulder. "Thanks again for babysitting. Have a good night."

When the door closed behind them, Onegus turned to Cassandra. "We should go too."

"No way. I want to hear all about Gabi and why she didn't come back with you as planned."

"Yeah," Alena said. "I want to hear that too."

Geraldine pushed to her feet. "I'll brew a fresh pot of coffee." She smiled. "You can't have juicy gossip without coffee and cake, right?"

Darlene laughed. "Absolutely."

After coffee was served, Darlene and Eric took turns recounting Gabriella's curious response to learning that her brothers and niece were immortal and that she could turn immortal as well.

"All because of a guy?" Cassandra asked. "He must have left one hell of an impression on her."

"Evidently." Darlene smirked. "She had it bad for him. I could see it in her eyes. When Onegus said that she would have to leave her phone behind, her entire attitude changed. Suddenly, she no longer wanted to go to the village with us and was okay with Orion compelling her to keep immortals a secret. It was a complete one-eighty."

"I need to find out more about that Uriel guy." Onegus took the coffee cup Geraldine handed him.

Orion eyed him with a doubtful expression. "How? Gabriella didn't tell us his last name. I don't think she even knows it."

"Roni can hack into the airline servers and easily find out who flew first class from Toronto to Los Angeles today."

"Do you know which airline she flew on?" Shai asked.

"No, but Roni can find that out in seconds. Gabi didn't use a fake name to book her flight, so that should be a piece of cake for him."

The guy who claimed his name was Uriel had probably lied about it. Uriel wasn't a common name, though, so maybe Onegus was seeing shadows where there were none. When people faked their identities, they usually used common names like Tom, Michael, or David and last names like Smith or Baker. The more common the name, the better.

It also wasn't a Doomer's name, but it would be a mistake to base his assumption on that alone.

Orion looked amused. "If you were so suspicious, you should have just asked Gabriella which airline she flew on and what her flight number was. She probably called that guy up as soon as she got settled in her hotel room, and he's probably already there. Gabriella is a looker, and any single man would jump to attention when getting an invitation from a beautiful lady."

"Guys." Cassandra lifted her hand. "Give the girl a break, will you? All she wants is a night of passion with a hot stranger. You are all jumping to conclusions about Uriel's identity just because of Gabi's stupid remark about him and his friends being as good-looking as you are." She waved her hand over the immortal males in the room. "Is it really so hard to believe that there are gorgeous male specimens among humans? And especially on a flight to Los Angeles—the mecca of actors and other performers worldwide?"

"It's also where the Brotherhood likes to hunt for unsuspecting females," Onegus said. "Although I have to admit that Gabi doesn't fit the profile of their typical victim. For starters, even though she's a beautiful woman, she's too old. Secondly, she has family that will notice immediately if she goes missing. Also, Doomers don't typically fly first class or travel in threes. That being said, Roni can do a quick search, find out who the guy is, and assuage my fears."

"What fears?" Cassandra asked. "You put Gabi in the clan's hotel, and knowing you, you've asked the front desk to notify you when someone visits her."

Onegus smirked. "Of course. That's why I offered to book her a room in our hotel."

Orion leaned back with his coffee cup. "Was I right? Is the guy already there?"

Onegus shook his head. "She ordered some stuff from a nearby liquor store, which was delivered to her room. Other than that, she hasn't had any other visitors."

"She probably ordered stuff in preparation for the visit," Darlene said. "Can we please stop talking about Gabi's love life?"

Cassandra snorted. "Says the woman who was making a list of possible suitors for Gabriella, with Max topping the list."

"That's different." Darlene pouted. "She needs an inducer, and I was looking out for her interests."

As the sisters argued about Gabriella and her future guy, Onegus pulled out his phone and texted Roni.

I need a quick favor. If you can do it tonight, great, and if not, tomorrow works as well.

The return text came in a few minutes later. *I'm hanging out with some new friends. If it's not urgent, I'll do it tomorrow morning. Send me the info.*

The new friends were probably some of the young Kra-ell purebloods and hybrids, and Onegus was glad that they were hanging out together.

Gabi's mystery man could wait.

Gabi

"I didn't know what you liked." Uriel started pulling things out of the paper bag. "I got a chocolate liqueur that the guy at the store said was a ladies' favorite and two bottles of wine, one red and one white. I also got mixed nuts in case you like salty things and a box of chocolates in case you like sweets."

With him sitting so close and smelling divine, it was hard to concentrate on what he was showing her.

He'd showered and changed, exchanging the white T-shirt for a gray one and the blue jeans for a pair of black ones, and Gabi couldn't decide which outfit looked better on him.

Easy, he was delicious in both, and she couldn't wait to see him in nothing at all.

"I like both sweet and salty," she murmured absentmindedly. "But that doesn't mean that I can indulge in either. They are both unhealthy for different reasons."

When Uriel's face fell, Gabi quickly added, "I don't need to be a good girl all the time. I can be naughty once in a while and snack on unhealthy things." She gave him a loaded look that left little room for misinterpretation.

Uriel seemed surprisingly unpracticed in the art of flirting, but perhaps he had never needed to develop the skill because women had just fallen into his lap.

Heck, she was a case in point. She'd called him up and invited him to her hotel room, and she'd done that with only the slightest indication that he even wanted to see her again.

Thankfully, Uriel had no problem understanding her double entendre if the gleam in his dark eyes was any indication.

"Snacking on me can be very healthy for you." He reached for her hand and brought it to his lips. "But I need to hear you ask for what you want."

Was this a sex game? Or was it just an insurance policy against later possible accusations of rape?

In today's litigious world, a guy couldn't be too careful, especially since he had snuck up to her room under false pretenses.

Given the devilish expression on Uriel's face, though, it was her first guess and not the second.

Well, if he wanted to play games, she was not going to refuse.

Gabi swallowed.

She wasn't shy about what she wanted, but she wasn't used to actually verbalizing her desires.

"I want you to kiss me." That should do it if he was after her consent. If he wanted to play dominance games, she wasn't sure how to proceed.

Gabi had no experience with that, and all she knew about the alternative lifestyle was from romance novels that probably got it all wrong, but if she was ever tempted to experiment, it was now with Uriel.

Just not anything that involved being tied up. She wasn't that dumb or horny. Although, with those muscles, Uriel didn't need ropes to immobilize her.

Strike the not-that-horny. She had never been so aroused just by talking to a guy and imagining what he was about to do to her.

"Where do you want me to kiss you?" he asked with that velvety smooth, sexy-as-sin voice of his.

"Right here." She tapped her lips with her pointer finger.

As a groan rose in his throat, the sound traveled right to where she was already tingling with need.

"Close your eyes," he commanded.

It was a shame to lose the magnificent view of his incredible face, but Gabi was all up for playing Uriel's game.

Despite him being a stranger, despite the sheer size of him and his muscles, and despite his evasiveness, she felt safe with him.

A small voice in the back of her head whispered that victims of serial killers had probably felt safe with them before they did not. Sociopaths were known to be great mimickers, and they could pretend to be very charming, fooling their victims into a false sense of security.

Despite the sinister whispers, though, Gabi trusted her instincts.

Uriel wasn't a serial killer.

He was keeping secrets, and there was probably no future for them beyond this one night, but she would be damned if she didn't enjoy it to the fullest for as long as it lasted.

When his large hand closed over the nape of her neck, she couldn't help the shiver that ran through her, and her lips parted of their own volition, but Uriel didn't immediately close the distance as she'd expected.

Instead, she felt him looking at her.

Did he need another invitation?

"You're so beautiful," he whispered.

A smile curved her lips. Men had called her beautiful before, but when coming from Uriel and spoken with such sincerity, it meant more to her.

"Kiss me," she murmured.

Instead of his lips, she felt his finger on her lips, wiping at her lipstick.

So that was his problem. He didn't want to taste lipstick.

"It's not going to come off, and you're not going to taste it." She was tempted to open her eyes but couldn't bring herself to disobey his command for some reason.

If she did, the magic would be broken, and that was the last thing she wanted.

He chuckled softly. "I wondered what it would taste like. I was hoping for cherries." He brushed his lips against hers ever so softly. "But you are right. It doesn't taste like anything. Maybe I need to give it another try." He swiped his tongue over the seam of her lips, demanding access which she gladly granted.

As he swooped inside, taking possession of her mouth, Gabi's eyes rolled back in her head behind her closed lids, and as his hold on her nape tightened, she moaned into his mouth, but it sounded more like a whimper.

His hold immediately relaxed, and he pulled back. "Did I hurt you?"

Was he kidding her?

Once again, she wanted to open her eyes and look at his face, but something prevented her from doing so. Was it her stubbornness to see this game play out as she'd expected?

"You didn't. That's the kind of sound I make when I'm turned on. Can you go back to kissing and stop worrying about hurting me?"

He cupped her cheek. "Only if you promise to tell me to stop the moment something feels uncomfortable."

Damn, Gabi wanted to open her eyes so badly that it hurt. "I promise. But I'm not as fragile as I seem."

"To me, you are." He took her lips, applying just the barest of pressure. "I don't want to accidentally cause you harm."

"Don't worry about hurting me," she murmured against his lips. "If I don't like what you're doing, I'll say the word cease."

He chuckled. "Why not just a simple stop?"

"Because I fully expect to tell you 'don't stop,' and I don't want any misunderstandings."

Karen

"**G**oodnight, sweetie." Karen kissed Idina's forehead.

"Goodnight, Mommy."

Karen tucked in the blanket again, looked at her daughter's angelic face, and smiled. Idina looked angelic only when she was asleep. When awake, she had a mischievous streak that bordered on mean, and the look she sometimes got in her eyes was a little devilish.

Tiptoeing out of the room, Karen didn't close the door all the way behind her and headed to the living room.

She found Gilbert brooding over a glass of whiskey that he seemed to be holding but not drinking from.

"What's the matter? Are you still upset about Gabi?"

"Yeah. I'm thinking back to how I was with her after our parents died, and I realize I let her get away with everything. I didn't hold her accountable for anything other than keeping up her grades in school."

"Oh, sweetheart." She sat on his lap and leaned her head on his shoulder. "You were just a kid yourself when you were tasked with raising your brother and sister. You've done amazingly well."

He shrugged. "I could have done better. I should have expected more of the two of them. But to be frank, Gabi did her share. She took on cooking for the three of us, which was a great help. She also helped with cleaning and the laundry. But emotionally, well, I didn't know how to handle her. She had temper tantrums and crying fits, and I humored her because I felt sorry for her. I feel like she hasn't grown up emotionally because of that."

Karen sighed.

It was so like Gilbert to take responsibility for everything, including things he had no control over. It was the eldest child syndrome taken to the umpteenth degree.

"Gabi has a certain personality, and I'm sure it was volatile even before your parents' deaths. You just didn't pay that much attention to her before. It's like Idina. Is her mean streak our fault? Do we encourage it in any way? We don't, and I hope she will grow out of it, but if she doesn't, I'm not going to blame myself or you for it. She was born a certain way, and all we can do is encourage the good and discourage the bad. The rest is up to her."

Being the stubborn ox that he was, Gilbert only pretended to accept what she was saying, but given his expression, he wasn't internalizing any of it.

"I shouldn't have let her marry that jerk. That was another mistake I made. It destroyed her self-confidence."

Gabi was confident in some ways and not so much in others, but that was true of most people.

"Would she have listened to you if you had told her not to marry her ex?"

Karen couldn't remember his name, and she didn't want to. The idiot did not deserve to be remembered.

"Probably not. I knew the type, and I warned her, but she said that I was generalizing and that her guy was not like the other basketball or football stars who slept with half the school. She thought he loved her."

"Did he?" Karen asked rhetorically. "You don't cheat on someone you love. But maybe he thought that he loved Gabi when he married her?"

"Probably." Gilbert sighed. "I've made my share of relationship mistakes, so I'm not one to talk. I thought my ex loved me, and I think she thought so for a while too. But then she started screwing her CFO, and when I confronted her, she didn't even deny it. She said she didn't love me anymore."

Karen had heard all of it before, but it was no less painful to hear again. Regrettably, the transition couldn't heal the scars that the woman had left on Gilbert's soul. But maybe plenty of time eventually would.

Cupping his cheeks, she lifted his face so he had to look at her. "I love you, and I will never stop loving you. Do you know why?"

"Why?" He seemed truly perplexed by that.

"Because I see you, every part of you, the good, the not-so-good, and everything in between, and there is not a single piece of you that I don't love. That's why my love for you is eternal. And that's even before the bond. I can't imagine our connection getting even stronger than that, but everyone says that it will."

He grimaced. "Yeah. I just hope our love can survive getting in bed with another couple. The idea repulses me. Perhaps I should ask Bridget to give me a tranquilizer so when the time comes for the other guy to bite you, someone can put me out of my misery."

"Don't be silly. You'll be fine. Would you prefer to wait until your fangs and venom glands are functional? Because I don't mind waiting. You were the one pushing to do it as soon as possible."

"I don't want to risk you." He put the full glass of whiskey aside and wrapped his arms around her. "I'm just in a bad mood, and everything seems bleak. I will do anything to keep you safe, even if that involves having another couple with us in bed and someone else biting you. I'm terrified of anything happening to you before or during the transition. I want all this to be behind us."

Gabi

The kiss must have been the longest Gabi had ever shared with a guy, and Uriel didn't seem like he was about to be done any time soon. Twice he'd released her mouth for a split second to allow her to take a breath, and then he'd gone back to ravishing it with such fervor that she was on the cusp of orgasm even though his hands still hadn't found her breasts or reached beneath her dress to touch her where she needed him to touch her the most.

If not for the sounds he was making in the back of his throat and his tight grip on her nape, she would have thought that he wasn't going to take it any further than kissing, but he was clearly as affected as she was.

Besides, they were not teenagers, and she'd made her expectations clear.

Suddenly, he released her mouth and her nape, gripped her hips, and flipped her around so her front was pressed against the rounded armrest, and he was behind her with his hands on her hips.

Goodness, that display of strength was hot, and so was the pose he'd put her in.

All he had to do now was to flip her dress up and expose her bottom that was barely covered and thong-style panties that by now were soaking wet.

When nothing happened, she wanted to turn her head and look over her shoulder to see what was keeping him, but as before, her eyes remained tightly closed.

When she felt his hands on the back of her thighs, she nearly moaned in relief, and as he smoothed them up toward her ass, pushing the skirt of her dress along the way, she sagged against the armrest and surrendered to the sensations.

"Perfection," he murmured as he exposed her bottom, which was bare save for the thin strip of fabric scarcely covering the center. "I hope you are not too attached to these." She felt his fingers pushing under the elastic, and a moment later, there was a tearing sound, and her panties were gone.

How had he done that so effortlessly?

And why did he want her with her back to him?

Was it part of the game?

Between commanding her to keep her eyes closed and turning her around, it seemed as if he didn't want her to see him.

Or maybe, maybe he wanted to keep it impersonal so she wouldn't get any ideas about this being anything more than a hookup.

The thought shouldn't be painful. After all, that was what she'd wanted, what she'd planned. It was supposed to be a one-time adventure before she embarked on—on what?

Her mind went blank, and a headache started pulsing at her temples. There was something she'd been planning to do, but she couldn't remember what it was. Something about moving to Los Angeles to be near her family, something she'd discussed with Gilbert and Eric during dinner, but she couldn't remember any of the particulars or why she'd promised them to think about it.

"You have a gorgeous ass." Uriel pulled her from her rambling thoughts, centering her on the here and now.

With his large hands closing over the sides of her butt cheeks, he pressed a kiss to each globe, and then he nipped her, once, twice, eliciting a yelp each time. The sting was a little uncomfortable but also arousing, and certainly nothing that required the word she'd promised him if it got too much for her.

The small bites had been playful, but Gabi had a feeling that Uriel was testing her with them to see whether she was averse to some sexual pain.

Evidently, she wasn't because those little nips had just gotten her wetter and needier. If he asked her now what she wanted him to do, she would tell him to get naked and feed her that hard length she'd spied before he'd ordered her to close her eyes.

It had been far too long for her, and she hadn't even realized how much she craved the touch of another instead of her own fingers or her trusty BOB.

Leaning over her, he kissed her neck, pulled her dress down, and then yanked it from under her knees, leaving her naked save for her bra, but not for long.

As his deft fingers did away with the clasp in a practiced move, she wondered how many women he had undressed during his young life to learn to do that so skillfully.

Most men, including her ex, fumbled around a bra clasp as if it was a bomb in need of defusing.

Whatever. Don't go there. He's not yours. Never was and never will be.

"What's wrong?" Uriel leaned over her again, palmed both of her breasts and then tugged on her nipples, scrambling her thoughts.

She stifled a moan. "You've gotten me naked, but you are still dressed."

"That's true. Do you prefer me unclothed?"

"Oh, yes, definitely, please, and thank you."

Uriel chuckled. "So polite." He rewarded her with a nip to her shoulder and then a lick to soothe the little hurt away. "And such a beautiful little liar."

Gabi

U riel was reading her like an open book, which should have flattered her but instead alarmed her for some reason.

Men were normally not that perceptive, and Gabi preferred it that way. Her thoughts were not always kind or sane, and she didn't need anyone inside her head, especially not a guy she'd just met.

Except, this was only a one-night stand, and she shouldn't worry about his ability to guess her thoughts and her moods so easily.

What was the worst that could happen? Uriel would tell his friends that he'd banged the crazy chick from the flight?

Who cared. They probably already thought that about her.

"You're still dressed." She wiggled her bottom, rubbing it against his erection.

"Patience, beautiful. First, I want to pleasure you so thoroughly that you will forget whatever is troubling you."

She smiled even though he couldn't see her. "I like your plan."

It would be nice to have a guy focused on her pleasure for a change, someone who actually knew what he was doing.

"Keep your eyes closed until I tell you that you can open them."

"Yes, sir."

Gabi was barely done saying the words when Uriel flipped her around, landing her flat on her back.

Lifting her arms, she found his neck and twined them around it, pulling him down for a kiss, but he kept the kiss light and continued down her throat, kissing and nipping his way to her aching breasts.

When he took her nipple between his lips, she arched up and moaned. "Goodness, Uriel. I wanted you to do this for so long."

He chuckled around her nipple and then bit it lightly before moving to the other one. It hurt, but in a good way, and as she threaded her fingers in his long hair, he bit the other one. This time it hurt even more, and she was sure he'd drawn blood, and as he started sucking on it, she had the crazy thought that her one-night stand was a vampire.

It was silly, but the idea of hooking up with a vampire fueled her desire to a whole new level.

I'm certifiable.

There was a difference between having a vivid imagination and actually convincing herself that what she was imagining was true.

When he slid lower, his intention was clear, and Gabi wantonly spread her knees wider to give him better access, and as his mouth made contact, she gripped his hair and arched off the couch.

It was so hard to keep her eyes closed.

She could feel his lips on her, his tongue lapping at her juices as if it was the best nectar he'd ever tasted. His growls and groans of approval reverberated through her body while providing a lewd soundtrack.

Gabi wanted to watch, but she didn't dare open her eyes.

What if she did, and he disappeared?

It was one more crazy thought, but she kept her eyes closed, nonetheless.

Not wanting to pull out his hair, she let go and gripped the couch instead, her fingernails digging into the soft velvet. "What are you doing to me?"

Instead of answering, he reached for her nipple and pinched it as he stabbed his tongue into her entrance and fucked her with it.

"Oh, my God," she croaked, her hips undulating with his lapping.

She'd never been eaten out and tongued like that before, and it was exquisite.

Pulling his tongue out, he replaced it with two fingers and then used it on the bundle of nerves at the top of her entrance.

Gabi was a hair away from climaxing, everything inside her coiling upon itself until it was so tight that she couldn't breathe.

When he pushed his fingers even deeper and hooked them inside of her while swiping his tongue just right over her clit, the coil sprang free, exploding from her with a moan that must have been incredibly loud, but she couldn't hear it because her climax was still roaring in her ears.

When Gabi's butt finally touched the couch again, her legs were shaky, and her throat felt hoarse as if she'd shouted her climax all over the hotel's sixty-ninth floor, which she probably had.

"Wow," she murmured. "Can I open my eyes now?"

"Not yet."

The sound of clothing being removed brought a smile to her lips.

"Finally."

When he climbed on top of her, the feel of his hard length against her entrance was a temptation she didn't want to resist. Putting her hands on his shoulders, she pulled him down for a kiss.

They kissed softly, like lovers who had known each other forever, their lips and tongues practiced in the dance of seduction they had perfected over the years.

But it was just an illusion, and tomorrow, Uriel would be gone, and she would move on.

As a tear slipped from her eye, he swiped it with his lips. "Why are you sad?"

"I'm not," she lied. "It's what I do after I orgasm so hard that I can't breathe."

He chuckled. "Such a pretty little liar."

Nevertheless, his erection twitched against her entrance as if in gratitude for her compliment.

Claiming her mouth with another kiss, he thrust his hips in one brutal move and seated himself deep inside her.

"Uriel!" She threw her head back.

"Did I hurt you?" he murmured against her throat.

Yes, he did, but she didn't want to tell him that, or he would stop. He was larger than anyone she'd been with before, but she was already getting used to the sensation, and the initial shock of his penetration was turning into pleasure.

"Don't stop," she whispered.

"I wouldn't dream of it." He gripped her hip and started thrusting slowly and deliberately inside her.

Gabi had a feeling that he was watching her face to gauge her reaction, and only when he was convinced that all she was experiencing was pleasure did he start going faster and deeper.

Her fingernails must have left grooves on his back, but that didn't slow him down one bit, and his groans of pleasure were turning more and more animalistic.

Just when she thought he was about to climax, he pulled out, flipped her around, yanked her ass up, and entered her from behind.

Wow, the guy couldn't make up his mind about how he wanted her—front or back or even sideways, but they hadn't done that yet.

Gabi had no problem with any of that.

It was refreshing.

Exciting.

Exhilarating.

From this angle, he was impossibly deep inside of her, and she wondered at her body's ability to accommodate him, but it was as if they were made for each other.

Except for that first shocking moment of penetration, they were a perfect fit.

Reaching around her, he feathered his fingers over her sensitive nub, applying just the right amount of pressure to heighten her pleasure without overstimulating her, and when she was about to explode again, she heard him hiss, and then he bit her shoulder so hard that she screamed.

The pain was gone almost immediately, the burn replaced by a cooling sensation, and Gabi wondered whether she'd imagined it, but her thoughts were obliterated as a climax exploded over her like a tornado, and it didn't end with just one. She wasn't sure whether it was a string of orgasms or the same one that came in waves, but with each new surge, she was catapulted higher to the clouds and beyond—the euphoric bliss indescribable.

Onegus

negus strode into the lab and headed straight for Roni's station. "Good morning." He pulled a rolling stool from the nearest desk and sat next to the young hacker. "Show me what you got."

"Nothing exciting." Roni clicked on his keyboard, and a grainy black-and-white passport photo appeared. "Uriel Delgado, age thirty-one, born in the USA to Portuguese parents, currently resides in Portugal and has Portuguese citizenship in addition to his American one."

"Can you make the picture sharper?"

"Sure." Roni clicked on his keyboard, and the passport picture filled the screen in moments.

"I'll admit he's a good-looking fellow, but Gabi's description was grossly exaggerated."

Roni arched a brow. "How did she describe him? Does it match the picture?"

"She didn't actually mention any particular features. Gabriella said that he was as good-looking as Orion and me, which naturally made us think that he might be an immortal, potentially a Doomer, although members of the Brotherhood are usually not as striking as Orion." Onegus felt awkward talking about himself as handsome, and the truth was that he wasn't in the same league as Orion's godly perfection, so it was okay for him to exclude himself from the comparison. "Their mothers don't have the luxury of being discriminating about the men who father them, and Navuh doesn't care about how his warriors look. In the past, it was all about brawn and cruelty; now, it's about brains."

Roni snorted. "The next generation of Doomers will probably look like me. I don't look like a descendant of the gods, and that's really annoying since I'm the great-grandson of a god, and I'm damn close to the source. I probably resemble my human father, and he must have been a very average-looking guy for me to come out like this." He waved a hand over his face. "He's still around, so theoretically I could track him down, but my mother doesn't want me to do that. She says it wouldn't do me any good to see him as he's old now and most likely married with several kids."

"True." Onegus nodded. "Most of us never knew who our fathers were. That's how it was for us until we started finding Dormants. At least you know you got your brains from your human father, and that's much more valuable than looks. You should be thankful for that."

Onegus would have loved to tell the kid that he was handsome, but the truth was that Roni was average looking, which must have rankled in a village full of gorgeous immortals.

"I agree." Roni smirked. "It's a great trade-off." The smirk turned into a frown. "But why couldn't I have gotten both? Just look at Kaia. She's brilliant and gorgeous, despite being a weak immortal who is far removed from the source, and she took a long time to transition despite being so young. I was the same age as she is now when I transitioned."

"I guess it's up to the Fates." Onegus really didn't want to get into a discussion about genetics. First of all, he didn't know much about it, and secondly, he was pressed for time. "What else did you discover about Uriel Delgado?"

"That's it. He left the States with his parents when he was six and hadn't been back for over twenty years. The first time he came for a visit was five years ago, and since then, he's been visiting quite frequently. If you want, I can find out which hotel he's staying at, and if he rented a car, I can find out the license plate number so we can track it."

Onegus looked at the photograph again. The guy could be an immortal, but he was most likely human.

"Does he have social media?"

Roni shook his head. "Nothing. But before you get your panties in a wad, that doesn't mean he's a fake. We create fake social media accounts for all clan members' assumed identities, and everyone who knows what they are doing does the same. If this passport and his other information is a counterfeit, someone has done an excellent job of it, and those kinds of people would have included a social media profile as well."

Onegus pushed to his feet. "So, what you are basically telling me is that if someone's info looks too complete, it's more suspicious than if it's lacking?"

"It depends. If it's a bad fakery, then less is less. But if it's a good one, then sometimes less means more, and more means less."

Onegus shook his head. "Now I'm even more confused. Is there any way you can hack into the Portuguese database to find out more about him? Tax returns, marriage certificates, etc?"

Roni grimaced. "I don't speak the language, and it will take time I don't have, but I can search for a local hacker to do the job for us. Do you want to spend time and money on this?"

Onegus glanced at the picture again. The guy looked like a typical Southern European, with dark hair, eyes, and olive-toned skin. He was good-looking, but that didn't mean he was an immortal. Human males could be just as handsome, especially since the advent of plastic surgery that could correct small imperfections. Should he spend any more time investigating a guy who seemed legit?

Gabi might see him once or twice, get her itch scratched, and then move into the village and start looking for an immortal to induce her. When she saw the selection available to her, Uriel Delgado would be of no more interest to her or anyone else in the clan.

"Nah. You're right. It's probably a waste of time."

Gabi

G abi wasn't surprised to wake up alone in bed. Uriel hadn't made any promises about staying the night, and she remembered his friend's comment about an early morning meeting.

Had he left a note, though?

Snatching her phone off the nightstand, it dawned on her that she'd passed out on the couch last night, which meant that Uriel had carried her to bed and tucked her in.

He'd also collected her phone from the coffee table and connected it to the charging cable on the nightstand.

That was so thoughtful of him.

Releasing a contented sigh, Gabi turned her phone on and checked her messages. As usual, there were several from her clients, probably asking about food substitutions and confessing to not following their prescribed diet, but before she read any of them, she scrolled until she saw the one she was looking for.

Last night was incredible. I wish I could have stayed in bed with you, but I had an early morning meeting. I'll get in touch later today, probably in the evening. Have a wonderful day, and thank you for the smile you put on my face. It's going to stay with me throughout the day.

"Oh, that's so sweet." Gabi hugged the phone to her chest and then reread the message two more times before typing a reply.

Ditto. I'll be smiling all day long too.

The rest of the messages could wait for after she'd used the bathroom.

Surprisingly, she wasn't sore. It had been a while since she'd been with anyone other than her battery-operated boyfriend, and her BOB was modestly sized and gently used.

Neither could describe Uriel.

It had been pretty intense with him, and she'd fully expected to pay the price for last night's fun today, but there was no discomfort whatsoever, which meant that in addition to carrying her to bed, he'd also cleaned her up before tucking the blanket around her.

It was so damn sweet that it brought tears to her eyes.

A glance around the bathroom confirmed her suspicions. There was a pile of used washcloths in the corner that hadn't been there before.

What a considerate guy—

Wait a minute.

She'd expected to be itchy and sticky because they hadn't used a condom.

Oh, hell. How stupid could she get?

She'd invited a stranger to her hotel room and had had unprotected sex with him?

It was his fault.

Every man she'd been with after her divorce had taken care of the condom part. She couldn't remember even one instance of having to remind a guy to put one on. Everyone knew that it wasn't safe otherwise. That was why it hadn't occurred to her to check whether Uriel was using protection.

She wasn't even on the pill!

"Way to go, Gabi. You might have gotten knocked up by a stranger."

But wait, her period had ended the first day of the conference, so there was no way she was ovulating.

"That's a relief." She put her hands on the vanity and made a disapproving face. "Dumb luck, Gabi. You were saved by sheer dumb luck."

Looking closer, she lifted her shoulder, expecting to see a bite mark, but her skin was as smooth and blemish-free as always.

"That's weird."

She could have sworn that Uriel had bitten her pretty hard, but she must have imagined it.

"Or maybe he got into my head and made me experience a phantom bite." She laughed at her reflection.

After what she'd learned yesterday evening, that wasn't such a crazy idea. Or maybe her mind had finally snapped, and she had imagined everything, including the sex god who'd made her black out from pleasure.

What the hell was that about, though?

She'd never blacked out from sex before, but it had been such a traumatic day that her brain might have short-circuited. It had started with the stress of anticipating the long flight, then its cancellation, then flying first class and drinking too much champagne while flirting with Uriel, and then Eric had pulled that fang stunt, and she'd fainted.

It was a miracle that she hadn't passed out before Uriel had even gotten to her room. She should have been exhausted. Heck, after the day she'd had, she should still be tired but felt great instead.

Well, except for the anxiety over contracting an STD, or the less likely but not entirely impossible pregnancy.

After a quick shower Gabi put on the hotel bathrobe, made herself a cup of coffee, and sat on the couch with her phone clutched in her hand.

She should answer her clients first, but she was too anxious to concentrate on them and typed a text to Uriel instead.

I had a great time with you last night, but this morning I realized that you didn't use protection. How could you have been so irresponsible? I blame myself, too. I should have paid attention, but I expected you to take care of it. I hope you didn't give me any sexually transmitted diseases or get me pregnant.

Gabi hesitated a moment before sending the text. There was a very slim chance Uriel could have gotten her pregnant, and she should have mentioned that pregnancy wasn't likely, but she was mad, and she wanted him to freak out the same as she had.

Then again, she was also at fault for not verifying that he used protection, but that only made her angrier.

Nevertheless, she hit send, lifted her coffee mug, and leaned back.

Jade

"**G**ood morning, Ingrid." Jade offered the designer her hand. "This is a very nice showroom you have here."

Photographs of interiors done in different styles hung on the walls, some from private residences and some from hotel rooms, and it was easy to see that the same person had been in charge of designing them all, whether the style was contemporary or traditional. Ingrid liked warm woods and light flooring, and the accessories provided colorful accents. Pictures, pillows, blankets, vases, and potted plants were strategically scattered throughout the rooms.

"Thank you." Ingrid smiled. "For the longest time, I worked from my place, and it was a pain having people come over to choose furniture or ask to be teamed with a different roommate. That's why I understand your pain, and it must be even more difficult for you because you live with a mate and a daughter. I only had a roommate who didn't mind the constant flow of people."

Jade nodded. "I feel like I've taken over Phinas's home."

"Let me show you the spare room." Ingrid led her down the hallway and opened the door. "I've already had the bed taken out, and I asked Onegus to send a desk and a chair from one of the classrooms. So, if you want, you can start using it right away."

The room was clean, and the wall art was probably there when it was still a bedroom, but it was more than she'd expected. All she needed to add were a few more chairs, or if she wanted to keep it more traditionally Kra-ell, she could get a few floor pillows.

"It's perfect. Thank you."

"I'm glad. Do you want to return to the showroom and look through furniture catalogs? I'm sure that in the long run, you will need more than a chair and a small desk. A conference table, perhaps?"

"I was actually thinking about floor pillows. That's how I traditionally conducted meetings before my compound was attacked."

"Of course." Ingrid looked slightly offended or maybe disappointed that Jade didn't want to invest time and effort into decorating. "Do you want me to take the desk out?"

"No, I'll use it when I need to do administrative work. The floor pillows are for meetings. I don't have time to look through catalogs. Can you pick something for me and tell me how much it will cost?"

Ingrid frowned. "I'd rather not. Floor pillows can be done in countless combinations of fabrics with different textures, patterns, and colors. I have several books with samples that you can flip through."

Evidently the designer didn't want to decide for her.

Perhaps some flattery was needed. "You have great taste and a lot of experience, Ingrid." Jade waved a hand over her outfit and smiled. "As you can see, I don't. There is a reason all my clothes are either black, gray, or olive. That way, I don't need to think about what I'm going to put on in the morning. Can you please decorate my office for me? I'm positive that it will come out a hundred percent better than anything I can come up with."

Ingrid let out a breath. "Can you at least give me some clues? What are your color preferences?"

"I like bold colors and comfortable, durable fabrics."

Ingrid tilted her head. "Do you like Moroccan decor?"

"I like the colors but not how busy the patterns are. Can you marry Japanese minimalism with a Moroccan color palette?"

The designer's eyes brightened. "Now I know precisely what you want. I'll have a design ready for you by tomorrow."

Jade hadn't wanted to make a big production out of it and hoped that Ingrid would just order a few items to make the room fit the way Kra-ell traditionally conducted meetings, but apparently, that was not how things worked with the designer, and Jade didn't want to start their relationship on the wrong foot.

"Thank you. I know how busy you are, and I truly appreciate you taking the time to help me furnish my new office."

Ingrid's smile grew wider. "You've given me a challenge, a new style that I haven't seen anyone attempt before. I will enjoy playing around with it."

As the front door chimed, announcing a new visitor to the design center, Ingrid offered Jade her hand. "Welcome aboard, partner. I'll see you here tomorrow."

"Thank you."

As Ingrid went to take care of her customer, Jade took another look at her new office and then slipped out through the sliding door to the backyard and out through the side gate.

Security was not an issue in the village, and no one locked their doors. The fences around the backyards were for privacy, not security.

Glancing at her watch, Jade quickened her step. Talking with Ingrid had taken longer than expected, and she was late. Kagra would keep Rishana and Sheniya and the rest of the Kra-ell team busy, but that wasn't how Jade liked to run things. When she called a meeting, she always planned to be the first one there.

That was why Ingrid's offer was such a timely gift. Once the place was set up, Jade wouldn't need to rush from place to place to meet with people. It was far from perfect, and having a private area for her people to train and to gather in would have been better, but she'd promised herself to take things one step at a time and not obsess about the long list of items still pending on her to-do list.

Gabi

As the minutes ticked away, and there was still no response from Uriel, Gabi's chest tightened with anxiety.

Had she gone too far?

Had her text been too accusatory?

After all, it was her responsibility to protect herself, and she shouldn't delegate it to anyone else.

Letting out an exasperated breath, she closed her eyes and dropped her head back on the overstuffed cushions of the couch.

It would be a shame if this was how things ended between them.

Uriel was supposed to be a one-night stand, but last night had just whetted her appetite, and she wanted one more taste. Not that it would be enough, but given that there was no future for them, perhaps it was better to pull the Band-Aid off sooner rather than later.

Regrettably, Uriel wasn't immortal, and it was a shame because she really liked him.

It wasn't just because of his gorgeous face and great body. He was sweet and considerate and didn't fit the stereotype of the hot bad boy. So, he was a little bit of an airhead and had forgotten to put a condom on, but she was guilty of the same thing, so she couldn't hold that against him.

When her phone pinged with an incoming text, Gabi was so startled that the device almost flew out of her hands. She fumbled to hold on to it but then couldn't focus her eyes to read the text.

She had to squint to make out the words.

I'm sorry. It didn't occur to me that I would need one. I'm clean and can't get you pregnant, so you have nothing to worry about.

Gabi reread the short text to make sure she hadn't misunderstood anything.

Why couldn't he get her pregnant?

Was there something wrong with him?

And why hadn't it occurred to him that he would need protection?

Had he thought she'd invited him to her hotel room to chat?

No one was that naive. He was probably lying to avoid taking responsibility for his mistake. He'd gotten carried away the same way she had and had forgotten the condom, and he might be clean or not, but he was probably just making up the stuff about being infertile.

Damn, she hated liars.

She'd had enough of that with Dylan, who had lied to her about everything and denied having affairs until she'd shown him the proof.

When she'd started suspecting him and confided her suspicions to her brother, Gilbert had hired a private investigator to follow Dylan around. It had been shocking to discover how many women her ex had been screwing on the side, especially given that, at the same time, he had also been having plenty of sex with her.

It was a wonder that he'd managed to hold on to a job and an even greater wonder that he hadn't given her an STD.

Dylan was a sex addict, which was one of the things he had said in his defense, explaining his addiction as an unquenchable thirst for love.

Gabi groaned.

If Uriel was a liar, it was best she'd discovered it sooner rather than later. She had no room in her life for liars.

"Focus, Gabriella, and repeat until you get it through your thick skull—Uriel is just a hookup, not boyfriend material, and not future husband material."

It was her rotten luck to find a man who was a nice guy in addition to being a sex god, but who she couldn't have even if he was honest because she was about to jump down the rabbit hole.

He could, however, be a hookup for one more night.

Taking a deep breath, she typed a message back.

I'm glad you are clean, and I'm sorry about your fertility issues, but if we meet again, please bring a condom with you. I don't think I can order them from room service.

Hopefully, the humor would take the sting out of her demand.

The three dots appeared immediately, and she didn't have to wait long for his reply.

I wish I could call you instead of answering with a text, but I'm in the middle of a meeting, and my friends are giving me dirty looks. I'm so glad you want to see me again, and I didn't blow my chances with you by admitting to being a moron with a low sperm count.

"Oh, my goodness. He really is infertile."

Or he could be perpetuating the lie.

In either case, his answer was so sweet that it was moving. What hunk in the history of hunks would have admitted those things to a woman he'd just met?

None that Gabi had ever met, and she'd met many in her personal life as well as in her practice. Cleveland wasn't Los Angeles, but it still had actors and models, and some of them needed help maintaining their ideal weight, so they came to her for help.

Gabi texted back.

Call me when you are done with your meetings. I want to see you one more time tonight before I leave tomorrow.

She had a flight back home on Wednesday, which meant that she had only one day left to visit her family in their village. She had to check out of the hotel tomorrow morning and spend the rest of her short vacation with them. After all, they had been the reason for her braving the flight over.

Jade

Phinas's dining room had never been as full of people as it was now.

Jade was grateful he was at the downtown office and didn't have to witness the Kra-ell invasion of his home. He'd told her a hundred times, if not more, that she should think of the house as theirs, not his, but she had trouble doing that. She hadn't chosen a single item of decor, hadn't changed the location of any of the plants, and hadn't even taken more than a tiny section of his closet.

Phinas was not a fancy dresser by any stretch of the imagination, but he had at least four times as many articles of clothing as she did.

"Anyone want any more?" Kagra lifted her empty glass of vodka with cranberry. She was handing it out as if this was her house, but Jade didn't say a thing.

Her second-in-command had a way with people that Jade lacked, and if a bottle of vodka smoothed things over, it was well worth it. The problem was that Jade couldn't order it online and would have to ask someone to get it for her.

None of the Kra-ell had cars, which was probably why the four young males Kagra had recruited for the mission were so eager to go.

Vrog and Aliya had their own reason for being excited about the mission, but it probably had more to do with visiting Vrog's former school than curiosity about the scouts. Even though it was no longer his, Vrog was proud of it, and he wanted Aliya to see what he had managed to build.

Sheniya and Rishana looked suspicious and sour as usual. They had both arrived on Igor's pod, which made them the oldest members of the community, and that might have been the source of their animosity, especially Sheniya, who thought that the faint traces of royal blood she carried entitled her to special treatment.

She had begrudgingly accepted Jade's position as Igor's prime and later the new community's leader only because Jade's triangle was darker than hers. That alone was enough for Jade to doubt the female's intelligence. Having faint traces of royal blood was meaningless, and it wasn't what made Jade a good leader.

Still, Sheniya's dark triangle, however faint, might convince the scouts that they were dealing with someone who was in charge.

Sheniya leaned back with the fresh drink Kagra had handed her. "Finally, you realize how important blood is." She turned her eyes to Jade. "All that talk about meritocracy becomes nonsense when proof of royalty is stamped on one's tongue." She extended the appendage and flipped the tip in a show of agility.

Rishana laughed. "Is that how you are going to greet the scouts? You're going to waggle your tongue at them and say, I have royal blood, therefore you must obey me?"

The males and Kagra chuckled, but Jade kept a straight face.

Sheniya turned to her. "That's a good question. What am I supposed to tell them?"

Jade hadn't thought it through yet. "That depends on the last time they were awake and what they knew. I have to assume they didn't know about the ship's arrival or would have looked for us. You can tell them what happened to the ship but don't tell them about Igor. It will be interesting to find out whether they knew about the assassins hidden among the settlers."

"Why would they?" Rishana asked. "They were sent by our queen, and the assassins were planted by the Eternal King. The scouts could only know what she knew."

Jade shrugged. "I'm no longer sure of anything. For all we know, the Eternal King could have also planted spies among the scouts."

"Not possible," Sheniya said. "The scouts were hand-picked by the queen. She knew each of them in person."

That was true. They had been selected from the queen's guard, so unless the Eternal King had created clones of those guards, the scouts were bound by vows of loyalty to the queen.

The question was how Sheniya knew that. The scouts' identities hadn't been public knowledge, and Sheniya shouldn't have known they had been selected from the queen's guard unless she knew one of them personally.

"How do you know who the scouts were?"

"One of them was my uncle. My mother told me to look for him when I got to Earth." Sheniya lifted her drink and threw it down her throat. "Not many Kra-ell warriors reach old age, but if they do, it's their family's responsibility to take care of them. It was up to me since I was the only family my uncle would have on Earth. Maybe I will still get to fulfill my duty."

That had sounded reasonable enough.

The queen's guard was usually selected from those who had some traces of royal blood in them, and Sheniya's uncle fit the profile.

"That's very honorable of you," Vrog said.

Sheniya shrugged. "It's my duty. We are all bound by it."

Pavel raised his hand. "I have a question."

"Go ahead."

"What are the four of us supposed to do?" He waved a hand over himself and the other three males. "Are we there to protect Sheniya and Rishana? And who are we supposed to take orders from, the Guardians or Kagra?"

Jade thought that Kagra had explained their duties, but evidently, she hadn't.

"We know the location of the signals, but for all we know, the pods could be buried deep underground, and you will have to dig them out. Also, we don't know what state the scouts are in. They might need to be transported to a hospital."

"We might also search for another pod in Lugu Lake," Vrog said. "That's where Aliya grew up, and it seems like there might be a pod there as well, but the excavation site is booby-trapped, and the humans digging there are being very careful. We can do a better job, but whether we get to do that or not is up to the guy with the digging permit."

"Who's that?" Pavel asked.

"Kalugal," Kagra said. "But let's not get carried away. The excavation site in Lugu Lake will probably mean another mission for us."

"Hold on." Pavel lifted a hand. "How large was the scouting team? Did they arrive in two pods? And why would the pods land in two different places? They didn't crash land."

Those were valid questions, but again, Jade didn't have the answers. "We weren't told how large the scouting team was and what exactly their mission was. I find it odd that they didn't make any effort to find the gods, who had already been settled on Earth by then. But this is not the time for speculation." She glanced at her watch. "You are departing for the clan's landing strip in five hours, and we need to go over the chain of command and the conduct I expect from you." She looked pointedly at Sheniya and Rishana. "If you screw up this mission, it will be a long time before the immortals let us join forces with them again, and that includes the war on trafficking, which many of our people wish to take part in. I want your behavior to be exemplary and leave an impression of professionalism, courtesy, and dedication. I don't want to hear about any immature squabbles or temper tantrums. Am I clear?"

"Yes, Mistress." Vrog bowed his head.

"It's yes, Jade, and I'm not worried about you." She kept her eyes on the two females. "Vow it, or you are not going."

Gabi

G abi got dressed in a state of funk.

The excitement over meeting Uriel again was tinged with sadness because it would be their last time together, and that confused and alarmed her.

Why was she mourning the end of what was basically a pleasant hookup?

Ugh, who was she kidding?

Uriel had rocked her world, which hadn't happened with any of the men she'd dated since her divorce. Thinking back to her dating history over the last eleven years, she couldn't bring up even one that she would have wanted to see again, and it wasn't because they had all been so terrible.

Some were nice men who could have been great for someone else, just not for her. A lot of it had to do with how broken she'd felt after the divorce and her trust issues. Even though she was fully aware of her faulty reasoning, Gabi had deemed every guy she'd gone out with guilty of duplicity until proven innocent.

Yeah, that hadn't worked out great for her, which was why she was still single.

Perhaps she should go shopping to lift her mood.

She needed some sexy lingerie, and perhaps also a pair of slim-fitting pants and a nice loose blouse, or maybe a tight skirt that showed off her legs. None of the dresses she'd packed for this trip were designed to entice or make her look sexy. Their purpose was to make her look professional, which was also fine for visiting family but not for going out with a hot guy, even if they never left her hotel room.

On the other hand, wearing a dress last night had proven expeditious. It had been very easy to take off. So maybe she should go for a casual dress that was sexier than what she had brought with her but still comfortable and easily discarded.

The problem was that she couldn't fit any additional clothing in her carry-on, so if she bought more clothes, she would have to leave them in Gilbert or Eric's home. Except, once she was in the mall, she would not remember that she was planning on moving in with her brother in the near future, and she would either not buy anything or get a suitcase.

Whatever. She could use the new suitcase to store her purchases.

When her phone rang, her heart accelerated, hoping it was Uriel, but then she realized it wasn't her regular phone ringing, but the one Gilbert had given her yesterday.

She pulled it out of her purse and smiled at her brother's photo on the screen. "Good morning, Gilbert."

"Good morning, Gabi. How was your night?"

"It was great." She affected a sugary tone. "Thanks for asking."

"Did he show up?"

She chuckled. "A lady doesn't kiss and tell."

"So, the answer is yes. You're a big girl, Gabi, and you deserve to have fun, but I hope you are being careful. Safety first."

Gabi winced. She hadn't been careful, but Gilbert didn't need to know that.

"Of course."

"Good. I'm glad that you are cautious. So, are you ready to visit your family in our new home?"

Realizing she remembered everything she'd learned about immortals was a relief. "I was afraid that Orion's mind trick would make it impossible to talk about you-know-what over the phone."

"He excluded everyone who was with you in the restaurant from the prohibition, but it's never a good idea to speak about those matters on a device that is not secure or a place that might not be safe. As it happens, the hotel you are staying in belongs to the clan, and your room is free of listening devices and surveillance cameras, but you need to be careful when you do so from anywhere else. Always use the clan-issued phone."

"Got it."

The thing looked like a standard iPhone, just without the logo, and was programmed to respond only to her. It only unlocked after scanning her face and locked the moment her face wasn't in front of it. The immortals took security seriously, and rightfully so.

If the secret ever got out, they would be hunted and experimented on to discover the secret of their immortality.

"We've gotten distracted," Gilbert said. "You still didn't answer whether you want me to come to pick you up?"

She felt a little guilty about postponing her visit by one more day, but then she was about to move in with her family in the near future and would get to see them all of the time, so it wasn't a big deal.

"I want to stay in the hotel for one more night, but I'm coming to your place Tuesday morning and staying overnight. My return flight is Wednesday afternoon."

"Are you spending the day with that guy?"

"No, I'm only seeing him in the evening, but I want to do some shopping. Do you think Karen would like to join me?"

"She's at work, but maybe she can meet you for lunch. Call her. And use the new phone. Her number is already in your contacts list, and so are the phone numbers of everyone else in the family."

"Awesome. I'll give her a call right now."

"I wish you could stay longer," Gilbert said. "You finally get up the courage to come, but it's only for three days, and you spend two of them away from us."

Got guilt?

"I know, but I'm about to move in with Eric and Darlene and spend so much time with you that you will get sick of seeing me all the time."

"Never. You have no idea how excited I am about you joining us here. Our family wasn't complete without you."

"Oh, that's so sweet. How about you, Eric, and Darlene join Karen and me for lunch? We can meet somewhere in the middle so it's convenient for everyone. I'll call Kaia too. Cheryl is at school, right?"

"No, she's actually on her summer break."

Gabi winced. "I forgot. Is she doing anything interesting over the summer?"

"Yeah, she's working on her Instatock account."

Gabi was the worst aunt ever. She knew how important that app was to Cheryl, and she hadn't even asked about it.

Talk about self-absorbed.

All she could think about was how difficult it was to wrap her head around what they were telling her and about her infatuation with Uriel.

She should have asked her nieces how they were doing, Kaia about the project she was working on and Cheryl about school, and she should have asked Karen about her new job. And what was Gilbert doing with his properties? And Eric with his jets?

"I'll call Cheryl too. Maybe she'd like to take a break from building her social media empire and hang out with us for a little bit."

"Call Karen first and see if she's available."

"I'll do that. Talk to you later, Gilbert. I love you," she tacked on at the end.

"I love you too, Gabi."

Kian

After a quick stop at the lab and a chat with William and Roni, Kian joined Onegus in the conference room. "The good news is that there were no more signals. If the team doesn't find anything at Chengdu, which is likely, I want them to continue to Lugu Lake and help Kalugal with the excavations over there. He's actually planning to take Jacki and Darius and several of his men and fly directly there."

"I don't know whether to hope that they find something or that they don't." Onegus pulled a bottle of water from the fridge and opened it. "In any case, it will be an interesting experiment to see how well the Kra-ell get along with the Guardians."

"Indeed." Kian pulled out a chair and sat down. "Especially since Jade regards the two females as troublemakers. If they can behave and follow orders, then working with the Kra-ell should be a viable option."

"Yeah, well. I have a problem with including warriors that haven't gone through Guardian training in combined missions. I have the same misgiving about Kalugal's men."

Kian arched a brow. "They did remarkably well in Karelia and on the decoy ship. I think that they have proven their worth."

"They did, and I appreciated the help, but I would like them to train with our men. I brought it up with Kalugal, and he said that they don't have time. That's nonsense. All I asked for was one weekend a month. I'm sure they can spare the time."

"They probably don't want to." Kian glanced at his watch to check how much time he had left before his next meeting. "They are not eager to join missions. The only reason Kalugal volunteered their help in Karelia was that he didn't want to be left out of the loop. Now that he's a council member, he probably won't be as quick to volunteer his men."

Onegus chuckled. "Yeah, most likely. Kalugal views them as a resource, and he's not the sharing type."

"Right." Kian leaned back. "I spoke to Roni, and he told me about the snooping he did on the guy Gilbert's sister had met on the plane. Why did you consider him worthy of investigation?"

Kian was surprised that Onegus had even requested that of Roni based on a remark she'd made about the guy's looks. The chief had good instincts, and if he felt the need to investigate, then he had a good reason to do that.

Onegus shrugged. "She gushed about how incredibly good-looking he was and compared him to Orion and me, so naturally, I got suspicious. Doomers are usually not that striking, but there could be exceptions. I should have known that she was exaggerating. I've seen his passport photo, and the guy is handsome, but he's not in Orion's league. He also seems to be who he claims to be. They spent half the night together, and he left early in the morning. When he visited her, he pretended to be the delivery guy, but that's not a big deal. He stopped by the front desk on his way out and apologized, saying that he didn't want to get the receptionist in trouble. That's not something a Doomer would have done."

"Did you have him followed?"

"Why would I? If we follow every human a clan member hooks up with, we would need triple the number of Guardians we have. Gabi's fling is not a priority."

"Yeah, I guess you are right. When is she coming to the village?"

"She told Gilbert she would come tomorrow morning. I guess she wants to spend another night with her guy. But then she's flying back to Cleveland to finalize her affairs there. When she's ready to move into the village, Eric and Darlene are going to host her for as long as she needs." Onegus smiled. "I don't think it's going to be long at all. Gabriella Emerson is a looker, and she has a fiery personality. There will be plenty of suitors for her to choose from."

"It's up to the Fates and what they have planned for her." Kian turned his gaze to the door, which he had left open. "Who did Yamanu choose for his team?"

"He's taking Peter, Franco, and Jason."

"Is Mey going?"

Onegus shook his head. "Not this time. But if they don't find anything in Chengdu and the team continues to Lugu Lake, they are going to do so without Yamanu. He will book a commercial flight from Chengdu and come home."

"I can understand that. Who will take over leading the team in his absence?"

"Peter. He needs to gain experience as a team leader, and the Lugu Lake excavation is a low-risk mission that's a perfect learning opportunity."

Gabi

As the Uber driver stopped in front of Gino's, Gabi thanked the lady and stepped out.

The place was packed, but Karen had told her that they had a private room reserved on the second floor for special customers, and that was where they were meeting.

Two of Karen's friends from the university were joining them for lunch, but Gabi couldn't remember why. Did they work in the same department as Karen?

Karen was a system administrator, and she used to work for a large defense contractor, but she'd taken a pay cut to work at the university because they offered in-house daycare, and she preferred to have Ryan and Evan close by.

Despite never having kids, Gabi could understand that, and she was super excited to see her nephews. They must have grown so much since she'd last seen them.

Regrettably, Idina was in preschool, Kaia was too busy at work and couldn't get away, and Cheryl had made prior plans to hang out with friends.

Darlene was coming, though, and Gilbert had said that he and Eric might stop by after lunch and join the ladies for coffee.

"Hello." She smiled at the host. "My name is Gabriella Emerson, and I'm here for the private party on the second floor."

"Oh, yes, Signora Emerson." The guy grinned as if she was his favorite person in the world. "Follow me, *per favore*." He grabbed a menu and gestured with his hand toward the stairs.

If he wanted her to follow him, he should have gone ahead of her, but whatever. Given his lascivious smile, he wanted to look at her ass while she climbed the stairs.

Men lived for those small thrills, and she didn't begrudge them.

Well, to be fair, women did the same thing. If she was a restaurant hostess and Uriel was a client, she would have followed his fine ass up the stairs and admired it all the way.

The rickety stairs groaned under her feet as if she were still a hundred pounds overweight, or rather like a two-hundred-pound guy was climbing them behind her.

The host looked like someone who enjoyed food.

When they got to the second floor without the staircase collapsing under their combined weight, Gabi released a relieved breath and scanned the room for familiar faces. Her gaze got snagged on a stunning brunette holding a baby and grinning with a set of teeth that belonged in a commercial for dental work.

In fact, everything about the woman was commercial-worthy.

Gabi wasn't a fashionista, but she could recognize luxury brands when she saw them, and what the woman was wearing was head-to-toe Prada. She'd seen that exact same outfit of olive blouse and black trousers in a fashion magazine she'd bought for the clinic a couple of weeks ago.

Was the gorgeous brunette a famous actress? Or maybe the trophy wife of a famous Hollywood producer? But then, what was she doing with Karen?

"Gabi." Karen pushed to her feet and came over to give her a hug. "Let me introduce my friends." She walked over to a pretty blonde woman who was feeding an adorable baby girl with a spoon. "This is Syssi. Syssi, this is my sister-in-law, Gabriella."

Karen and Gilbert weren't officially married, but Gabi and Karen had always introduced one another as sisters-in-law. It was easier than getting into an explanation for why Karen and Gilbert had three kids together but hadn't gotten married yet.

The woman smiled and offered Gabi her hand. "It's so nice to finally meet you. I've heard a lot about you."

Gabi arched a brow. "You did? From Karen?"

What reason did Karen have to mention her to her coworkers? Neither of them looked like they needed a nutritionist.

Syssi glanced at Karen. "I thought Gabi was told."

"She was." Karen looked at the waiter. "It must be the effect of what Orion did to her."

The name sounded familiar, but Gabi couldn't remember where she'd heard it. A handsome face popped into her mind, dark hair, intelligent blue eyes—

"Alfonso," the brunette said. "Can you please tell Gino to get my favorite wine and bring it up? I'm in the mood to celebrate."

"Of course, Signora Amanda." He bowed, folding nearly in half and confirming Gabi's suspicion that the brunette was someone famous.

Karen waited until his footsteps faded before walking up to the woman. "This is Dr. Amanda Dokani. She heads the neuroscience lab in the university, and Syssi is her research assistant."

That was odd. How had Karen become friends with the two ladies if they didn't work in the same office as she did?

"It's a pleasure to meet you, Gabi." The professor smiled again. "This is my daughter, Evie, and the sweetie in the highchair is my niece, Allegra."

"The pleasure is all mine." Gabi waved at the older baby, who was watching her with eyes that seemed too old for the young child they belonged to.

"Oh, now I get the connection. You all have kids in Evan and Ryan's daycare." She looked for her nephews. "Where are they?"

"Over here." Karen pointed behind the table. "On the floor."

Gabi rushed around and gasped. "Oh, my goodness. Look at you! You are so big!" She crouched next to the boys, who were eyeing her with curiosity. "You don't remember me, but I'm your Aunt Gabi, and I'm so sorry I didn't visit you more often."

"Ga?" One of them lifted a toy truck and offered it to her.

"Thank you." She took it and glanced at Karen. "What am I supposed to do with it?"

Karen

K aren laughed. "You can make *vroom-vroom*
sounds." She demonstrated. "Or you can
admire the truck for a moment, say it's very
cool, and return it."

To Evan's great delight, Gabi did both.

"We need to do something about the block," Amanda
said. "Otherwise, it's not going to be any fun." She
pulled out her phone and scrolled through the contacts
with a manicured long fingernail. "Here you are." She
chose the number. "Hello, Orion. I'm sorry to bother
you, but Gabi is here, and she's confused. Can you please
modify your phrasing so she can remember everything
around us?"

As footsteps sounded on the stairs, they all turned
toward the landing, but it wasn't Gino or one of the
waiters. It was Darlene.

"Sorry for being late. Traffic was a bitch."

"Can you guard the entrance for a moment?" Karen motioned for her to stay where she was. "We need Orion to modify his instructions. Gabi doesn't remember what we told her because Amanda and Syssi are strangers to her."

"Right." Darlene nodded. "Go ahead. I'll tell you if anyone comes up."

"Here you go." Amanda handed the phone to Gabi. "Talk with Orion."

Eyebrows arched, she took the phone. "Why?"

Amanda waved her hand. "Just humor me."

Gabi put the phone against her ear. "Hi, Orion. Do I know you?"

Karen was the only adult in the room who couldn't hear what Orion was telling Gabi, but watching the woman's facial expression, she could see exactly when the memories resurfaced.

"Damn, this is confusing," Gabi told Orion. "How long will I have to live with this dual existence? It's like I have a split personality, and one half does not know what the other half knows. I can't go on like that."

A couple of seconds later, she nodded. "Tonight, I'm going to say goodbye to him, and tomorrow morning I'm coming to the village. Once that's done, I hope I can keep the memories whether I'm in company or alone."

A few moments later, Gabi nodded again. "Awesome. Thank you." She handed the phone back to Amanda. "I feel sorry for people who suffer from a split personality disorder. It's so confusing."

Amanda took the phone and put it on the table beside her bread plate. "It's no longer called multiple personality disorder. We now call it a dissociative disorder." She smiled. "It's not my field of expertise, so I can't really say much more about it, but I get how disorienting it must be for you."

Darlene abandoned her station by the door and came over to give Gabi a hug. "What I want to know is how it went with your mystery man last night."

"Oooh." Amanda clapped her hands. "A mystery man. That sounds exciting. Do tell, darling."

Karen took pity on Gabi, who looked like a deer caught in the headlights. "Before we get Gabi to entertain us with all the juicy details, let's introduce you properly." She waited for Gabi to sit down. "Syssi is the wife of the clan's leader, and Amanda is his sister, and she's also a council member."

Not sure whether she was allowed to tell Gabi about Annani, Karen looked at Amanda. "Should I continue?"

Amanda shook her head. "Let's keep some of the details for later. Poor Gabi looks like she's been hit over the head with a frying pan."

Gabi patted her head. "Is my hair that flat?"

As Amanda started to apologize for her comment, Gabi laughed. "I was just joking. I know what you meant, and the truth is that I have a headache." She rubbed her temples. "I get it every time I try to remember things I'm not supposed to remember around strangers. Since you are a neuroscientist, can you tell me whether I should worry about brain damage?"

Amanda looked unsure. "If it was to last much longer, I would have said that it was potentially harmful, but since it's only until tomorrow, you're probably safe. What I don't understand is why Orion felt the need to make you forget what you learned when you were around strangers and remember it when you were alone or with your family."

Gabi let out a long-suffering sigh. "It's because of a stupid comment I made about the guy I met on the flight being good-looking enough to be an immortal. They right away jumped to the conclusion that he was indeed an immortal, and perhaps even one of the enemy immortals." She scrunched her nose. "Dumbers? Is that what they are called?"

"Doomers," Darlene corrected. "It's an acronym for the Brotherhood of the Devout followers of Mortdh."

Gabi tilted her head. "That doesn't make Doom. It spells BDFOM." She chuckled. "It sounds like something kinky."

"The name is actually the Brotherhood of the Devout Order of Mortdh," Syssi said. "And there is nothing funny about them, but it's kind of funny that the first letter of the last four words of their bombastic name spells doom in English."

Gabi

G abi was about to ask about those Doomers, the clan's enemies that Syssi seemed very concerned about, but as the waiter came up with two bottles of Amanda's wine and two baskets of bread, she forgot what she was about to ask.

Once their server was done taking everyone's order and departed, she suddenly remembered what Onegus and Orion had said about them.

They were led by a guy named Navuh, who was up to no good. Trafficking was one of the things mentioned. They also had said that he wasn't generous and wouldn't have paid for his men to travel in first class. He also had sons who weren't actually his but who he claimed as his, and those sons might fly first class, but not all three at the same time.

Or were there more than three?

The sons were good-looking because their mothers were close to the source, whatever that meant, and they were also well-educated and therefore polite.

Uriel could very loosely fit that description.

He was good-looking and had a good vocabulary, so perhaps he was well-educated and polite. He was also a wonderfully generous lover, and she doubted the son of a misogynist would be into giving more pleasure to their female partners than receiving.

Navuh had to be a misogynist to deal in trafficking, right?

It wasn't possible to be one way in public and another in private. Of course, people could pretend, but that didn't change who they were at their core. She couldn't imagine a cheater like Dylan being honest in his business dealings, or someone that was a hundred percent loyal to his wife cheating on his business partners.

So yeah, she might be seeing the world in black and white while it was many shades of gray, but that only meant she was right most of the time and not all of the time, and that was good enough.

Amanda trained her impossibly blue eyes on her. "Fess up, sister. I want to hear all about the yummy hottie you met on the plane."

Gabi glanced at the baby girl who was chewing on a piece of baguette while watching them with her smart eyes and listening as if she could understand every word.

"It's okay." Her mother winked. "Allegra is good at keeping secrets."

The girl nodded, pulled the chewed-up piece of bread out of her mouth, and offered it to Gabi. "Yum."

Amanda laughed. "Yes, sweetie. The baguette is so very yummy."

Allegra gave her aunt a cute smile, shoved the bread back into her mouth, and resumed chewing.

Babies were fascinating, adorable, and very kissable, but they were also a lot of work. At some moments, Gabi craved a baby with excruciating intensity, and at others, she was glad to be single and childless and to have all the freedom to do what she pleased whenever she pleased.

Choices, choices. Life was all about making choices and hoping not to make the wrong ones.

"We are waiting." Amanda tapped the perfectly manicured fingernails of one hand on her opposite arm.

"There isn't much to tell. Uriel is gorgeous, sweet, polite, accommodating, and great between the sheets, but I'm probably not going to see him again after tonight." The thought brought tears to her eyes, but she managed to keep them at bay. "Although he looks like a god, he's human, and from what I was told, I need to find an immortal male to induce me. I don't suppose I can keep a human lover on the side, can I?"

Amanda shook her head. "If you don't bond with your inducer, which might happen, you can keep having hookups with humans after you turn immortal, but you can't have a long-term relationship with them. You will become stronger, your hearing and eyesight will improve dramatically, and you will heal from scrapes and bruises in moments instead of days. It's possible to hide all those things from a casual lover, but it's nearly impossible to hide them from someone you live with or even see on a regular basis."

Gabi hadn't known about all the perks that came with immortality that Amanda had just mentioned, and they sounded exciting, but would they help alleviate the heart-break of saying goodbye to Uriel forever?

Get a grip, Gabi. You've known the guy for less than twenty-four hours and had sex with him once. You are not saying goodbye to the love of your life.

So why the hell did it feel like she was?

Syssi cleared her throat. "Did you ask him what he does for a living?"

It was an obvious attempt to steer the conversation in a less depressing direction, and Gabi was grateful for it.

"Uriel said that he and his friends are flea market flippers and were hunting for treasures in Korea and other countries in the area, but somehow I doubt it. I think the three of them are starring in a movie or a show about flea market finds, and Uriel was staying in character."

"Why do you think that?" Amanda asked.

"Well, for starters, they came from South Korea, which everyone knows is where people go to get plastic surgery, especially men who don't want people to find out that they had chin implants to make their jaws look like they can cut stone, or hair transplants, or nose jobs, and whatever else. Secondly, flea market treasure hunting is not so lucrative that they could fly first class. And thirdly, they were flying to Los Angeles, the world capital of movie making."

Perhaps the story she'd painted in her mind had lost some of its vividness with each retelling because it sounded flimsy to her now. She knew nothing about the real business of flea market treasure hunting, and the fact that Uriel and his buddies were gorgeous and had just returned from South Korea didn't necessarily mean that they had undergone procedures there.

"It could be true," Amanda said. "Orion deals in antiques, and he finds undervalued treasures all over the world. He says that the Orient has recently emerged as a fertile hunting ground for great finds, so it's entirely possible for Uriel and his friends to find undervalued bargains that they can sell for a nice profit in the West."

Darlene

As Darlene listened to the exchange, she debated whether to tell Gabi about Roni's investigation and what he had discovered about Uriel.

Gabi would probably get upset that Onegus had asked Roni to do that, and there wasn't much to tell because none of the things Roni had discovered were incriminating in any way. But perhaps she would find it interesting that Uriel lived in Portugal, and it would ease her mind that he wasn't an actor.

Perhaps he was a wannabe actor, but he wasn't yet, and it wasn't likely that a movie studio was paying for his first-class ticket. Uriel was either making good money flipping flea market finds, or his parents were rich and were paying for him to travel in style.

"I have some information on Uriel," Darlene said. "But all of you must swear you won't tell anyone I spilled the beans."

Syssi grimaced. "You know how hard it is to keep secrets from our mates. Can I tell Kian?"

"He probably already knows what I'm going to tell you. It's just that Roni wasn't supposed to tell me, and if I tell Gabi, and Onegus finds out, he will be furious, and I don't want him to get mad at Roni."

Gabi lifted her hand. "Wait a minute. Are we talking about the same Roni, who is your son from a previous marriage? How did he find out information about Uriel?"

There was still so much that Gabi didn't know, and there hadn't been time to tell her.

"Yes, it's the same Roni, and he's the clan's hacker. Whenever they need to dig out information about someone, he's the guy they turn to."

Gabi pursed her lips and nodded. "Impressive. He must be really smart."

"He is, and it's not thanks to my ex. His father was a fling I had while temporarily separated from my husband." Darlene snorted. "For long years, I regretted returning to my husband and not pursuing a relationship with Roni's father, but it was all decreed by the Fates. I was supposed to meet Eric."

"Well." Amanda waved a hand. "Don't keep us in suspense. What did Roni find out about our mystery hunk?"

"His name is Uriel Delgado. He's thirty-one, was born in the US to Portuguese parents who returned to Portugal when he was a young boy. He hasn't been back to the States until about five years ago and has been visiting frequently since. He doesn't own or rent a residence in the States, and he doesn't have a car registered to his name."

Gabi's lips were still pursed. "How old was he when his parents took him to Portugal?"

"I think he was six. Why?"

"His English is perfect, but I could tell he was the child of immigrant parents. There was only a shadow of an accent in his English, and I couldn't tell which language contributed to it. Now I know why. Portuguese is so strange. It doesn't sound like Spanish."

"It's part of the Ibero-Romance group of dialects that evolved from colloquial Latin," Amanda said. "It has common roots with Spanish, but they are two separate languages."

Syssi frowned at her. "It never ceases to amaze me how much you know about so many topics."

Amanda laughed. "I had a long time to learn all those tidbits of information. Compared to you, I'm ancient."

"How old are you?" Gabi asked. "Or is it a rude question to ask an immortal?"

"It's not rude. I'm a young immortal. I'm only two hundred and fifty years old."

Gabi's eyes widened. "That's young? How old is the oldest member of your community?"

"That would be my grandfather," Darlene said. "He's over seven thousand years old."

"Wow." Gabi shook her head. "That's older than human civilization."

Amanda smiled. "That's because our ancestors were responsible for the creation of human civilization. Humanity would have eventually gotten there, but without their help, it would have taken much longer."

While the gods had been discussed extensively over dinner the day before, no one had told Gabi that some of the gods were still around. Gabi was under the impression that only their immortal descendants remained, and she was under compulsion to keep it all a secret. Nevertheless, they all seemed to share the same feeling that she shouldn't be told more while she was still hanging out with Uriel.

Logically, it didn't make sense to keep suspecting him of being an immortal after Roni had found his birth certificate, his parents' identities, and where he lived—the guy seemed to be legitimately human, and even Onegus didn't feel the need to investigate him any further. And yet, Darlene's gut feeling to exercise caution persisted.

"Well, at least I now know Uriel's last name." Gabi reached for the wine bottle and refilled her glass. "For some reason, he didn't want to tell me what it was." She took a sip. "Did Roni find out whether he was married?"

Darlene shook her head. "Roni doesn't speak Portuguese and is unfamiliar with their bureaucracy. He asked Onegus whether he wanted to hire a local hacker to find out more about Uriel, but Onegus didn't deem it a priority."

Gabi

Darlene threaded her arm through Gabi's. "I haven't been shopping in so long. Thanks for inviting me."

After lunch, the others had returned to work, but Darlene had taken the rest of the afternoon off to accompany her to the mall.

Gabi smiled. "Thank you for driving me."

"It's my pleasure. Let's check out the sale at Nordstrom." Darlene leaned closer to whisper in her ear, "They have a very nice lingerie department, but if you prefer a specialty store, I think they have a Frederick's in this mall."

The stuff they sold at that store looked like it was made for strippers or porn stars, and Gabi's tastes were demurer.

"Nordstrom is good enough."

"It is." Darlene nodded sagely, but the corner of her lips twitched in a suppressed smile. "To quote Eric, sexy lingerie is a waste of money because all he wants to do is take it off as fast as he can."

Gabi winced. "Please. I don't want to think about my brothers and sex."

"Pish posh. We are all grownups. When you come to live in the village, you will discover that immortals don't have human hang-ups about it."

What village and what immortals? Was the village a movie theater name, and there was a new movie about immortals Gabi had agreed to watch but had forgotten about?

As a headache pounded against her temples, she pulled her arm from Darlene's and rubbed at it. "What are you talking about?"

"Oh, right. Sorry about that. Forget I said anything."

Gabi was more than happy to do that. The headache was making her nauseous, and she needed to sit down.

"Do you mind if we take a break for coffee? I've gotten a sudden headache."

"Sure, no problem. Nordstrom has a great coffee shop." Darlene guided her back toward the entrance. "Sit down, and I'll get us coffees. How do you like yours?"

"Non-fat small cappuccino, please." Gabi scanned the small sitting area, but all the tables were taken.

"Sugar?"

Gabi shook her head and immediately regretted it as her headache had worsened. "No sugar and no artificial sweetener either." She spotted a couple getting up and rushed over to secure the table.

She heard Darlene chuckling and murmuring something under her breath, but with how noisy it was in the mall, she couldn't hear what it was.

Whatever.

It was probably something along the lines of how miserable a nutritionist's life was because of all the dietary restrictions. Her friends who didn't work in nutrition and fitness made similar comments, but Gabi no longer bothered to explain that it was a state of mind. Everyone made their own choices about how they wanted to live their lives and what they wanted to put in their mouths.

To her, coffee tasted great without any sugar, and it wasn't even a question of sacrificing anything. The hardest part wasn't the restrictions. It was always being mindful of portion size and nutritional value.

But people were judgmental, and they either thought that everyone who didn't make the same choices as them was doing things wrong or that she was trying to preach to them to adopt her ways.

Heck, no.

People paid her good money for that advice, and the only ones she'd tried to convert for free had been her brothers, but they had ignored her and continued eating like they were immortal.

Damn, the headache had just gotten worse.

Was it because it always made her angry when her brothers dismissed her on account of her being the youngest?

No, the cause of the headache couldn't be anger because she hadn't been mad at anything that Darlene had said. Strangely, the trigger seemed to be the word immortal.

As a piercing pain shot through her eyes, Gabi winced.

Evidently, she was allergic to that word even when she was just thinking it. Reaching into her purse, Gabi searched for the small container of Motrin she kept for emergencies, and when she found it, she glanced at Darlene to see if she was any closer in line to getting coffee so she would have something to wash the pills down.

It looked like it would be a while, so she pulled out her phone to check her messages.

As usual, most were from her clients, and as she scrolled through them, she tried to convince herself that she wasn't disappointed that there were none from Uriel.

It was after four in the afternoon, and if he wanted to make plans for later, he should have called her already or at least texted her.

She was replying to a client's text when the message she'd been waiting for came in. Abandoning the half-finished text, she switched to his contact to read what he wrote her.

I'm still in meetings, which is why I didn't call. Can you go out to dinner with me at seven?

Gabi forced herself to count to twenty before replying so he wouldn't think she had been so anxious to hear from him that she was constantly checking her messages.

My hotel has a restaurant with a great view of the city, and the food is good.

His reply arrived a moment later. *I'll meet you there at seven.*

"Someone looks in a much better mood." Darlene put a paper coffee cup in front of her. "Got some good news?"

Gabi smiled. "Uriel texted me. He's meeting me in the hotel's restaurant."

Darlene sat down and removed the lid from her coffee. "Who suggested the hotel? Was it Uriel or you?"

"I did." Gabi smiled sheepishly. "The distance to my room was a deciding factor."

Annani

Annani looked around the living room of her modest village house and sighed.

It was a nice room, but it was too quiet, and she missed Kian and Syssi's place. However, she would have been alone there this time of day as well, so feeling down made little sense. Her son and his wife were at work, and Syssi took Allegra with her to the university, but in the evenings the house filled up with baby sounds and cooking smells, and later with Kian's gruff voice that turned softer the longer he was home.

Staying with them had been very enjoyable, but it was time for her to resume her duties.

"I need to organize my schedule," she said aloud, even though she had only the Odus for company. "I need to make new appointments with clan members and also start meeting with the Kra-ell."

Oshidu walked over to her and bowed. "Should I retrieve your appointment book, Clan Mother?"

"No, thank you. I need to think of what I want to do first."

"As you wish, Clan Mother." He bowed again. "May I offer you a fresh cup of tea?"

"Yes, that would be lovely. Also, if you do not mind, put on some music for me. It is too quiet in this house."

"Of course, Clan Mother."

She did not need to specify which music she liked. Her Odus had stored every selection she had ever made in their memory banks, including what she liked to listen to with different activities.

When she needed to think, classical or instrumental music was best. Lyrics tended to distract her because she always pondered whether there was meaning behind them or if they were just a selection of words that went well with the melody and rhymed at the appropriate places.

With Tchaikovsky's Violin Concerto playing in the background, Annani started a mental list of people she needed to see.

Kaia still needed some help with the ghost of her previous incarnation, but it was not urgent. Nathalie and Andrew were taking fertility potions in the hopes of conceiving again, and she wondered how that was going, but it was not polite to inquire on matters of that kind over the phone.

Then there were the new immortal and Kra-ell couples that she wanted to meet for an afternoon tea and learn about the difficulties they were facing. She was very curious about how those pairings were working out.

The Fates' touch was evident in Jade and Phinas's union and Vanessa and Mo-red's.

On the face of things, the Fates' agenda was clear.

It seemed they wanted the immortal descendants of the gods and their old enemies to get along and show their ancestors that they had been wrong about the strict prohibition on such pairings.

Annani suspected that the Fates' tapestry had a much deeper and more intricate design than any god or mortal could discern. What if their intent was a new super race of people who exceeded the best genetic design the gods could master?

Was it possible that the Fates were behind keeping the twins in stasis long enough for the new pairings to produce offspring powerful enough to stand in their way?

Except, if that was the case, they would have paired Toven with a pureblooded Kra-ell female to achieve maximum results, or perhaps even paired Annani with a Kra-ell male.

Could one of these Kra-ell be the reincarnation of her Khiann?

Annani hoped that was not the case.

It was not that she thought them unattractive, but they just did not look like her Khiann.

Ever since she had been given the prophecy about Khiann's reincarnations fathering her seven children, she had always searched for men who resembled him. Tall, broad-shouldered, blue-eyed, and with a charming smile.

The Kra-ell were just too different.

Did she truly believe that each of her five children had been fathered by a reincarnation of Khiann, though?

Annani let out a sigh. The mortal males had all shared physical characteristics with him, and also some of his other attributes like innate leadership, intelligence, and moral decency, but none had been even a fraction of the whole that was Khiann.

They had not been together long, and since his death he might have grown to mythical proportions in her mind, but he was still her one true love, and she doubted she could fall in love again, even with his reincarnation, unless the new Khiann was an exact replica of the old one.

Getting to know David and realizing how little he had in common with the prior incarnation of himself, whom she had personally known, had driven the point home.

The entire purpose of reincarnation was to allow the soul to grow and change. Even if she found her Khiann as a new incarnation, he would not be the same male she still loved with every fiber of her being.

Had she given up hope of ever finding the perfect replica of him?

No. She could not do that. That sliver of hope was what kept her going.

Still, even though she did not expect to find Khiann among the Kra-ell, it was time she met with them. The question was whether to organize a big event with all of them gathered in the large assembly hall or invite them to her place in small groups of two or three.

Pulling out her phone, she called Kian.

"Mother, good afternoon."

"Good afternoon, Kian. Do you have a moment?"

"For you, always. But it will have to be quick. The team I'm sending to China is about to leave, and I'm giving them last-minute instructions."

"Then please call me when you are done. I want to discuss my introduction to the Kra-ell with you."

Peter

It had been two weeks since the day Peter had flirted with Kagra in the training center, but nothing had come of it. She'd been busy helping Jade prepare for the trial and training the females wishing to join the war on trafficking, and it was also possible that she was avoiding him intentionally, although he had no idea why she'd want to do that.

He'd been polite, not too pushy, and she'd seemed interested. She also hadn't been hanging out with anyone else or inviting males to her house.

Yeah, he'd been checking.

Was he a little obsessed with Jade's second-in-command?

Maybe a little was describing it too mildly. Something about her drew him to her like a moth to a flame, and it could very possibly be a sense of danger that he had never felt with any other female.

It was exciting, it was new, and Peter wasn't going to give up just because she was playing hard to get.

When he'd heard that Yamanu was seeking volunteers to join the team investigating the signals in China and that Kagra was going to lead the Kra-ell portion of the team, he jumped at the opportunity.

During the orientation Kagra merely acknowledged him with a nod, but he was a patient guy, and as the team members boarded the bus, he lingered by the stairs, waiting for Kagra to finish her conversation with Jade.

When she turned around and caught his gaze, he waved at the open bus door. "Ladies first," he said.

That earned him a crooked smile. "Who said I'm a lady?"

"Is mistress better?"

Her smile widened, and after giving him a sultry look, she started up the stairs.

Following, Peter enjoyed the captivating sway of her hips. Was it his imagination, or was she deliberately exaggerating her movements?

As he scanned the bus, he was happy to see that everyone had already paired up, leaving Kagra with no choice but to select a seat that left the one next to her vacant, seemingly reserved for Peter.

The Fates must have been smiling upon him.

Settling beside her, he respected her personal space, ensuring his thigh wasn't touching hers.

From everything he'd heard about the Kra-ell, he knew that the females expected the males to wait for an invitation, much as it had been in Safe Haven, and he had to wait for Kagra to initiate. He'd given her enough not-so-subtle hints that he was interested, so if she found him attractive, she should feel free to do so.

Heck, he was more than interested. At this point, he was obsessed and guilty of stalking.

Had she noticed he'd been hanging around the café when she was? Or that his training schedule had somehow coincided with hers? Or that his nightly walks just happened to include the path near her house?

"This must be my lucky day," he said to start a conversation. "I get to sit next to you."

"You think?" She gave him the half smile that always made him think she was hiding a secret.

"Yeah, I do."

He loved Kagra's snarky attitude. She was so different from every woman he had ever dated. Eleanor was the only other female he'd been interested in, whose assertive character and no-nonsense attitude were similar to Kagra's, but Eleanor lacked Kagra's charm and sense of humor.

There was a lightness to Kagra that belied the hard life she'd had in Igor's compound.

As the bus door closed and the engine engaged, Peter experienced an unexpected surge of excitement mixed with nervous anticipation, making him wonder whether it was about the mission or the female sitting next to him.

The clan's airstrip was forty-five minutes away, and Kagra was his captive for the duration. A lot could be achieved in that span of time, and he intended to take advantage of every moment.

As the bus windows turned clear again, revealing the scenic route they were traveling, Peter affected a dramatic sigh. "We never got to dance, after all."

She turned to look at him. "I expected you to invite me to a party in your house, but you never did."

That was true, but only because she hadn't shown the slightest interest in him. What was the point of organizing a party and going to all that effort if she didn't show up?

"Would you have come?"

She shrugged. "If I had nothing better to do. Jade keeps me very busy these days."

"I know. All the preparations for the trial and Igor's interrogations kept her busy, so she had to lean more heavily on you to keep your people occupied and out of trouble."

Kagra seemed surprised that he knew that. "Yeah, I'm glad that's over. By the way, your psychologist marrying Mo-red was a gutsy move. She looks like such a straight shooter, a goody two-shoes as you say, and I didn't expect her to do something so underhanded to save him."

"Vanessa is a straight shooter, but she also loves Mo-red. Wouldn't you have done the same if you were in her goody shoes?"

Her lips curved in that half smile that he adored. "Love is a foreign concept to me, but I would have used every loophole to save one of my consorts. It would have been expected of me to protect them, but even if it wasn't, I cared for them."

The mention of Kagra's paramours soured Peter's gut. But maybe she was referring to the males of her tribe who Igor had murdered?

"What is a consort? Is that like a lover?"

"It's more than that." She sighed. "The way we live here on Earth is not the traditional Kra-ell way. If I were back home, I would have a group of three to five consorts that would be my personal harem, for lack of a better word. It would be my responsibility to ensure they each had a chance to father a child with me, but I could have a favorite if I chose to. In Jade's compound, the lines were blurred. The males were allowed to have sex with humans and father hybrid children, and the pureblooded males were shared among the adult females. But Jade and I agreed not to engage with the same males."

That was interesting. "Why?"

She shrugged. "We are both very competitive females, and it wouldn't have been healthy for our relationship to squabble over the males. It was better to keep our harems separate." When he cringed, she lifted her hands. "I only use that word because there is nothing better to describe the relationship. I could call them my boyfriends or husbands, but that wouldn't be accurate either."

"What about Igor's compound? Did you have consorts there?"

She shook her head. "The males I engaged with weren't my consorts because I didn't select them to be mine." She closed her eyes. "We didn't have much choice. None of us did. We did what we had to in order to survive, and I tried to find joy in it despite the tragedy of the past and the sad circumstances of the present."

He regarded her with even more appreciation than before. "You are an incredible female, Kagra. I admire your strength."

A flicker of surprise danced across her face as if she hadn't expected praise from him. "Thanks." She arched a brow. "That's what I'm supposed to say when someone compliments me, right? I should just thank them?"

"Yes. You are catching on quickly." He needed to change the subject and move to more pleasant topics. "So, tell me. What do you do for fun?"

Again, she looked surprised, and after a brief pause, she waved her hand at the window. "I love nature. In Karelia, I escaped into the wilderness whenever I could. We were allowed to hunt, and Jade and I used hunting as an excuse to let off steam and run like the wind. It rejuvenated my spirit and reminded me of the beauty outside the compound walls."

He wasn't sure whether she meant it seriously or was being sarcastic. "You must feel stifled in the village. I mean, since you have livestock to feed off, you don't need to run to hunt."

She shrugged. "I also don't have excess steam to release. Life is good in your village, and I'm excited about building a new Kra-ell society free from the traditional rules of conduct. We are making new rules as we go along, and it's fun. Instead of letting the past shape our future, we are building a new one as we want it to be." As her eyes sparkled with excitement, their color flickered between blue, green, and purple. "It's like the difference between remodeling an old house and building a new one. You are not constricted by the preexisting foundation."

"That's actually an excellent analogy. But I have to wonder—what do you know about remodeling?"

She laughed. "I have a new addiction. Do you know the show *Fix that Dump*?"

"I've never heard of it."

"It's about remodeling versus rebuilding. A team of five experts evaluates old run-down houses and decides whether something is salvageable or if it's better to demolish and start from scratch." A smile lifted one corner of her mouth. "If you want, we can watch an episode together. Do you have Netflix on your phone? Mine is useless outside the village."

Peter would have preferred to keep talking, but if he showed interest in the show she liked, it could lead to many more shared viewings that might then lead to other things.

Like dancing.

"I sure do." He pulled out his phone. "What is the name of that show again?"

"*Fix That Dump*!"

Gabi

"Come on." Gabi yanked on the hairbrush. Once again, it got snagged as she pulled it down, trying to smooth the flyaways that refused to be tamed.

The hairdryer supplied by the hotel just wasn't strong enough for her stubborn hair, and she was impatient because she was running out of time. Maybe she should just braid it. Uriel had no problem with how she looked the day before, so there was that.

She had a sexy new outfit and even sexier lingerie underneath. This time, however, she decided not to put on the red lipstick. For some reason, it had bothered Uriel yesterday, so today, she was going for the nude look.

Well, her lips were nude, but she'd used plenty of makeup on the rest of her face.

Would she still need as much when she turned immortal? Amanda was the most beautiful woman Gabi had ever seen, and she'd had makeup on. That was probably due to the perfect canvas it had been applied on and many years of practice. The woman, or rather female, was two hundred and fifty years old, which was considered young for an immortal.

"That's what your future holds." Gabi smiled sadly at her reflection. "You should be grateful and happy instead of moping over a guy." She braided the ends of her frizzy hair and secured the small braid with an elastic hair tie. "You should also hurry up and finish getting ready. You don't want to keep him waiting."

She also should get a pet so people would not wonder about her sanity when she talked to herself. Gabi did that often, and it wasn't because she lived alone. She'd been doing that ever since she could remember.

"What can I do?" She smiled at her reflection. "I'm such a great conversationalist."

Perhaps she should tell Uriel about it tonight, so he wouldn't feel as bad when she told him she wouldn't be seeing him again.

Gabi didn't want to do that, in fact, she hated it, but it was the right thing to do.

He was thirty-one, seven years younger than her, and lived in Portugal. So even if she wasn't about to turn immortal and was returning to her normal life in Cleveland, a relationship wasn't an option.

Regrettably, there was no alternative, and tonight would be the last.

Hey, maybe she could ask Orion to make her forget Uriel?

Should she?

The idea of forgetting him and their time together seemed even worse than the pain of remembering him and wondering about what could have been if the universe wasn't against them becoming a couple.

With a sigh, Gabi stepped into her new shoes, took her purse, checked that she had the room key in her wallet, and headed out the door.

To get to the restaurant, she had to take the elevator to the lobby downstairs first and then take the rocket elevator up to the top floor where the restaurant was located.

At least this time she was ready for it and held on to the side rail throughout the ear-popping fast ride.

Her legs were surprisingly steady as she approached the hostess's desk.

"Hi, I have a reservation for two under Gabriella Emerson."

The hostess smiled. "Your party is already here." She walked around the station. "I'll take you to your table."

"Thank you."

Excitement thrumming through her ribcage, Gabi scanned the restaurant for dark, longish hair, cheekbones chiseled from granite, and a radiant smile. She didn't have to look for long.

As soon as Uriel saw her, he rose to his feet and pulled out a chair, waiting for her to reach him.

He looked even more stunning in a gray suit, a black dress shirt, and no tie. A movie star if ever she saw one.

It seemed like it took her forever to cross the twenty feet or so between them.

"Hello, Gabriella." He leaned and kissed her cheek. "You look stunning tonight."

"Ditto." She sat down and let him push her chair in. "It should be illegal to look that good," she murmured.

Behind her, the forgotten hostess chuckled. "Can I get you some wine or a cocktail while you look over the menu?"

"Yes, please." Gabi looked up at her and would have smiled if the girl's eyes weren't eating Uriel up. "I would like a Southside, please."

"Of course." The girl was still staring at Uriel. "And for you?"

"I'll have what she's having."

Gabi stifled a chuckle. "Good choice," she croaked. "We would also like a basket of bread, please."

Not for her, but Uriel would probably love to have some.

"Naturally." The hostess finally took the hint and walked away.

Uriel's smile was just as brilliant as Gabi remembered. "What's a Southside?" he asked. "I've never had it."

"It's made with gin, simple syrup, lime juice, and mint leaves. It's like a Mojito just with gin instead of rum. It's on the sweet side, so it's considered a girly drink, but look on the bright side, it's not going to grow unwanted hair on your chest."

Uriel looked confused. "What kinds of drinks do that?"

Was he teasing, or had he really not gotten the joke?

"The manly kind, of course. Straight vodka, whiskey, tequila. Manly men drinks."

He laughed. "Oh, now I get it."

It was strange that he hadn't gotten the reference right away, and there was something in the back of her mind that knew why he hadn't, but when she tried to tug on the misty string and pull the thought through the hazy curtain, her head started aching so badly that she let go of it.

Uriel frowned. "What's the matter?"

"Oh, it's nothing. I get these headaches from time to time. They suddenly come out of nowhere and then disappear just as fast."

The crease between his eyes deepened. "You should get it checked out."

"Yeah." She rubbed her temple. "I'll call my doctor when I get home."

"When is that?"

Gabi thought she'd told him she was leaving the next day. "I'm flying back Wednesday afternoon, but I promised my brothers to spend time with them tomorrow, so I don't know if I'll be able to get away, but I'll definitely try."

Uriel looked sad. "Then we have to make the most of today."

She had a feeling that there was something she was forgetting, but as the headache assaulted her again, she relinquished the thought.

Eric

"Catch." Darlene tossed a pillowcase at Eric, which he caught with ease.

In preparation for Gabi's one-night stay in their guest room, Darlene had insisted on washing all the linens even though no one had ever slept in that bed, and they were clean. But Eric was a smart man and knew not to get into arguments he had no chance of winning.

"I'm excited about Gabi staying with us, but I want to give you fair warning." He stuffed the pillow inside the case. "She is a sweetheart ninety percent of the time, but the remaining ten she can be a handful, especially when she gets in a mood."

Darlene smiled. "I think a ninety-to-ten ratio is better than most."

"Yeah, that's true. But Gabi's ten can get intense. It's like she's holding things in until she can't anymore, and the smallest thing can trigger an explosion."

Darlene put down the pillow she was trying to force into a too-tight pillowcase.

"First of all, Gabi is only going to be with us for one day, and most of it is going to be spent touring the village and visiting people. She will have no reason to get upset. Secondly, what do you mean by her getting in a mood? Does she get depressed? Angry?"

"Both." He took the pillow she'd been wrestling with and slowly forced it into the case, careful not to tear it. "It's hard to explain. Gabi has a heart of gold. She will never say no to a friend who needs help, and she is generous to a fault with money she doesn't have." He smiled. "She pretends to make a fortune, but I know she doesn't. It's not easy to make a lot of money as a nutritionist unless you have movie stars singing your praise to the press. But I digress. She's not the mellow type. She's emotional and assertive, and when you combine the two, they sometimes become explosive. Like vinegar and baking soda."

"They foam up, not explode, but I get what you mean. Is it really that bad, though? No one is perfect, and we all have our pct peeves and character flaws. I'm not assertive enough, and I hate thinking about all the years I let people walk all over me because I wanted to avoid conflict. I admire Gabi for fighting for what she wants."

Eric walked back to the other side of the bed and fluffed the pillows. "It gets her in trouble. There is a good reason she chose to have her own business and stay small with no additional employees. Eventually, she would have picked fights with them and either fired them or just lived with the bad dynamics."

"Is that why she got divorced? Was she fighting a lot with her ex?"

"No." Eric walked around the bed and put his arm around Darlene's middle. "The bastard was a serial cheater and a liar. The thing is, Gabi divorced him eleven years ago, and she's still single despite being beautiful and smart, having her own condominium that is almost free and clear, and a small business that supports her perhaps not lavishly but well enough. I don't pry into her love life, but I assume that she has no shortage of men to choose from, and yet she hasn't had even one serious boyfriend since she got divorced. She sees a guy once, twice, and that's it. She moves to the next one. That's no way to live."

Darlene chuckled. "You lived like that for a long time, and until you met me, you were perfectly happy with your player ways."

"I wasn't happy." He pulled her into his arms. "I was getting by." He kissed her on the tip of her nose. "What say you we go to our bedroom and test how fresh the bedding is?"

"I washed it last Thursday." She affected a frown. "But we've been very active in that bed, so perhaps we should change the linens before Gabi gets here. I don't want your sister to think that we are slobs."

"Fates forbid." He stifled a smile. "Not to be wasteful, though, first we need to mess up the bedding some more, so it will need washing for sure."

"Absolutely." Darlene nodded sagely, took his hand, and led him toward their bedroom.

Gabi

S omehow, Uriel had managed to pass the entire evening without telling Gabi even one fact about his childhood or his parents, or where he lived when he wasn't traveling.

He'd kept her entertained with anecdotes of his bargain hunting all over the world, which Gabi doubted were real and not part of a script he'd memorized for a movie, but she didn't want to spoil their last evening together by poking holes in his stories or challenging their veracity. Besides, just hearing him talk and looking at those perfect lips of his was making it difficult for her to think about anything other than taking him to her room and having her way with him.

She was on her third Southside, which was one of the best she'd ever had, and Uriel had been matching her glass for glass, but the difference was that she was woozy while he was not.

Well, he had at least a hundred pounds on her, if not more, so he was obviously not as affected.

Still, despite the alcohol overindulgence, her brain remained as sharp as ever, and when Uriel finally overdid it, telling her a story about a pair of shoes he'd found in a secondhand clothing store that had belonged to a Korean princess and was worth tens of thousands of dollars, Gabi found it so unbelievable that she could no longer hold her tongue.

"You know what I think?" She lifted her glass and took a sip.

"What?" He held his glass up but didn't bring it to his lips.

"I don't think that you are really a flea market bargain flipper. I think that you are an actor, and so are your friends, and that you've been cast in a show about bargain flipping, and because the three of you are method actors, you stay in character and pretend that you are flippers in real life."

Leaning forward, he gave her a panty-melting smile. "All of us are actors on the stage of life. Perhaps you are not really a nutritionist from Cleveland who is visiting her family in Los Angeles but an actress playing the role of Gabriella Emerson, the brave hero of God, galloping to the rescue of her eldest brother? Maybe your method acting is so immersive that you can't remember who you really are?"

"Galloping?" She laughed. "I flew over, and as you've witnessed firsthand, it required a lot of bravery on my part." She shook her head. "You are doing it again. You're answering my question with another question."

He frowned. "Was there a question in there? You asked if I wanted to know your thoughts, and I asked what? Then you told me what you thought, and I answered with what I thought about what you thought."

Gabi laughed again. "Goodness gracious, you are giving me a headache." She drank the rest of the Southside. "I need another one." She lifted the glass to signal the waitress.

Uriel arched one dark brow that was so perfectly shaped that it had to be painted on or plucked to perfection. "Are you sure you want another one?" He leaned forward. "I have an early morning meeting tomorrow, and I was hoping we could retire to your room and spend the next few hours enjoying each other. After tonight, we might not see each other again for a while."

"Just for a while?"

This was the end of their time together. She would never see him again, and it hurt more than it should.

"Don't be sad." He reached over the table and wiped a tear that had slid down her cheek. "I'll come visit you in Cleveland."

"Promise?"

She should feel lighter, but she didn't. There was something she was forgetting that would make it impossible for Uriel to find her, but she couldn't remember what it was.

What the hell was wrong with her?

Was this a dream? Was that why she felt like there were gaps in her memory?

"I promise. I'm just not sure when I will be able to get away. My friends and I are working on an important deal, and I don't know how long it will take to finalize it."

"Is that what your early morning meeting is about?"

He nodded. "I wanted it to happen later in the day, but my friends are impatient and want to proceed as soon as possible."

When he lifted his hand to signal to the waitress, she arrived immediately. "Would you like another drink?" she asked Uriel, whose glass was still half full, while ignoring Gabi's empty one.

"No, thank you. We are ready for the check," he said.

"Of course." She pulled out a leather folder and put it on the table. "Whenever you are ready."

Uriel snatched the thing, opened it, and put three one-hundred-dollar bills inside. "No change."

When had he pulled out his wallet?

Gabi hadn't seen him opening it.

Had he been holding the money in his pocket?

And who paid with cash these days?

People with shady deals, that's who. Flipping flea market finds, my ass.

"Thank you." The waitress smiled sweetly at Uriel. "I hope to see you at the Seventy-Second again soon."

"I hope so too." He rose to his feet and offered Gabi a hand up.

Forcing a smile, she took it.

This was not the time nor place to let nasty Gabi out to play. Usually, she kept her temper on a tight leash, but sometimes the trigger just flipped the switch on, and she had to react even though she was aware that the impetus might exist only in her head.

Uriel could have a thousand legitimate reasons for paying cash, and she shouldn't jump to conclusions and accuse him of imaginary crimes. He traveled all over the world, and many places still didn't accept credit cards. He had to have cash on him.

"Did she annoy you?" he whispered in her ear as he pressed the button for the elevator.

"Who?"

"The waitress who was trying to flirt with me. I didn't encourage her, but it probably still angered you. If the roles were reversed, I would have been growling at the waiter, if not worse. And then I left her a big tip, which must have made you really mad."

Gabi hadn't seen the bill, so she didn't know how big the tip was, and if he hadn't mentioned it, she wouldn't have cared.

"How big was the tip?"

"More than twenty-five percent." Uriel pulled her into his arms as soon as the elevator door closed behind them. "I just didn't want to wait for the change."

Well, that was actually a very good reason to leave a big tip.

"I don't care about that, and I didn't care about her flirting with you. What got me angry was—"

He kissed her, and Gabi forgot what she'd gotten upset about.

Kagra

Peter was persistent, but surprisingly, Kagra wasn't annoyed with him, perhaps because he didn't strut and posture to get her attention like the Kra-ell males would.

Rishana and Sheniya had been casting her dirty looks, but their disapproval had only prompted her to respond to Peter's flirting with more enthusiasm.

She was finally free, and no one was going to dictate to her who she could hang out with or who she invited to her bed.

"Kagra," Pavel called from the last row on the plane. "They have Russian dubbing for the movies." He lifted the earphones. "Every seat has one."

"Awesome," she answered in English. "But I suggest that everyone watch in English. Most of you need to work on your language skills." She frowned at Rishana. "Are you watching the movie with Russian dubbing?"

"*Chto*?"

Kagra motioned for her to remove the earphones. "You need to learn English. Don't listen to the movie in Russian."

Rishana shrugged and put the earphones back on. She probably was still listening in Russian, and Kagra didn't want to make a scene in front of Peter and the other Guardians. She would deal with her later.

"How come you speak such good English?" Peter asked.

"I wasn't as fluent before your people liberated us. But I have a good ear, and I learn fast."

For some reason, her answer made him happy. "Immortals learn languages quickly too. Evidently, we are genetically similar."

"Of course, we are. Otherwise, we wouldn't be able to produce children together."

"True that." Peter's sultry look invited a comeback, but Kagra had to be careful about what she said in front of her people.

She cast a quick glance around to make sure no one was eavesdropping on their conversation.

Aliya and Vrog were cuddled under a blanket and talking in hushed voices, which was kind of cute but also disturbing. Her people didn't cuddle, and although Vrog looked human, Aliya didn't, and it was just odd.

Thankfully, Jade was more circumspect about touching Phinas in public or even in the house they shared while Kagra or other Kra-ell were there.

Pavel and the other three purebloods were all watching movies on the monitors mounted on each seat, Rishana and Sheniya did the same, and the Guardians were mostly doing stuff on their phones and tablets.

Yamanu was humming quietly, and although she could barely hear him, there was something soothing about the faint melody. Maybe it was one of his many talents.

The guy was incredible, and it was a shame he was taken. She would have liked a tumble in bed with him. She also liked Dalhu, the former Doomer, but he was also taken.

That was the trouble with the immortals. They didn't share.

Peter was single, and he was obviously interested, but he was too interested, and she wasn't looking to repeat Jade's mistake. All she wanted was good sex with a male who knew what he was doing and wouldn't expect her to fall in love with him.

Peter shifted in his seat, making her wonder whether he had to change positions because he was aroused. "So far, there is only one kid who was born to an immortal female and a hybrid Kra-ell father, which means that both parents are part human. We don't know whether purebloods and immortals are compatible." He smiled devilishly. "But I would sure like to try."

Damn, it was difficult to keep him at arm's length without offending him, especially since she really liked him. Just not as much as he liked her.

"Do you have children?" Kagra asked, pretending not to get the sexual innuendo.

"Not that I know of. I hope I don't. If I ever have children, I want to be part of their lives, not just the sperm donor."

She nodded. "That's what the fathers of my sons were. The difference is that they knew they were the fathers, but I wish they hadn't."

"Why?"

"Because we are connected through the sons we share, and I don't want to be connected to them. They didn't do anything to help raise my sons, and they don't deserve to be part of their lives."

Peter regarded her with his smart, dark eyes. "I thought that was the Kra-ell way—the tribe raised the kids, not their individual parents."

"I was born on Earth, but Jade was pretty traditional in how she ran her compound. The children belonged to the mothers, and the fathers' role in raising the children was limited. Some were better than others, though." She didn't want to talk about it. The loss felt less acute now, but it still pained her to think about all the people she'd lost— her father, her brother, and the other males. It was better to feel angry. "Igor spat on the Kra-ell traditions, and he didn't want the males to be involved in raising the children at all. He embraced human patriarchal attitudes."

"I'm sorry." Peter put a hand on her arm. "Would you like to watch another episode of *Fix That Dump*?"

She would have watched a show about the lives of ants just to take her mind off the past.

"Do you get Netflix up here?"

They'd watched one episode on the bus, but now they were several thousand feet in the air and flying over the ocean.

He grinned. "Yes, I do." He lifted his phone to show her that he had reception.

"Then what are you waiting for? Let's watch."

Gabi

The short walk from the elevator to Gabi's room could have gotten them in trouble if any of the other guests had stepped out into the hallway.

Uriel was holding her up by her ass, her legs were wrapped around his narrow waist, and the skirt of her dress was hitched all the way up her hips, so she was practically exposed, and they were kissing.

Somehow, he'd managed to get them to her door and leaned her against it, holding her up with one hand while reaching his other hand out. "Give me the key."

"It's in my purse," she murmured. "Where the credit cards are."

"Got it." He pulled out her wallet and handed it to her.

She found the key and touched it to the reader while he got the handle and pushed the door open.

Uriel didn't bother turning the lights on as he carried her to the bed and laid her on top of the cover.

"I want you so much." She held up her arms.

She must have been really drunk because it looked as if he was moving too fast for her to catch his movements, and when he was done, his suit jacket, dress shirt, and pants were draped over the desk chair, and his magnificent body was clad only in a pair of tight-fitting boxer shorts that left very little to the imagination.

His bulge was just as massive as she'd remembered, and she had a flicker of apprehension before also remembering how perfectly they had ended up fitting and that, in the morning, she hadn't been sore at all.

As he came into her arms, his incredible body moving with the powerful fluidity of a puma, he didn't climb on top of her but rather lay beside her and pulled her to him. Her breasts were pressing into his bare chest through the fabrics of her dress and bra, but her hips were exposed, and it was skin-to-skin below the waist except for their underwear.

Impatient, she wrapped her arms around him and tried to roll on her back, but trying to move Uriel was like trying to move a boulder, and he wouldn't budge until he was good and ready.

"Patience," he murmured against her lips and then proceeded to kiss her softly as if they were just starting their sensual dance and not ready for the main act to commence.

The two elevator rides, one from the restaurant down to the lobby and then the second one from the lobby up to her room, had provided enough of an opening act, and Gabi was primed and ready to go.

When she groaned, he rolled her onto her back and propped himself on his elbows. Hovering only inches above her, with his hair falling like two black curtains on both sides of his impossibly gorgeous face, he was distorting her reality.

She cupped his cheek, which was covered in a five-o'clock shadow. "How can you be so beautiful?"

"Beauty is in the eye of the beholder." He leaned down and kissed her eyelids, forcing her to close her eyes.

Feeling the hard length that was still trapped inside his boxer shorts pressed against her inner thigh, Gabi spread her legs to make room for him.

He shifted, letting some of his weight press her into the mattress, but she knew he was still bracing most of it on his forearms, or he would have squashed her.

Running her hands from his shoulders down to his arms, she tried to memorize the feel of his smooth skin, the powerful muscles underneath it, the way he felt on top of her, and as she opened her eyes and looked up at him, she was in awe of the creator's scalpel and the magnificent male animal it had crafted.

"Uriel," she whispered his name as if it was a prayer, and with a name like his, perhaps it was.

Names had power, and Uriel was the light of God.

He took her lips in another kiss, and as she surrendered to it, she was acutely aware of the fact that they were running out of time and that they had to make every second count.

Perhaps the same thought had run through his mind because his kiss got harder, more demanding, his tongue dueling with hers, probing and licking.

When he let go of her mouth, it was only to pull her dress off, free her breasts from the bra, and yank her panties off.

Fully bared before his eyes, the cool air from the air conditioning vent tightening her nipples into hard points, she undulated her hips in blatant invitation.

His nostrils flared, and she could have sworn that a glow was coming from his dark eyes, but it must have been the reflection of the moonlight shining through the expansive windows of the hotel room.

"I want you," she said in case her previous hint wasn't clear enough. "All of you."

He blinked, and the glow was gone, and then he lowered himself on top of her in slow motion, his arms bowing as he suspended his mouth over her aching nipples.

Remembering the night before and how he'd demanded that she ask for what she wanted him to do to her, she groaned. "Don't tease me. Kiss them."

Smiling like the devil he was, Uriel didn't do what she asked. Instead, he feathered kisses over her collarbones and sternum, teasing her mercilessly before finally swiping his tongue over one turgid peak.

"God, yes." She pitched her head back, and as she churned her hips under him, she was annoyed that he still had his boxer shorts on.

That thought didn't last long.

As he latched onto her nipple, sucking and licking it, she lifted her legs and wrapped them around his hips for better friction.

Uriel let go of her nipple with a pop, but instead of giving its twin the same agonizingly pleasurable treatment, he slid his mouth down her body, kissing and licking along the way.

"Oh, yeah," she breathed. "I definitely want that."

His growl of approval was delicious, the vibrations going straight to her core.

Peter

Peter had watched the episode of *Fix That Dump* with just enough focus to make occasional remarks and to be able to talk about it later.

Running a parallel script in his mind, he wondered whether Kagra's charm and playfulness were just a cover and that underneath, she was hurt and damaged like the other Kra-ell. She hadn't lost children like Jade had, but she must have lost her father and other males she cared about.

He should avoid asking her questions about her life before coming to the village.

But then, how would he get to know her?

He didn't even know how old she was or how she'd become Jade's second-in-command despite being Earthborn.

The other thing he needed to figure out was the mixed signals she was sending him. When he was teasing and playful, she was teasing and playful back, but when he expressed more serious interest in her, she backed away.

Well, that should have been as obvious as a new day, but he hadn't been thinking in Kra-ell terms. He'd been thinking in immortal terms.

He needed to approach Kagra as someone who was looking for some fun but didn't want to commit. Or he should just treat her as he had treated any of the human females he had hooked up with over the years. He'd never pretended to want more than one night of pleasure with them, and if the lady wasn't okay with that, they'd parted with no hard feelings.

But if he did that with Kagra, he would be pretending in the other direction. He wanted more than one night of passion with her, but he would be fine starting with that.

Perhaps that was how he should approach it.

One step at a time.

"This is amazing." Kagra waved a hand at the screen. "How do people come up with such pretty combinations? I would have never thought a pink fluffy pillow could liven up a space like that." She turned and smiled. "Can I tell you a secret?"

"Always." He leaned closer, excitement bubbling in his chest.

"I love this shit. I love decorating, and that's why I was finding excuses to hang around Ingrid's design center and chat with her. When she offered us the spare room in the center for our headquarters, I jumped at the opportunity and convinced Jade to take it. Now I will get to hang around there whenever I want."

This was the last thing Peter had expected from Kagra, which was an excellent lesson to be learned. People were multilayered, and it was a mistake to assume that the face they showed the world was the only one they had.

"Did you decorate your new home?"

She shook her head. "Jade has just gotten access to our money, and we are in the process of getting fake documents and opening bank accounts for everyone. Bottom line, I don't have the money to spend." She leaned forward to glance at the other Kra-ell on the flight and then leaned back and sighed. "Even when I have the money, I doubt I will use it to redecorate the house I'm staying in. Ingrid did a great job with it, and I would just mess it up. Besides, decorating doesn't go with my persona." She waved a hand over herself. "I'm a tough warrior, not a designer."

"Can't you be both?"

She arched a brow. "Do any of your Guardian friends have artistic hobbies?"

"Yeah. You know Magnus, right?"

She nodded.

"So, he retired from the force a long time ago, and for many years he was into men's fashion and other things that most of the Guardians wouldn't have considered very manly. But he didn't care about their opinions and did what he loved doing."

"Why did he get out of the fashion business?"

"He answered a call like the rest of us." Peter smoothed his hand over his goatee. "I was retired as well. When the world had become a more peaceful place, there was no more use for a large Guardian force, and many of us retired and turned to different occupations. But then Bridget summoned us back and offered us a worthy reason to join the force again. The clan decided to wage war on trafficking, and we were needed."

There was understanding in her big eyes that only a fellow warrior could have. "I bet you and your friends were thrilled to be needed again. It's no fun to feel like the skills you've honed over years and years of sweat and blood are suddenly obsolete. It would have been devastating to me."

"Really? Even if you could attend a design school and become an interior designer or even an architect?"

"I would love to do that as a hobby, not a job. My ultimate goal is to one day lead a tribe of my own."

That was another surprise. "You would leave the village?"

She winced. "No, I love it in the village. But maybe we could organize our community as smaller tribes." Leaning back, she closed her eyes. "I don't know. Branching off on my own used to be all I wanted, all I dreamt about, and then our compound got sacked, and my dreams and aspirations were put on hold. But now that I think about it, they are not really what I should aspire to. I need to find a different goal."

He leaned closer to her and whispered conspiratorially, "It could be designing homes."

"I don't even know whether I have any talent."

"I have an idea." He smiled. "How would you like to decorate my house? I'm tired of it looking exactly like all the other houses in the village. I want something different, and I have the money to get it done. I just need someone with a vision."

She slanted him a look. "Is that a ploy to get me into your bed?"

"No, it's a genuine offer, but if you happen to find yourself in my bed, I won't throw you out."

She laughed. "Good to know."

Gabi

Gabi lay panting, spent from the string of orgasms Uriel had wrought out of her, but as he brought his fingers to his mouth and sucked on them, her arousal flared again.

How could one man be so damn sexy?

A satisfied smirk lifting one corner of his lips, he put his fingers back where they'd been a moment ago and started stroking her again.

She wanted to tell him that she was too sensitive and couldn't take it anymore, but then he lowered his head and teased her nipple with the tip of his tongue, and when her hips arched off the bed to meet his fingers instead of pulling away, he took her mouth in a scorching kiss, and she came again.

Leaning away, he grinned. "Was there something you wanted to say?"

Was the guy made of granite?

How come he wasn't inside her already? His erection was sticking over the elastic of his boxer shorts, and the tip was beaded with pre-cum. Which reminded her that they needed a condom.

Maybe that was why he wasn't inside her yet?

She'd demanded that he bring them, but perhaps he'd forgotten? Or maybe he hated using them?

Well, tough. It was a mood spoiler to remind him to put it on, but even if he was as clean as he claimed, she didn't want to get pregnant—

Or did she?

Gabi was thirty-eight, and her biological clock was ticking. Once it had become clear to her that she wasn't going to find the man of her dreams because she couldn't bring herself to trust any guy she dated, she'd considered using donor sperm to have a baby on her own. Then she'd realized that, without a support system, she couldn't raise a child and also run her business, and she had given up on the idea.

But perhaps she could move to Los Angeles to be near her family and let her brothers help her. She really shouldn't wait much longer, and she couldn't have asked for a more magnificent sperm donor than Uriel.

He'd claimed he couldn't get her pregnant because of his low sperm count but, somehow, she doubted that was true. He was too virile and too masculine to have such a problem.

The logical part of her brain knew that it was nonsense and that one had nothing to do with the other, but her hormone-saturated brain had its own ideas, and they were more appropriate for a cavewoman than a twenty-first-century college graduate.

All it perceived was—a big, healthy man with big muscles—strong, healthy babies.

Gabi put a hand on Uriel's wrist. "I want you inside of me without any barrier between us. I'm willing to take the risk if you are."

"Are you sure? I brought a big pack of condoms."

It gladdened her that he hadn't forgotten and that he had considered her wishes, but she was still convinced that taking a risk on him was the right thing to do.

She had no illusions about him being a part of the baby's life, but she'd given up on having a partner she could trust enough to commit to a long time ago.

"I'm sure," she breathed.

As his expression turned feral, she had a moment of trepidation, but when he got rid of his boxer shorts between one blink of an eye and the next and gripped his erection, she was glad of issuing the invitation.

She wanted to feel that velvety length inside her, and without a trench coat taking away even an iota of the experience.

Supporting his weight with one arm, he positioned himself at her entrance and stroked the tip of his erection up and down.

She held her breath, waiting for the moment he would push inside her, and when he surged in with one brutal thrust, she gasped, not from discomfort, but from bliss.

As Uriel let loose, going hard and fast, Gabi's body greedily absorbed his thrusting, relishing the clapping and grinding of their bodies, and she didn't want it to end.

But then he pulled out, flipped her around, pulled her hips up, and surged in again. She felt owned and possessed, but it didn't bother her in the slightest. In fact, being aware of how temporary it was and that soon she would regain full ownership of her body made her sad and took away from the incredible experience.

His hands clamping her hips, he was shafting into her with such force that the bed was banging against the wall with each thrust, and as the coil winding inside her sprang free, it released a climax and a torrent of sensations that was so overwhelming she was gasping for air.

Behind her, Uriel stilled, and as his erection kicked inside her, she heard him hiss, and then he bit into her shoulder, and she orgasmed again.

Kian

A sense of unease had kept Kian awake long into the night, and as he wondered about its source, he wasn't sure whether it was connected to his mother's wish to start introductory meetings with the Kra-ell or to the team flying to China.

His mother hadn't decided yet whether she wanted to organize a grand appearance and a speech in the assembly hall first, and then start meeting small groups of Kra-ell to create a more personal connection, or the other way around. In either case, he shouldn't be worried because they were all under Toven's compulsion to do no harm and wore cuffs that would immobilize them with a neurotoxin if they dared anything.

Was he still wary of them because of the residual effect of Igor's attack?

It wasn't only about being under the guy's compulsion. The pureblood's physical strength alone was enough to give Kian nightmares. As someone who had felt physically superior to nearly everyone around him throughout his long life, it was a hard pill to swallow.

Still, the unease was more likely about the mission than his mother's plans.

He had been checking his phone for messages and had even called Morris a couple of times to make sure that the team was okay and that the jet was in the air.

Perhaps it was time to make another call?

Syssi was sleeping peacefully beside him, and he could hear Allegra's breathing through the baby monitor, and whenever he wanted, he could watch her sleep through the camera mounted in her room, but with that strange unease churning in his stomach, it wasn't good enough. He needed to check on her in person.

With a sigh, he glanced at his mate. Somehow, she'd managed to sleep through his tossing and turning. Not wishing to disturb her, he'd called Morris from the bathroom, but this time he was going to make the call from his office and call village security as well.

After that, he could make a couple of cappuccinos and surprise Syssi with coffee in bed. It had been a long time since he had done anything to spoil her, and Kian felt guilty for neglecting her.

His plan had been to be all hers during the wedding cruise, but with everything that had happened since the idea had been originally hatched, he doubted they were going to sail anytime soon, and certainly not with the entire clan. They would have to break it up, which defied the whole purpose of having Alena's wedding on a cruise ship.

They wanted the entire family to be there, and since Alena was the de facto Mother of the Clan, that was the whole clan.

After carefully slipping out of bed, he tiptoed into Allegra's room to check on her.

His daughter's sweet little face tempted him to kiss her rosy cheeks, but she was a light sleeper, and if he touched her or made a noise, she would wake up and would be cranky the rest of the day.

After tiptoeing out of her room, he walked over to his office to call Morris again to confirm that everything was fine on that front.

The jet had taken off at six in the evening the day before, and it should land at about eight in the morning, but that was three hours from now, and Kian knew that he wouldn't be able to sleep until it landed safely.

He was turning into a damn mother hen.

What if the sense of impending danger had nothing to do with the flight but with the mission itself?

Nah, that wasn't likely.

Even if they found the scouts, and even if they were hostile, the team could handle them. The Kra-ell settlers hadn't arrived with any advanced weapons, and Kian had no reason to think that the scouts who had arrived before them had anything better.

From what he had gathered so far, the gods' mode of operation was not to land a craft on Earth but rather to dispatch pods from a large spaceship that didn't enter Earth's atmosphere, and those pods didn't have room for much more than their occupants. Then again, a pod loaded with supplies might have been dropped along with the settlers.

However, he wondered how they were supposed to get picked up. The large spaceship had to have a smaller vessel capable of passing through Earth's atmosphere, landing, and taking off to reach the mother ship.

Kian wasn't a rocket engineer, but he knew that was not an easy feat to pull off. The amount of fuel required was staggering, but even though the gods probably had a very different way of fueling their vessels, it still had to be costly or dangerous to land on Earth and take off. Otherwise, they wouldn't have bothered with pods to drop off their people.

He pulled a bottle of water from the minibar fridge, removed the cap, and took a long swig before calling Morris.

"Good morning, boss. Everything is fine, and we are still in the air."

Thankfully, Kian's anxiety hadn't influenced the veteran pilot, and he sounded as calm and collected as ever.

"Good to know. Call me when you land."

"I will. Morris out."

Next, Kian called the security office. "Good morning. How are you guys doing?"

"Good morning, Kian. Jarmo and his crew are at the barn, tending to the animals, but other than that, there is nothing to report. Everything is still quiet."

"Excellent. No news is good news. Let me know if anything seems out of order, and I mean anything."

"Are we expecting trouble?" the Guardian asked.

"No, but I have an uneasy feeling."

"Got it. Do you want us to raise the alert level?"

"No, just stay vigilant."

"Always, boss."

After ending the call, Kian leaned back in his chair, took another big gulp from the water, and turned to look at the rising sun through the sliding doors of his home office.

"What is it going to be this time?"

Gabi

G abi opened her eyes, turned on her side, and put her hand on the pillow beside her.

It was cold, which meant that Uriel had left right after she'd passed out from bliss. This time, they had done it on the bed, so he hadn't needed to carry her from the couch, but she wasn't sticky, meaning he'd cleaned her before leaving.

Strangely, she didn't feel embarrassed. If their roles were reversed and he passed out from bliss while she remained awake, she would lovingly clean him up too.

Lovingly was the wrong qualifier, though. She was in lust with Uriel, not in love. She didn't know enough about him to be in love with him. Perhaps tenderly was a better word.

The memory of the evening they had spent together was bittersweet.

She'd had a great time. Both in and out of bed, and now that she remembered what her subconscious had been trying to tell her, she had even less reason to regret the decision not to use a condom.

While Uriel had been with her, she hadn't remembered that she was about to close or sell her business in Cleveland and move into the immortals' village with her family. She was supposed to find an immortal to induce her transition, but she didn't need to hurry because she was relatively young and in great shape. During lunch, Karen, Darlene, and the other immortal ladies had told her about how low fertility was for immortals and that she should mentally prepare to wait decades to have a baby. They had a doctor in the village who gave out potions that were supposed to help with conception, but no one knew whether they worked. So far, Syssi and her husband were the only success story, and the others were still waiting to conceive.

If by some miracle she'd gotten pregnant, which was almost as unlikely as her winning the lottery, she could raise the child in the village, surrounded by aunts and uncles and cousins, and in the meantime, she could find a nice immortal nerd to bond with and to induce her transition.

It was a fantastic plan, but the one thing missing in the beautiful picture she'd painted was Uriel.

With a groan, Gabi turned on her back and draped her arm over her eyes to stop them from tearing up.

She was going to miss him.

He'd promised to visit her in Cleveland, and he might have even meant it, but life would come up with ways of keeping them apart, and if he ever ended up visiting the city that had been her home for so long, he wouldn't find her there because she would be in the hidden immortal village in California.

Reaching blindly for her phone, Gabi patted the nightstand until her hand landed on it and brought the device in front of her eyes.

There was no message from Uriel, which was so disappointing that annoying tears leaked out of her eyes. There were two messages from the same client asking if it was okay to substitute Eggs Benedict with Canadian bacon for her prescribed morning omelet of two eggs and a cup of spinach.

What did Melinda expect the answer to be? *Go ahead, honey. Enjoy your Eggs Benedict*?

"People are so dumb," Gabi groaned. "Actually, they just like playing dumb."

Melinda Ratcliffe was an attorney, and to become one, she'd had to pass the bar, so she couldn't be stupid. She just wanted Gabi to allow her to cheat on her diet, and later she would blame her for not losing any inches from her hips.

Talk about wanting to have your cake and eat it too.

If that was an option, Gabi would have no business and no income, but she could also turn immortal and keep Uriel as her lover.

Except, he hadn't even left her a message, which was a message in itself. It was over, and there was no reason to drag the pain out.

Then again, he might have been in a rush and forgotten.

Ugh, she needed to talk to someone about this, someone who could help her get her emotions together and who wasn't a member of her family.

Was it too early to call Becky?

Her trainer should be in her gym already, but if she was coaching a client, she might be unable to talk. Perhaps calling Suzi or Mira would be better?

Nah, they were both good friends, but they wouldn't tell her what they really thought, like Becky would. They were too nice and wouldn't want to hurt her feelings. She also didn't want to tell them she was moving to Los Angeles. Not yet, anyway.

She would have to tell them eventually.

Becky was a straight shooter, and she had no qualms about hurting someone's feelings if it was for their own good.

The problem with that plan was that as soon as Becky got on the line, Orion's compulsion might cause Gabi to forget about moving to Los Angeles and why she couldn't be with Uriel. Not that she could tell her friend anything about immortals and how they affected her future plans, but at least she wouldn't have big gaps in her memories.

When she'd spoken with Gilbert on the phone before, she'd remembered everything, but when she'd met Karen and Darlene in the restaurant, she'd forgotten again, but that could have been because of Syssi and Amanda who had been strangers to her at that point.

Oh well, she wouldn't know until she tried.

After a visit to the bathroom and a cup of coffee from the coffee maker, Gabi sat on the couch and called Becky.

The phone rang for so long that she was about to end the call, but then Becky's voice came on. "Gabi? Are you back in town?"

"I'm in Los Angeles, visiting my brothers."

"Oh, right. I forgot that you were going there straight from the conference. How did it go with the flight?"

"Better than I expected. My flight was canceled, and I got a free upgrade to first-class another flight."

"That's amazing. Those tickets are three times more expensive than coach. Did you get gourmet meals and free booze?"

Gabi chuckled. "The meal was far from gourmet, but I got plenty of free champagne. I also got to sit next to the most gorgeous guy I've ever seen, and I mean ever. You know how crazy I am about Henry Cavill, and he has nothing on Uriel."

"Really?" Becky sounded skeptical. "Did Uriel also have a jaw implant?"

They had joked about the actor's jaw being impossibly big and square, but none of the gossip magazines confirmed that he'd had anything done. Supposedly, it was the result of weightlifting.

Becky had even joked that she needed to up the weights in her routine.

"I suspect that he did. He and his friends came from a trip that included South Korea, and all three looked like a walking commercial for some luxury brand for men."

Gabi continued to tell Becky about the two nights she'd spent with Uriel, how he had been so intently focused on her but had left each time in the middle of the night because of early morning meetings.

She didn't tell her about moving to Los Angeles, even though her memory of immortals had thankfully remained intact. It was premature, and she hadn't come up with a good enough reason to explain her move to her friends and clients.

"The guy is a beautiful butterfly," Becky said. "Nice to look at but not lasting. You had your fun, and whether you want to move on or not, you have no choice. Neither of you lives in Los Angeles, and from what you've told me, the guy evaded answering personal questions. For all you know, he might be married."

"He's not."

Darlene's son hadn't found evidence of Uriel having a wife, but he'd also admitted to having limited access to government records in Portugal.

"Why, because he didn't have a wedding ring?" Becky asked sarcastically. "Lots of guys don't wear them. Also, he might not have a wife, but he could have a steady girlfriend he's cheating on, and that's just as bad."

"Yeah. I didn't consider that." Roni wouldn't have been able to find out about a girlfriend even if he could easily hack into Uriel's official records.

"Keep your fun memories of him and move on," Becky said. "That's my advice, but you will do as you please." She chuckled. "I don't think you've ever followed my advice. You only use me as your sounding board."

"I ask for your advice because you will not try to sugarcoat anything for me. You are always the voice of reason." She laughed. "I'm the unreasonable one who sometimes chooses the wrong thing to do."

"At least you admit it. That's the first step in recovery. When are you coming back?"

"Wednesday night."

"Should I pencil you in for Thursday morning?"

"No, I have a full day of consultations. But you can pencil me in for Friday morning. Our usual time."

"Will do. I thought you would like a make-up session for the ones you missed."

"No, thanks." Gabi chuckled. "I had plenty of exercise the last two nights."

"Yeah, well, but not for the right muscle groups," Becky said. "Be strong, Gabi," she continued in a more serious tone. "Don't call him, don't message him, just let him go."

"Yeah, you're right. Bye, Becky. I'll see you Friday at eight."

As she ended the call, Gabi leaned back and released a long breath. Was she going to take Becky's advice?

Probably not.

It just didn't feel right.

Kian

Kian finished making the cappuccinos and was ready to go back to bed when his phone pinged with an incoming message.

Putting the cups on the counter, he reached into the pocket of his robe to retrieve the phone and frowned at William's picture on the screen.

As he read the message, alarm bells went off in his head. *Call me as soon as you can.*

It wasn't about the plane crashing because William wouldn't have known about that before him, and the only other thing that came to mind was the damn signals.

Were they broadcasting again?

Choosing William's contact from the list, he held the device to his ear, and the moment the call was answered, he barked, "Report."

"The signals are on again, and they are broadcasting steadily. No more winking in and out. We need the Odus to decipher the location, and I really hope the signals are still coming from Chengdu."

So that was what the uneasy feeling had been about.

In a way, it was a relief. He could deal with whoever was broadcasting those signals and what they represented, but he couldn't control weather conditions in China and ensure the safe landing of the jet carrying his team.

"I'll get the Odus. Meet me at my office in half an hour."

William let out a breath. "Here we go again."

"Indeed."

By the time Kian got to his office accompanied by Okidu, Onidu was already there and coffee was brewing.

William looked exactly the same way he had Monday morning when they had met for the same reason—his hair was disheveled, his billowing T-shirt was a remnant from the days he'd been much larger, and his feet were in the same pair of blue Crocs.

"Good morning, boss." He opened his laptop. "I recorded the signals, but since they are still broadcasting, I will just run the live feed." His fingers flew over the keyboard.

As before, Kian couldn't hear anything, but he knew the Odus heard it just fine, given their trance-like frozen mode.

It was spooky to see them like that, their robotic nature suddenly so evident and disturbing. He much preferred seeing them animated and displaying signs of sentience. Thinking of them as constructs was disturbing, and if he cared to be honest with himself, it had been one of the reasons he hadn't pushed for faster deciphering of the journals.

Humanity hadn't yet developed the materials necessary to build Odus as lifelike as Okidu and his brothers, and what the clan could accomplish with what was available were either robotic creations that looked like machines or mannequin-like at best. Despite having the same neural network as the original Odus and the same capacity for sentience, they would be regarded as less because of their appearance.

"Should I write down the coordinates?" Okidu asked.

"Please do." William handed him a sheet of paper and a mechanical pencil.

"Thank you, master." Okidu scribbled a list of numbers in his neat handwriting. "Here you go, master." He handed William the page.

William looked at the numbers and frowned. "This is not good." He typed in the coordinates and turned the screen toward Kian so he could see the location on the map. "All three signals are coming from the same place, and it's not from Chengdu."

"Indeed." Kian pulled out his phone and called the chief.

Onegus answered immediately. "Good morning, Kian. What's up?

"The three signals are back, and they are not coming from China this time. They are right here in our backyard. The implications are obvious, and as much as I hate to do it, we have to implement the lockdown protocols here and in the keep. Once that's done, please come to my office."

The signals were not originating from the scouts who had been sent thousands of years before, and this was a new threat.

There could be only one reason the signals were that close. Whoever was emitting them must have followed Igor's signal to the keep, and for some reason, they wanted that to be known.

Otherwise, why hadn't the signals been broadcasting continuously?

Why had they been activated in China, deactivated, and then activated again right here under his nose?

Locking down the keep wasn't optional, but locking down the village as well was an extreme measure. Until they figured out what and who they were dealing with, Kian wasn't taking any chances.

"Roger that," Onegus said. "I'll implement the protocol and head to your office."

Ending the call, Kian turned to William. "Can you please zoom in on the precise location?

He nodded and did as Kian had requested. "They are about ninety miles due east from us, located in a wilderness area at the foothills of Mount Baldy."

"It's like they are taunting us." Kian raked his fingers through his hair. "Obviously, they know how to turn the signals on and off, and they kept them off until they got in position. They turned them on to let us know that they are here."

As the door opened and the chief walked in, his eyes zeroed in on the screen. "I know the area." He walked up to the laptop and leaned closer for a better look. "The actual location is very hard to access. It's a mountainous canyon surrounded by sheer cliffs and accessible only through a very narrow dirt road."

Kian wondered why Onegus was familiar with the Mount Baldy area, but that was immaterial at the moment.

"Would you like some coffee, master?" Okidu asked the chief.

"I would love some, thank you."

"We need to find out what is out there and who we are dealing with," Kian said, "But we need to do that cautiously. I think those signals are meant to draw us out. Whoever was emitting them followed the signals from the Kra-ell, and since we failed to remove Igor's tracker before bringing him to the keep, they discovered that location. I'm just glad that the village wasn't compromised."

Onegus nodded. "I agree that it's a trap and with your decision to initiate the lockdowns. I alerted Anandur and Brundar, and they will be here any moment now. You know the protocol. If the alert level is raised to red, you need to have them by your side at all times."

That reminded Kian that Syssi and Allegra were alone and unprotected in the house. Not that anyone or anything could get into the village, and even an aerial attack would be difficult to pull off with all the safety precautions William had incorporated. Nevertheless, he would feel better knowing that Okidu was there to shield them.

Onidu needed to go home as well.

He turned to the Odus. "Thank you for your help, but you should return home and resume your duties." He looked at Okidu. "The village might be in danger, and I count on you to defend Syssi and Allegra." He shifted his eyes to Onidu. "Same goes for you. Your job is to defend Amanda and Evie."

"Yes, master." Both the Odus bowed and headed for the door.

"Don't leave their sides for any reason," he added.

Okidu hesitated by the door. "What should I tell Mistress Syssi?" he asked.

It was early, and Syssi was probably still sleeping, but she would wake up soon and prepare to leave for the university.

He needed to notify everyone about the lockdown without creating panic.

They had an alert system, but sounding the alarm would freak everyone out.

"I'll call Syssi shortly," he told the Odu.

"Thank you, master." Okidu dipped his head and walked out the door.

Kian turned to Onegus. "We need to alert everyone without creating panic. Any suggestions as to how we should handle that?"

"I'll send a broadcast text to everyone," William offered. "They will see it when they wake up."

"Try to make it sound like locking the village down is only a precaution because the keep's location was compromised."

Kian wasn't sure that William was the best person for the task, but he didn't have time to compose the text himself, and he would probably do a much worse job than William.

"We can use our high-altitude surveillance drone," Onegus suggested. "Although it has the range, we shouldn't fly it from here because it will have to go through the airspace of three international airports. I suggest dispatching a team to drive it closer to the area and fly it from there."

"That's an excellent idea." Kian tapped his fingers on the conference table. "Make it so. Also, wake Roni up and have him hack into the FAA's global tracking system so our drone remains undetected. If whoever sends the signals can access the network, I don't want them to know we are flying a drone to spy on them."

Onegus looked as if he wanted to say something but decided not to. "I'll wake Charlie up. He's the best at flying drones."

The chief probably thought hacking into the FAA's global tracking system was taking it too far, but Kian had just gotten confirmation that his paranoia was not only entirely justified but not far-reaching enough to think up all the possible doomsday scenarios reality was throwing at him.

As Onegus got busy, Kian turned to William. "Do you have a backup for the specialty monitors and receivers in case they malfunction?"

"I do."

"Good. I know you have alerts on your phone and laptop whenever a signal goes on, but I also want someone in the lab babysitting the equipment twenty-four-seven."

William nodded. "I'll put Marcel in charge of assigning people to the job."

"Good choice. Can you reroute the signals to the war room?"

"Of course."

"Excellent. Make it so. I want to hold an emergency meeting in there."

It was time to assemble the troops, so to speak.

Onegus paused his phone conversation with Charlie and turned to Kian. "What do you want to do with the team when they land in China? Do you want them to refuel and turn around? We might need Yamanu here."

By the time they were back, the crisis might be over. "Not yet. Have them investigate the location the signals came from before. Maybe they will find clues to help us figure out what and who we are dealing with."

Kian typed a message and sent it to Turner, Kalugal, and Jade to come to the war room at their earliest convenience.

Onegus ended the call and lifted his hand to get Kian's attention. "I suggest alerting security in Alaska and Scotland as well. They don't need to go into lockdown mode, but they should take precautions just in case."

"I'll call them." Evidently, Kian's paranoia didn't go deep enough because he should have thought of that before Onegus brought it up.

After Igor's capture, Kian had hoped for peaceful times ahead, but he should have known better. Igor-caliber assassins were waiting to be revived from stasis, and now three mysterious signals had appeared within days of them bringing Igor to the keep.

Gabi

After talking to Becky, Gabi's mind had been too busy running in circles to go back to sleep, but it was still too early to call Gilbert to get her.

She'd tried watching television, but nothing could hold her focus, especially since she kept glancing at her phone, hoping to see a message from Uriel.

Perhaps Becky was right, and she should at least try to forget about him.

Yeah, good luck with that.

Running always helped clear her mind, and the hotel probably had a gym with some treadmills she could use, but she didn't have gym clothes or running shoes. Also, she wouldn't be alone in the gym, which would make her memories of immortals disappear again, so that wouldn't be very helpful anyway.

If the hotel had a pool, though, she could go for a swim. She'd gotten a new bikini on her shopping trip with

Darlene, along with a matching cover-up, and her flip-flops would do just fine as footwear.

Picking up the receiver, she called the front desk.

"Good morning, Ms. Emerson," a cheerful lady answered. "How can I help you?"

"Good morning. I was wondering whether you have a pool in the hotel?"

"We have an exercise pool in the gym."

Gabi had seen commercials for those pools but never used one.

"Is that like a small pool with jets you're supposed to swim against?"

"It's more like a current than a jet. It allows you to work on your strokes without moving forward."

"Have you tried it?"

The woman laughed. "I have not. It scares me. But many of the hotel's guests enjoy it. You should give it a try."

"I think I will. Where is the gym?"

"It's on the sixty-second floor next to the spa."

"Thank you. I'll tell you how it was after I'm done."

"That would be great. Enjoy your swim, Ms. Emerson."

"Thanks."

After ending the call, Gabi walked over to the closet, took the bikini and the matching cover-up out of the shopping bag, removed the tags, and put everything on.

"Not bad." She admired herself in the mirror from several angles.

The bikini was dark blue with a slim golden line on the edges that made it look sporty and elegant at the same time. The bottoms provided adequate coverage for her ass without looking like it belonged on a grandma, and the top was like a good bra, giving her breasts the slight push-up they needed.

Good nutrition and exercise could only go so far, and some signs of aging could only be addressed by plastic surgery. Luckily, Gabi's plan to get breast implants for her fortieth birthday was obsolete. After her transition, her breasts would go back to being as perky and as lovely as they had been in her early twenties.

Hopefully.

She was still thinking about all the things that would improve after her transition when she got to the gym, but as soon as she stepped inside, she couldn't remember what she'd been thinking about on her way there.

The place was packed, and every treadmill was taken, and so was the exercise pool.

The attendant smiled politely. "The current session is about to end in a few minutes, and the next reservation is for half an hour from now. Should I put your name down for the one in between? They run twenty-five minutes each."

"Please do. My name is Gabriella Emerson. I would have called ahead if I had known that reservations were needed."

The guy smiled politely again. "The gym is small, so reservations are a must even for treadmill time. They should have told you that at the front desk when you checked in."

She hadn't done the checking in because Gilbert's friend had done it for her. He'd even handed her the key.

Why had Gilbert brought him to the family dinner?

As a headache pierced her temples, Gabi rubbed at them with her thumbs.

"Are you okay?" the guy asked.

"Yeah, it's just a headache. It will clear up as soon as I start moving."

"You can wait over there." He pointed at a row of three chairs next to the pool. "Mr. Clark's session will be over in four minutes."

"Thank you." Gabi walked over to where he had pointed and sat down.

Watching the guy in the pool battling the current, she wasn't sure she could manage it unless the force of the jets was adjustable. His muscular arms powered through the stream, and as his torso lifted from side to side, she got a good view of his chest muscles as well. It was a nice view, but it wasn't nearly as magnificent as Uriel's.

You need to forget about him.

As the session ended and the guy climbed out of the pool, his powerful body dripping water, Gabi waited for that spark of attraction she should have felt for such a fine male specimen, but there was nothing. It was like looking at a store mannequin and admiring how well it was made.

I'm so screwed.

Gabi lifted her phone to check if a message had come in without her noticing it, even though it wasn't likely given that the device had been clutched in her hand the entire time, and she would have felt the vibrations.

There was nothing.

Yep, I'm royally screwed.

Jade

Dawn had barely broken over the horizon, the darkness slowly giving way to light, but it was still cold, and Jade zipped up her light jacket before breaking into a light jog.

It was funny how quickly she'd gotten used to the balmy weather of Southern California. Compared to how cold it was in Karelia, this was a warm summer day, but good things were easy to get used to.

They were also worth protecting.

The team should be landing in Chengdu soon, and she hoped they would proceed straight to the location of the signals instead of checking into a hotel first. She had to know whether the signals had originated with the scouts and if they were still alive or could be awoken from stasis. Talking to them might shed more light on the real purpose of the settler expedition, because Jade doubted it had been about the Kra-ell establishing a colony on Earth.

The Eternal King hadn't been the only one with plots within plots. The Kra-ell queen had been a shrewd manipulator as well.

When her phone buzzed in her jacket pocket, she pulled it out and wasn't surprised to see that it was from Kian. He was probably letting her know that the team had landed safely.

Instead, the text was an urgent summons to his office.

Jade slowed down to reread it. It didn't say why he wanted her to come as soon as she could, only that her presence was required.

Putting the phone back in the pocket, Jade changed direction and jogged the other way.

The team couldn't have discovered anything yet, so it had to be about something else, and since the biggest trouble-makers were away on the mission, it wasn't about her people causing problems in the village either.

Could it be about more signals coming online?

Or maybe Syssi had had a vision about the twins?

Jade had heard the rumors about Kian's mate predicting the Kra-ell years before the first contact was made with Emmett.

Well, that wasn't accurate. The first contact had been between Stella and Vrog, and the result was Vlad, but Stella hadn't told anyone that her son's father was a hybrid alien she'd hooked up with while traveling the world.

Still, Syssi hadn't known that the Kra-ell were real until the clan found Veskar aka Emmett, but she'd written scripts about them for that Perfect Match thing.

Jade hadn't tried it out yet, and she probably wouldn't unless Phinas wanted to. She wasn't a fan of living out fantasies but would do it for him.

Love was a great motivator for doing things a sane person wouldn't have done otherwise. The queen must have loved Ahn to have a forbidden affair with him, and then she was saddled with hybrid twins she had to hide from the world because both the gods and the Kra-ell would have wanted to kill them if they found out about their mixed parentage.

The thing was, they'd looked perfectly Kra-ell when Jade had seen them entering their pods. Perhaps they were so powerful that they could use a shroud that even Kra-ell were not immune to. But if they could do that, why hide behind veils?

Maybe they couldn't maintain the illusion for long.

Yeah, that made sense. It also meant they were probably not as powerful as their grandfather feared.

As Jade rounded the bend and the café came into view, she was surprised to see several males sitting at the tables and drinking coffee in paper cups that came from the vending machines and eating prepackaged pastries. Usually, this early in the morning, the place was deserted.

She recognized some of them from the ship, which meant that they were Guardians, which also meant that village security had been beefed up.

Something was definitely going on.

With a sense of foreboding adding urgency to the summons, Jade took the stairs to the second floor of the office building two at a time and then strode down the hallway to Kian's office.

The door was open, and as she walked in and saw who else had been summoned, her sense of foreboding was confirmed.

If Kian had called her, William, Kalugal, Onegus, and Turner for a meeting at six in the morning, it wasn't to discuss trivial matters.

Most ominous of all was the presence of Brundar and Anandur. She had never seen Kian shadowed by his personal bodyguards while in the village before.

"Good morning, Jade," Kian greeted her as the others nodded. "Grab a seat. Would you like some coffee or water before we begin?"

"Thanks, but I'd rather get right to business." She sat down.

"My apologies for dragging all of you out of bed so early, but this couldn't wait. The signals are back, and this time they are coming from our backyard, so to speak—a canyon near Mount Baldy. We initiated lockdown protocols here and in the keep, and we alerted all other clan members currently residing in Scotland, Alaska, and elsewhere. Until we identify the source of these signals, we have to assume that this is an assassins' force that was somehow activated as a result of moving the Kra-ell here or because of Igor's capture and that, for some reason, their trackers are an older technology, or that the Odus misinterpreted the difference in the signals. They appear to have the ability to turn the trackers on and off at will, which means that they are not the same type as the ones the settlers and even Igor had."

"Let me recap," Turner said. "Sunday, the signals came from China, winked out, came back on again, and winked out again. The assumption was that they originated from the scouting team that had been dispatched ahead of the settler ship. Now the signals are coming from the Mount Baldy area, and they just popped up here with nothing between here and Chengdu. We assume that they belong to the other assassins that were smuggled among the settlers and that they are a slightly different technology with the ability to be turned on and off. Did I get it right so far?"

When Kian nodded, Turner looked at William. "Have they moved since they were first located in the Mount Baldy area?"

William cleared his throat. "They haven't. After the system pinged my phone, activating the alarm I'd set up, I identified the signals, but I needed the Odus's help to locate where the signals were coming from. After the Odus provided us with the coordinates, and those trackers kept broadcasting, I was able to triangulate the signals with our other receivers and keep track of them. They haven't moved. But just to confirm, we can have the Odus do another round of deciphering."

"How far from here is Mount Baldy?" Jade asked.

"It's about seventy miles from the village," Onegus said. "We are sending a drone to investigate the area before we dispatch Guardians."

Kian nodded. "It might be a trap, and I won't send our people without utilizing every precaution available to us. We are dispatching a small team with a van to launch a high-altitude surveillance drone. Charlie will remotely pilot the drone, and Roni will tend to the FAA's tracking system while we are at it."

Jade tilted her head. "Why can't you just send a small drone that flies under the radar and doesn't register on the FAA tracking system?"

"I don't want the assassins, or whoever these people are, to realize they are being watched. A small, low-altitude drone in a remote area will be clearly visible to humans, let alone Kra-ell, who possess superior vision and hearing."

Leaning back in his chair, Kalugal braced his elbow on his other arm and leaned his chin on it. "If these are the assassins from the ill-fated settlers' spaceship, where are the rest of their pod members? In my opinion, we are dealing with something or someone entirely different but somehow connected to the Kra-ell or to Igor or both."

"Like who?" William asked. "Who else could it be?"

Jade had no clue. It didn't make sense for the assassins to have a different kind of tracker than the settlers, especially given the fact that Igor's tracker was the same as everyone else's on the ship. No one from Anumati could have arrived so quickly, either. The scouts were still the best candidates for the signal origins, but then how did they get from China to Los Angeles without their trackers transmitting in the interim?

Unless...

Unless some of the survivors had woken up a long time ago, removed their trackers so they would stop broadcasting, and then put them in again to send a message. But then, how had they known where Igor and the people he had held captive in his compound had been taken?

"It might be related to what I suspect was Igor's ability to communicate telepathically," Kian said. "And to his so-called tasting of my blood. If his primary objective was the assassination of all the legitimate heirs to the throne, and if he was somehow able to broadcast telepathically across space and time, his handlers now know that he found a direct descendant. I have human blood mixed in, but they might assume that Ahn has other descendants who are purely gods."

"They couldn't have gotten here so fast," Jade said.

"Probably not," Kian agreed. "But for all we know, the gods could have activated resources that they already had on Earth. Igor might not have been aware of being watched."

Leaning forward, Turner lifted his coffee mug. "The how of the signals' sudden appearance is certainly interesting, but for now, we need to focus on the who and what and neutralize the threat. Unless we get proof to the contrary, we must assume that each signal point is at least as dangerous to us as Igor, and since we could barely handle one, we need to figure out how to deal with three Igor-caliber adversaries at once."

Kian

"My thoughts exactly," Onegus said. "My guys are mapping out all the locations the Kra-ell passed through while their trackers were still active, and the same goes for the gerbils that hosted them after we removed them from the Kra-ell. If we assume that the originators of the new signals can trace the trackers, and that's why they are here, all the locations those trackers passed through need to be either fortified, evacuated, or used as honey traps to draw them in. Fortunately, we made sure that no trackers made it to the village. But that still leaves the keep, our warehouse downtown, and Safe Haven."

"We are assuming that the three signals represent three people," William said. "But if the signals were turned on deliberately to flush us out, there might be many more of them who don't have trackers and are not broadcasting. The assassins might have followed the Kra-ell trackers until they were all deactivated, so they know the general location of where that was done, but they don't know who did it and where they are now. They most likely figured out that we can trace the trackers, and that's how we found Igor's compound and the Kra-ell, and since they don't know where to find us now, they are luring us in with a limited number of signals, hoping we will assume that we are missing a few Kra-ell settlers and want to collect them as well. "

William wasn't a strategist, but he was a smart guy, and his assumptions made sense, but they were incomplete. "If they saw the damage we did to the compound, they probably assumed that we took the Kra-ell by force, and to do that, we needed to have a large force with advanced weapons." Kian pushed to his feet and took his nearly empty coffee mug with him. "If they suspect the truth, that the Kra-ell rebelled and we only assisted in their liberation, they would also suspect that we have a strong compeller to free them from Igor's compulsion. But in either case, the fact that we found the Kra-ell and freed them from their trackers indicates that we are familiar with the technology and that we are capable of identifying the signals and deciphering their location."

Merlin along with Hildegard had flown to Helsinki to remove the trackers from the students who had been away at the university at the time of the attack, but unlike Sofia, the others hadn't been deemed important enough to receive the alien trackers. They had been implanted with man-made ones.

Kian refilled the mug with coffee from the carafe and returned to the table. "Also, they must assume that three signals are not going to get our panties in a wad and that we will not think twice about sending a team to investigate."

Onegus chuckled. "That's exactly what we have done. To achieve their goal, they should have remained in China instead of coming here."

"They couldn't be sure we would take the bait when the signals were far away." Kian put the mug on the table. "In fact, I was inclined to let it go. Still, they might have split forces, and some are still in China. We've alerted the team in Chengdu, and they know that the signals have moved here, but we also need to let them know we suspect there could be more than three people behind the signals."

"Right." Onegus pulled out his phone. "They should be landing shortly, and I don't want them to proceed to the location. I'm putting Yamanu on the line so he can participate in this discussion."

Kian nodded. "Good idea."

Jade's doubtful expression indicated that she disagreed. "That only makes sense if those other assassins figured out that they have trackers implanted in their bodies and removed them before the technology to build the receivers became available. Otherwise, Igor would have found them. He went after any signal he detected, and I believe he was telling the truth when he said that he collected all that had come online."

Kalugal tilted his head. "I'll tell you why that's not likely. If those were indeed other assassins from the ship, who knew how to track the signals and decipher them, they would have joined forces with Igor as soon as they found him. They wouldn't have been watching from afar to see what he was up to. They had their orders the same way he did, and given that the gods bred them for that purpose and programmed them for a specific task, they wouldn't have been able to resist contacting Igor. But if those are not the assassins, then who could they be?"

Frowning, Jade turned to Kian. "You said something before that got me thinking. What if you are right, and the gods have hidden assets on Earth that they can deploy quickly? I don't understand what purpose a hidden cell of gods could serve after determining that the exiled gods were gone, and if they were sent to observe Igor, why didn't they intervene with what he was doing?"

"We can speculate all we want," Kian said. "But without collecting more intel, we won't get any smarter. Let's take a short break and continue this in the war room.

Syssi

As soon as the cobwebs of sleep receded, or maybe even before, Syssi sensed that Kian wasn't with her in bed, which worried her.

Not too long after they had gotten married, he had promised not to leave their bed before she was awake, because she hated waking up alone, and also so they could spend their mornings together. They were a bonded immortal couple, so on the face of things, they didn't need to work on keeping their marriage healthy because it was a given, but she thought it was important to grant their union a priority status.

It was so easy to get all bogged down with work, especially for Kian, and to neglect all the things that brought him pleasure, like spending time with his wife and daughter. As an immortal, he lived with the sense that there would always be time for that later, but it was an illusion, and it wasn't good for him.

First of all, Allegra wouldn't stay a baby for long, and that window of opportunity for father and daughter to bond would be missed if Kian didn't prioritize spending time with her. Secondly, the more Kian allowed himself to get sucked into the vortex of the never-ending issues and problems facing the clan, and the less quality time he spent with his family, the more agitated and dejected he became.

For the sake of everyone in the village, it was important to keep Kian's life balanced.

Touching his pillow confirmed that he had gotten up a long time ago. Sometimes he got up to check on Allegra and returned within seconds, but that wasn't the case today.

He might have thought that she hadn't noticed he couldn't fall asleep for hours or that he'd left the bed a few times and returned a few minutes later, but not from Allegra's room. She'd heard him talking in a hushed voice from the bathroom and had figured out that he'd been checking up on the team he'd sent to China.

They were still en route, and it wasn't like Kian to be so worried about the flight. Morris was a capable pilot, and the clan maintained its jets expertly, so a malfunction wasn't likely.

Perhaps he'd gotten more information about the signals at night?

He was probably in his office, and she could make them both cappuccinos and bring them there so they could at least salvage that part of their morning routine.

After a much-needed visit to the bathroom, Syssi checked Allegra's room first. Finding her daughter peacefully asleep, she walked down the hallway to Kian's office.

When she didn't find him there, she sat behind his desk, picked up the receiver, and called him.

"Good morning, my love," Kian answered. "What are you doing awake this early?"

"That's what I want to know. Where are you?"

"I'm on my way to the war room from an emergency meeting in my office."

Her stomach twisted in knots. "What happened?"

"The signals are back, and this time they are broadcasting from an area about an hour away from the village. Right now, that's all I know. I'll call you as soon as I know more. In the meantime, the village is in lockdown, so you can stay in bed longer because no one is leaving."

"Does Amanda know?"

"She will when she wakes up and checks her messages. I have to go, love. I'll call you later."

As the call ended, Syssi put the receiver down and leaned back in Kian's chair.

Why had he ordered a lockdown?

Three signals meant three people. Even if they were assassins, the Guardians could deal with them.

What wasn't Kian telling her?

Could the Doomers be involved somehow? Was it possible that they had discovered one of the missing pods?

She wouldn't put it past them to kill the twenty Kra-ell in the pod, dig out the trackers from the bodies, and then use them to lure Guardians into a trap.

Navuh hadn't launched a direct attack on the clan in far too long, and he was overdue.

No, that wasn't a likely scenario.

Lokan would have warned them of an impending attack, and even if he didn't know about it, Andrew would have known if a large group of foreign nationals had entered the city and would have checked them out.

But that was provided they had arrived at one of the major airports. If they had landed somewhere else and had used ground transportation to get to Los Angeles, Andrew wouldn't know about them.

Fates, Syssi hoped it wasn't the Doomers.

Even with all their genetically enhanced features, a few Kra-ell assassins worried her much less than Navuh and his legions of vicious warriors.

Kian

The call from Syssi had kept Kian out of the war room for a couple of minutes, and as he entered, the others were already seated around the table.

He'd hoped not to see that room for a long time, but he should have known better. It was like a game of whack-a-mole. He would barely get one crisis under control when a new one popped up.

As Anandur distributed water bottles, Kian sat down next to Kalugal.

Given the situation, he would have preferred a few shots of whiskey, but it was too early in the morning even for an immortal who had been born and raised in Scotland.

Kalugal removed the cap from the bottle Anandur handed him. "Since my men are stuck in the village along with everyone else, they might as well help out. I'm placing them under Onegus's command."

"Thank you." Kian gave him a nod of approval. "I appreciate the offer, but I hope we won't need the reinforcements. Can't your guys work from home? You have everything you need in your house to run your empire from here."

"True, true." Kalugal's lips lifted in a barely-there smirk. "But someone told me that my men have gotten soft and need more training. Not that I accept the unflattering assessment. They made me proud in Karelia."

Kian sincerely doubted that Kalugal's reason for volunteering his men was that he wanted them to train. That could have been achieved by talking to Bhathian, who was in charge of the training, and coming up with a schedule of classes for the men.

"A skill is like a knife." Kian removed the cap from his bottle. "If it's not regularly honed and sharpened, it becomes dull."

"I agree," Jade said. "My people train regularly, and a group of pureblooded females has joined the Guardians to train for the rescue operations. Other than the former prisoners, every adult member of the Kra-ell community is at your disposal."

Considering, Kian nodded. "Thank you, but don't share the particulars with them yet. Not before we know more." He turned to Kalugal. "Same goes for your men. I'm keeping it on the down low with my people as well. We don't want the civilians to panic."

Behind them, Turner chuckled. "With the village in lock-down, and all the able fighters on alert, that ship has sailed. Not knowing the nature of the threat, they will assume the worst, and you'll have the entire village banked up outside your office window, waiting to hear what's going on. I recommend bringing everyone up to speed and posting updates on the clan's virtual bulletin board."

That was atypical of Turner, who was always security first, but he had a point.

Kian glanced at William. "Did you send the group text already?"

William shook his head. "When? I haven't had time to do it yet, but I planned to follow your suggestion and keep it as vague as possible. I will only mention the keep's location being compromised and this being a safety precaution, without providing more details." He looked at Turner. "Should I say more?"

"No, that's good. Keep it vague, but not so much that people will imagine the worst." Turner pulled out his phone. "I need to alert my office that I cannot come in until further notice."

"Can't you work remotely?" Kian asked. "Your work involves saving lives, and I don't want them on my conscience. If your presence is essential at your office, I will make an exception for you and let you leave."

"It's fine." Turner waved a dismissive hand. "I can work from here. It will put more strain on my office staff, but they can handle it. Fortunately, I don't have anything urgent right now. My current mission is in the initial planning stages, and it's not a life-or-death situation, so I can make this my priority and start working on contingencies and strategies."

"That's good." Kian let out a breath. "I need your brain working on this, especially once we have more information."

Turner nodded. "On the way here, I thought about Jade's suggestion to fly a small surveillance drone, and I think that's a good idea."

Kian thought it was a terrible idea. "Why? That would alert them to our presence."

"Precisely." Turner tapped his pen on his yellow pad. "Think of it as a chess game. They made their first move, moving a pawn on the board, meaning the signals. We will respond in kind, sending a pawn of our own to signal that we are ready to play the game, meaning the small drone they will have no problem seeing. It's much better than sending in a knight or a bishop, don't you think?"

Syssi

After getting dressed, Syssi walked into the kitchen, where Okidu was expertly flipping an omelet.

"Good morning, Okidu." She walked up to the stove. "That smells good." Usually, he made her omelet from real eggs and Kian's from an egg substitute, but since Kian wasn't home, it was only real eggs.

"Good morning, mistress." He bowed. "Your breakfast is almost ready. I added plenty of spinach and feta cheese, just as you like."

"Thank you. I'm sure it's delicious, but I'm not hungry yet." When he looked mortified, she amended, "I need to check on Allegra, and when she wakes up, I will eat breakfast with her. Can you put it in the warming drawer for me?"

That brought a smile to his face. "Of course, mistress."

When he turned his attention back to the skillet, it dawned on Syssi that she wouldn't be heading to work this morning and that Amanda probably didn't know about the lockdown yet. Her sister-in-law was probably still asleep.

Pulling her phone from her pocket, she typed a message to her sister-in-law.

Good morning. I don't want to alarm you, but in case you don't know yet, the village is locked down, and we can't go to the university today. Do you want me to call the lab and let our team know?

There was no reason to expect Amanda to respond anytime soon, so Syssi placed her phone on the counter and replayed what Kian had told her. The three signals were now coming from a nearby location, and it could be a trap.

He hadn't said that, but he hadn't needed to. Obviously, those people had gotten nearer to lure the clan into a trap. Hopefully, it was as clear to Kian and his team as it was to her, and they were being careful and not sending Guardians to investigate without doing an aerial sweep of the area first.

Should she call him? Or maybe text him?

Would he be upset that she was telling him how to do his job?

Kian was usually good about taking advice .from her. Still, when he was stressed, especially about the clan's safety, he turned into a caveman, listening only to people he considered experts on security and strategy, meaning Onegus and Turner and sometimes Andrew.

He'd promised to call her as soon as he knew more, but he'd either forgotten or there was no new information, and she was so anxious that she was starting to hyperventilate.

Perhaps she should take a few minutes to relax before Allegra woke up to a stressed-out mom. A cappuccino would be a step in the right direction. Unlike most people, Syssi found caffeine relaxing rather than stimulating, and the ritual of preparing the perfect cup was calming in itself.

The familiar movements, the thumping sounds of the machine, the aroma permeating the room.

As she'd expected, preparing the cup had reduced her stress level by at least twenty percent, and as she took it with her to the family room and sat on the comfortable couch, she closed her eyes and imagined a placid lake bathed in moonlight. Usually, that was enough to calm her down, but not today.

Ravenous sharks lurked beneath the deceptively tranquil waters, and owls hooted ominously from the trees swaying prettily in the breeze.

Having a vivid imagination was a double-edged sword.

To achieve calmness, she needed to clear her mind from all thoughts, which was incredibly difficult, and she still struggled with it even after all the lessons she'd had with Madame Salinka and the many hours of practice since.

Setting the coffee down, Syssi started the slow, practiced breathing and repeated the meditative sound in her mind. After a while, she found herself floating aimlessly among the clouds with little or no thoughts at all.

Peace.

As the clouds thinned and the view below came into focus, some part of Syssi was aware that she wasn't meditating. This was a vision, but it lacked the ominous nature of most of her doomsday predictions.

She felt light as a feather and without a care in the world.

The canyon below wasn't pretty. The vegetation was sparse, the creek at its bottom was dry, and the soil looked parched, with cracked veins running through its dusty, yellow surface, but there was nothing unusual about it. This was Southern California on the cusp of summer. It hadn't rained in a while, and things had dried out pretty quickly despite the heavy rainfall of the preceding months.

As movement ahead drew her attention, she floated forward.

Below, three men were arguing, gesticulating with their hands, and getting in each other's faces like three bucks competing for the favors of one doe. She couldn't hear what they were arguing about, but it seemed important.

As she drew nearer, the men raised their heads and seemed to stare straight at her.

Even in the hazy dream-like world of a vision, Syssi knew they couldn't see or even sense her, but the impulse to fly away and hide was strong. They must be looking at something behind her, but she couldn't see it. She could only see them and the canyon they were in.

It wasn't the first time Syssi realized that she was being shown only a fraction of the experience, and that some things remained outside her perception without any rhyme or reason. Sometimes it was sounds, other times it was part of the scenery, and in still others it was any identifying features of the main players.

When one of the men lifted a strange-looking cylinder and pointed it at her, Syssi gasped and recoiled, thinking it was a monocular and that he was trying to get a better look at her, but then the one standing next to him grabbed his wrist and pushed his arm down.

At that instant, Syssi realized that the cylindrical tool was a weapon of some sort, and that the man who had pointed it at her was about to shoot something that was flying either behind or above her.

The third realization was that the weapon was not from Earth, and neither were the three males.

Gabi

When Gabi returned to her room, every muscle in her body was aching. Swimming against the current had been difficult, requiring the use of muscles she must have neglected during her workouts with Becky. Usually, she would have welcomed the ache because it meant that her muscles were getting stronger, but today it just added to the feeling of exhaustion that had nothing to do with physical activity and everything to do with the lack of a message from Uriel.

Even Gilbert hadn't called her yet, and there was no way he was still sleeping.

Leaving both her regular phone and the clan phone on the bathroom vanity, she stepped into the shower and made quick work of shampooing and conditioning her hair, washing the pool chlorine off, all while listening intently so she wouldn't miss an incoming call or message.

Except, none came during the shower or while she toweled off and blow-dried her hair.

It was after nine in the morning, and the day was wasted.

After making herself another cup of coffee, Gabi sat on the couch and looked at both phones, contemplating Becky's advice and whether she was going to listen to it or ignore it.

If life had taught her anything, it was that leaving the initiative to others was never a good plan. If she wanted Uriel or just wanted to hear from him, she should contact him and not wait for him to do it first.

On the other hand, what was the point of dragging this out when she would have to disappear soon?

Perhaps she should just say goodbye one last time?

Well, first she needed to call Gilbert and find out when he was coming to pick her up. Perhaps Uriel was done with his first meeting of the day and had time to meet her for breakfast?

But even if he could, it was such a bad idea. She was just prolonging their parting and making it more difficult for herself, but she couldn't help it.

She just needed to see him one last time, or at least try to.

Damn, why was it so hard?

He was supposed to be just a hookup, and he'd been a wonderful one. Why did she have to ruin it by wanting more?

Grabbing the white not-iPhone, she lifted it to her face to unlock it, found Gilbert's contact, and called him.

"Hi, Gabi," he answered right away. "How are you doing?"

"Great," she affected a cheerful tone. "I went for a swim in the exercise pool they have here in the hotel. I didn't know how hard it was to swim against a current. I'm aching all over. Anyway, when are you picking me up?"

He groaned. "I'm not. The village is in lockdown, and no one is coming or going."

Anxiety tightening a vise around her heart, Gabi forced herself to take a deep breath. "Please tell me it's a drill, and nothing terrible is happening."

The clan had enemies. The Doomers. What if they had launched an attack? What would happen to her family?

"It's nothing to worry about," Gilbert said. "A different clan location was potentially compromised, and Kian is not taking any chances with security, so he ordered both locations locked down. He's known to be a little paranoid, or a lot, so he's probably overreacting. I expect the village will open up in a few hours, but it sucks that we are missing out on the one day you had for us. Is there any way you can postpone your return flight? Can you at least stay over the weekend?"

His explanation alleviated some of her anxiety, but was he telling her the truth? Gilbert and Eric thought they were shielding her from worry by not telling her stuff, but it only made her worry more because she expected them to hide things from her.

"Tell me the truth, Gilbert. Are you really in no danger?"

"I told you everything I know. Do you think I would be asking you to stay longer if I thought I might be putting you in danger?"

He had a point.

It would take some maneuvering to reschedule the sessions she had arranged for Thursday and Friday, or she could turn them into virtual meetings. After all, she'd flown across the country to visit her family, and if she didn't get to do that, it would be such a waste of money and effort. So yeah, she'd seen most of them already, but it had been only a few hours, and she hadn't seen Idina yet.

Besides, if she stayed longer, she could see Uriel again.

"I'll check what can be done about the return flight. I can't go back without visiting the village, and seeing your new homes, and meeting the rest of Darlene's family. I didn't even get to see Idina."

"What about your clients?"

"I'll have to make up a good excuse for why I have to meet with them virtually and not in person and give them some sort of bonus in exchange for the inconvenience."

"That's great. We will have the entire weekend to spend together. Karen and the kids are going to be so happy."

"Don't tell them yet. I don't know if I can get a return flight Sunday evening or Monday morning at the same price, and secondly, what if your village remains in lockdown for more than a day or two?"

"All we can do is hope for the best. Check the flight situation and get back to me. Perhaps the lockdown will be canceled by the time you call."

"I hope so."

Well, at this point, she hoped the lockdown would remain in effect for a little longer. Otherwise, she would have no reason to postpone her return flight and wouldn't get to see Uriel again.

Kalugal

K alugal stared at the large screen mounted on the war room's east wall and the images the drone was broadcasting—rocks, dry soil, and a few scattered bushes.

"What are we looking at?" he asked.

"A lot of nothing." Kian groaned and leaned back. "I don't understand. The trackers are still sending signals, the Odus gave us the precise coordinates, and they are supposed to be right there, but there is nothing alive in that spot, not even gerbils."

"We can't be sure of that," Onegus said. "The resolution is insufficient to show very small animals, especially if they have the same coloring as the surroundings." He looked at William. "Could it be that some of the gerbils got away from our downtown warehouse before you removed the trackers from them?"

William shook his head. "All the trackers are accounted for. Merlin kept meticulous records, noting each tracker and who it had belonged to before taking it out. I compared our records, and they match. Well, we have four more trackers because we also removed them from Igor, Sofia, and the two hybrids that had been following her when she was at Safe Haven."

"Is there a way to enhance the resolution?" Kian asked.

"I'm running it through AI." William turned his laptop around so they could all see his screen. "There is nothing there."

The drone had spent over an hour in the air filming, and then it had to go back to change batteries.

"We should have sent two drones," Kalugal grumbled. "While one was recharging, the other one could have been filming."

"So we could stare at more rocks?" Kian rose to his feet. "They must have a way to activate the trackers without using a live host, and they buried them in the ground to set a trap for us while they are hiding and waiting to see who will show up. I wouldn't be surprised if they mounted several cameras nearby and are observing from afar."

That actually made sense.

Why risk a face-to-face confrontation if the objective was only to find out who they were dealing with?

"The drone was a long shot," William said. "But we can learn something from there being nothing." He smiled at Kian. "If they wanted to flush us out by luring us into the canyon just to record who showed up, then they don't have a large force. Otherwise, they would have attempted to capture whoever was sent to investigate so they could interrogate them to learn what they need to know."

"My thoughts exactly," Kalugal said. "Except, I don't know what they hope to achieve by taking pictures or filming other than to satisfy their curiosity. What were they hoping to see? Whether the people showing up were Kra-ell or humans? I'm sure they weren't expecting gods or immortals. Unless these people came with a huge force, which, as William astutely noted, is doubtful, it would be stupid of them to reveal their presence just to gather intelligence."

Knowing that someone took over a large and well-defended Kra-ell settlement halfway around the world and also outmaneuvered and entrapped Igor must have worried the signal originators. They needed to find out who was behind such a complex, large-scale operation.

They had followed Igor's signal to Los Angeles, and when his tracker stopped broadcasting, they'd become desperate and announced their presence.

It was such a stupid move that Kalugal was sure he and the rest of their team were missing a big piece of the puzzle and that they had gotten the situation all wrong.

Could it be that the signals' owners were not adversaries?

For the move to be calculated rather than stupid, they had to want to establish contact without making a move that would seem aggressive, and the only possible form of communication they could establish with the Kra-ell liberators was the trackers.

They were being cautious and wanted the parley to be done on their terms and on their turf.

If Kalugal was in their shoes, and he wanted to make contact with a superior force, hoping for an amicable reception but not certain of it, he would have orchestrated a meeting at a place and time of his choosing, and in circumstances that negated the other side's strength and size advantage.

He turned to Kian. "Let's consider a different angle for a moment."

"Like what?" Kian asked.

"What if these people's objective is to seek our cooperation and help? If we assume that the signal broadcasters are aware of what we did in Karelia and that we captured Igor, then they are also aware of our operational capabilities. Why announce their arrival if they want to attack? And if their plan was to kidnap one or more of us for interrogation, that also would have been better accomplished covertly. If they tracked Igor and the Kra-ell, they would know all the locations that the trackers broadcasted from, including Safe Haven, the keep, and the clan's downtown warehouse. It would have been much easier for them to lie in wait for a clan member to appear at one of those locations and grab them."

Kian nodded. "It occurred to me that if I was in their position and had adversarial intentions, I would not have advertised my presence. But then that's my preferred modus operandi."

"Mine too," Kalugal said. "And we are both smart guys, right? We shouldn't assume that these people are stupid, and that's why I think they want to meet. But since they don't know what we are about and how we will respond, they want to control the circumstances of this meeting in a way that levels the playing field and negates our superior numbers, or what they think are our superior numbers. There could be more of them than there are of us."

Syssi

"You should tell Kian about your vision," Amanda said. "What if it's connected to the signals?"

William had sent a text explaining that the lockdown was a precaution because the keep's location had been compromised, but he hadn't elaborated. Syssi had filled in the blanks for Annani, Alena, and Amanda as best she could, but she didn't know much herself.

"I don't want to bother him." Syssi handed Allegra a piece of bread to chew on. "You know what my visions are like. This could be something that happens hundreds of years from now or happened hundreds of years in the past. I don't even know if the vision was from a place on Earth."

It looked like Southern California, but it could have been an alien planet.

"What were they wearing?" Alena asked. "That could give us a clue."

Syssi frowned. "I don't remember. That's another thing about visions. Details that should be obvious are missing. They could have been wearing space suits or jeans. The only thing that was clearly visible to me was that weapon, and it didn't even look like a weapon. It looked like a monocular, not a gun, but I knew it was dangerous." She looked at Amanda. "Besides, we need to get busy. Alena came over to babysit Evie and Allegra so we could put in a few hours of work, and we are wasting her time."

Alena shrugged. "I don't mind just chatting with you two. It's not like I have anything more interesting to do."

"La-la," Allegra said.

Alena smiled. "Yes, sweetie?"

"We-we."

Syssi laughed. "She knows who she can bribe to let her watch her favorite show, *The Wiggles*."

When her phone rang with Kian's ringtone, she glanced at Alena. "Can you watch Allegra for a few minutes while I take this?"

"Of course." Alena waved her away. "Go, talk to Kian and get him to tell us what's going on."

"I'll do my best." Syssi pushed to her feet and walked over to the bedroom to talk in private.

Closing the door behind her, she accepted the call. "Hi, love. How is your day going?"

"Much better now that I hear your voice. It's a balm for my frayed nerves."

He'd said that so many times before that it shouldn't have affected her as much anymore, but she still loved hearing it.

"I'm glad I can help in some way." She sat on the couch. "Do you have time to talk now?"

"Yeah. I took a short break, and I'm out in the hallway, pacing back and forth. I need to compose a text to let everyone know what's really going on, and I thought that you could probably do a better job of phrasing it in a way that wouldn't induce panic but would be less vague than what William sent earlier."

"To do that, you need to tell me more. All I know is that the signals that previously came from China suddenly appeared nearby."

"They are coming from a location near Mount Baldy. We sent a team with a drone to investigate, but there was no one there. I'll have to summon the Odus again to check whether the signals are still coming from the same location. If they do, then our mystery visitors buried the trackers in the ground to lure us there, but we don't know for what purpose. The drone circled the entire area, so we knew that no one was there to ambush us, and it was not like there was anywhere to hide. It's pretty barren, and the bushes are only big enough to hide a gerbil, and probably not even that."

Syssi frowned. "The alien trackers need live hosts. So maybe they are inside a small animal, and the poor thing is tied to one of those bushes, or maybe in a cage that is covered in dirt."

"I didn't think of that, but I guess it's possible. It's also possible that the older model trackers were more versatile and could operate without a live host. They were also able to turn them on and off at will, which is not how the newer ones work."

"How did they know where to find us?"

"The keep's location was compromised when we brought Igor in without removing his tracker first. We thought he was the danger, and once we had him, we no longer needed to worry about the trackers. I'm just glad that I didn't allow any of them in the village."

"So, if the village location hasn't been compromised, there is no reason for a lockdown here. We are not in danger."

"I can't risk it before I know what and who we are dealing with. Especially not with my mother here."

Kian was always worried about Annani, but Syssi doubted that the goddess was his main concern this time.

"Right." She pushed a strand of hair behind her ear. "She's quite peeved at you for not telling her about the signals. After the text from William, I told your mother and sisters what I knew, but it wasn't much."

"I didn't have time to talk to her. All the usual suspects are in the war room, and we are trying to figure out what to do next. Can you tell my mother that I will call her as soon as I know more?"

"Of course."

"And can you also compose a message explaining the situation?"

"Sure. Amanda is here, and she can help me with that. Alena is babysitting Allegra and Evie, so we can do some remote work."

"Thank you. You are the best."

"Yeah, yeah." She laughed. "By the way, I had a strange vision that may or may not have something to do with your signals."

There was a long moment of silence before Kian spoke. "Did you force it?"

Syssi rolled her eyes. "I promised you that I wouldn't do that, and I didn't. I was anxious because you'd left before I woke up, and when I called you, you sounded stressed, so of course, I got stressed as well. I didn't want Allegra to pick up on those negative vibes, so I meditated, and the vision just came."

"Oh, so it's my fault."

Her mate sounded like he was chewing on gravel, which was sexy when they were playing their kinky games, but intimidating and annoying at other times.

"Will you stop and listen?"

"I'm all ears." He still sounded like he was chewing rocks.

"I was meditating and doing some breathing exercises to relax, and that actually helped. I felt calm and collected."

"When did the vision start, and what did you see?"

"Oh, so now you want to hear all about it when a moment ago you sounded like you wanted to spank me for being a naughty girl."

He chuckled. "Is that an invitation?"

"No. I'm upset with you, but since you are under a lot of pressure, I'll forgive you this time."

"You always forgive me," he said softly. "I don't deserve you."

Kian

"You deserve everything, my love. Everything I have to give and more."

That hit Kian straight in the chest, and he lifted his hand to place it over his heart. "I'm so blessed, and I don't know what I did to deserve winning the lottery of life with you. You make it all worthwhile."

"We are both blessed," Syssi said. "Now, do you want to hear about my vision or not?"

"Yes, please. Although, frankly, I would rather come home and take you to bed."

He was still hard like a hammer from their little kinky exchange and thankful that he had stepped out of the war room to make the call, not just because his slacks sported a tent but also because he was overwhelmed with gratitude and love, and he probably looked like a sap right now.

Syssi laughed. "What is different about today? That's how you end every conversation with me."

He frowned. "Do I?"

Was he that predictable?

That unoriginal?

"Well, not every conversation, but most."

Kian sighed. "That's because I always want you, but since I can't have you right now, tell me about your vision."

"You said that the signals are coming from somewhere near Mount Baldy, right?"

"Yes."

"And you also said that you flew a drone over the area and didn't find anyone, right?"

"Well, technically, Charlie flew the drone, but yeah. There was nothing but rocks and dried-up bushes. Where are you going with this?"

Was he missing something that Syssi found obvious?

"Just bear with me for a moment. Are the signals coming from a canyon that's not near any paved road?"

Kian's blood chilled in his veins. "Is that a guess? Or do you know that for a fact?"

She laughed. "I'm a seer, darling. I've seen that canyon. You probably think that you are dealing with Kra-ell assassins, either from one of the pods or from another ship, and you are assuming that their sudden appearance here is related to either Igor's capture, the Kra-ell's move here, or both."

For some reason, Syssi was dragging it out. He would have thought that what she'd seen in her vision was so terrible that she needed to prepare him for it, but she sounded way too cheerful for that to be the case. In fact, she sounded as if she was almost amused and was trying not to offend him by revealing what she'd seen.

Could it be that William had miscalculated, and what they were getting from the canyon were the signals from escaped gerbils?

Did gerbils hibernate?

Maybe they had been in hibernation and had just awoken. Or maybe the gerbils had been eaten by a larger animal who had then gone into hibernation and had just woken up.

"I don't want to sound impatient, but just tell me already. I can't stand the suspense."

"Okay." She let out a breath as if she was disappointed that he hadn't given her the time to prepare her story for maximum impact. "While I was meditating, I found myself flying over a wilderness scored by deep canyons and ravines. The vegetation was sparse and seemed very similar to what we see in the mountains surrounding the village during the summer months. In one such canyon, I saw three men arguing about something. One of them held up what looked like a slim monocular, but I knew that it was a weapon, and I also knew that it was not manmade. Unless it was a movie prop made to look like an alien weapon, it was indeed of alien origins."

Kian stopped in his tracks. "Can you describe it in more detail?"

"It looked like a slim metal cylinder with a lens at the end. I didn't see telescoping parts, but it grew longer when the man held it up and aimed at an object that didn't register in my vision. For a moment, I thought that they could see me, but they were all looking at something behind me. I didn't know what it was, but it might have been your drone. When the one holding the weapon trained it on the thing that they saw that wasn't me, another one held onto his wrist and prevented him from shooting it."

"Hold on. I need to text Charlie to tell him to do another fly-by."

"But you said that the drone didn't see anything."

Kian finished typing the text. "I think that your vision was precognition, and you saw a couple of hours ahead. Three guys in a remote canyon not too far from the city, looking up at a drone and holding something that looked like an alien weapon, is too much of a coincidence. They have to be the ones we are looking for. When they all looked up towards you, were you close enough to see their faces? Any distinct features?"

There was a long moment of silence. "Hold on. I'm closing my eyes."

He frowned. "Did you see them or not?"

"Visions are funky, Kian. Sometimes they are clear, sometimes they are not, and sometimes details become clearer later on. I saw their faces when I was hovering above them, but they didn't register. But now that I close my eyes, I can see them clearly."

"Well?" he prompted.

"They were definitely not Kra-ell assassins." Syssi sounded very certain of that.

But who else could they be?

Their original suspicion had been that the signals originated from the scouts, but there would be no difference in appearance between them and the assassins. They both had to look the same as other pureblooded Kra-ell, and they were hard to confuse for anyone else. They didn't look human, but then Jade and her consorts had traveled the world and had done business with humans using minimal disguises like dark sunglasses and clothing that had hidden their extremely narrow waists.

"Perhaps they were disguised to look more human? Who other than the Kra-ell could have had those alien trackers and emitted signals?"

All of a sudden, Kian knew the answer to his questions, but it was too outrageous to consider seriously.

"Well, weren't the trackers implanted in the Kra-ell by the gods?" Syssi asked rhetorically. "After all, the technology was developed by the gods and implemented by them as well. How else would the Odus know how to decipher the signals from those trackers?"

"Are you telling me that the three men you saw in the canyon were gods?"

"That is exactly what I am saying. I know a god when I see one, and the three men in the canyon were stunningly beautiful and inhumanly perfect. Also, I don't think that their intentions are nefarious. I am not sure what I am basing this on, and I might be biased because we are related, which kind of makes us on the same team, but I have a strong feeling that they are friendlies, not adversaries."

Syssi had never been wrong before, but she might be this time.

"We know that not all gods are nice people, but we have an innate bias towards beauty. We are programmed to perceive it as something good. We must proceed with extreme caution and assume a defensive position as if we are facing adversaries, including keeping the village locked down until we can confirm that these males are friendly and mean us no harm."

From all he had learned about the gods recently, Kian expected the worst rather than the best.

"I trust your instincts, my love, and I agree that we should proceed with extreme caution, but we should not be the aggressors unless we are forced to be."

"I can promise you that we won't shoot first and ask questions later, but I can also promise you that we will be armed with everything we have and ready to use it if need be."

"That's smart. Perhaps you should bring the noise cannon to the canyon. I still remember what that thing did to a large group of immortals. If not for the drones and other precautions, those supposedly weak humans could have picked us off like flies and driven us away to their testing facility."

Kian felt his fangs punching over his lower lip. "I don't like to think about that evening, but you are absolutely right. The noise cannon could be a formidable weapon against gods with sensitive hearing. They heal incredibly fast, but a few seconds might make all the difference."

Syssi chuckled softly. "My intention wasn't to rile you up, just to offer one more defensive idea. I know that you need to get back to the war room, so I won't keep you. Keep me updated if you can and try to come home before Allegra goes to sleep tonight. She needs a hug from Daddy to have good dreams, and so do I."

And just like that, his fangs had receded, and a smile replaced his snarl. "I will do my best to get home in time to kiss Allegra goodnight and to take her mommy to bed. You might find it hard to believe, but I'm more excited about that than discovering three new gods, even friendly ones."

She laughed. "You're so bad."

"I know. But you love me anyway."

"I do."

Gabi

G abi read over the text she'd written to Uriel.

Something came up, and I won't be spending the day with my family after all. I also changed my return flight from Wednesday evening to Monday morning, and since I will be staying four days longer than I originally planned, I thought it would be nice if we could hang out together some more. You never told me how long you would be staying in L.A., but if you're going to be here over the weekend, we could go to the beach or visit The Huntington Library, and if you have a car, we can even drive up to Solvang and visit some wineries.

There was so much more she wanted to say to him, but first, she needed him to respond to her text so she would know that he was still interested.

She was already going out on a limb by contacting him, she wasn't also going to admit that he had rocked her world and probably ruined her for any other man.

Or male.

She doubted the immortals Darlene had gushed over could compete with Uriel. He was simply incomparable.

Her hand shook only a little as she pressed enter, and the text was sent.

Now it was only a matter of waiting, but as she looked at the screen, the three little dots didn't appear. He wasn't texting her back.

Perhaps he was in a meeting and couldn't answer.

The text was marked as delivered, but that didn't mean he'd read it, only that it was on his phone, tablet, or any other device capable of accepting texts.

When over two hours had passed with no return text, Gabi had to accept that Uriel was ghosting her.

But why?

Why was he acting like that?

After the two nights they had spent together, he could at least come up with a good lie to let her down easily. He could tell her that he had to fly back to Portugal because of an emergency back home, or that he'd heard of a hidden treasure in Nepal or some other exotic location and had to leave right away to chase it.

She would have known that he was lying, and he would have known that she knew, but it would have been better than this silence.

What if something had happened to him?

As images of car crashes and armed robberies zipped through her mind, her chest constricted with panic, and she had trouble catching her breath.

A brave warrior of God, my ass. She used anger to quash the panic.

Gabi was mad at herself for always imagining the worst, mad at Uriel for being a jerk, and mad at whatever circumstances had forced the immortals' village into lockdown.

How did they even do that? Was there a big wall around the village and a moat filled with hungry sharks, and a bridge that they could lift to prevent anyone from coming in or leaving?

She'd always had a vivid imagination, but most of the time, it didn't produce anything fun. It was mostly about imagining the worst thing that could happen and getting a panic attack.

Becky had said she should speak to a psychiatrist and get something to help with her anxiety, but Gabi hated the idea of chemicals altering her mind.

It wasn't logical since everything in the body was affected by hormones and by gut bacteria, and those were all chemicals, but they were naturally occurring, and they usually worked gradually. She didn't want to take a pill and become instantly carefree and cheerful.

That just wouldn't be her, and she didn't want to lose her identity, no matter how screwed up that identity was.

Would she still be so fearful when she became immortal?

Probably not.

Knowing that her brothers were immortal now and she wasn't going to lose them had already slashed her usual anxiety by at least half, probably more, and if she found an immortal male she could fall in love with, her fearfulness would be all gone.

What scared her more than anything was losing the people she loved.

Maybe Uriel was doing her a favor by ghosting her.

She didn't need to fall in love with a human and live in constant fear of losing him.

When her phone rang, she snatched it off the table and answered it without checking who it was.

She just knew it was Uriel.

"Hi," she said. "I thought you were ghosting me."

"I'm sorry I couldn't answer right away. What happened to your plans to spend the day with your family?"

"My brothers can't make it." She couldn't tell him the real reason because she was under compulsion to keep everything about immortals and their village a secret. Besides, the truth was more unbelievable than any lie she could make up. "They had a business emergency. I didn't ask for details because they wouldn't have told me. They still think of me as their baby sister who needs to be shielded."

He chuckled. "Yeah, you told me. What about the rest of your family? Your nieces and nephews? Don't you want to spend time with them?"

Damn, how could she possibly excuse that?

"I do, but it's not going to be the same without my brothers. I changed my return flight, so I could see all of them together once that emergency is over." She paused and took a deep breath. "And also, so I could spend time with you."

Gabi held her breath as she waited for him to say something, anything.

It seemed like long minutes had passed until he did. "I would love to spend more time with you, but right now, I don't know when I can. The business deal my partners and I are working on is very complicated and might involve travel."

Gabi swallowed.

It sounded just like the kind of polite excuse she would have devised to let a guy down easily.

"When will you know?"

"It could be by tonight, or it might take a few days. I'll call you as soon as I can."

"Okay." She swallowed the lump in her throat. "I just want you to know that I enjoyed being with you. Whatever happens, I'm glad that I met you, and I'm glad we had those two nights together. I will remember them fondly."

Again, there was a long moment of silence. "Is that a goodbye?"

"You tell me."

"Not if I can help it."

GABI & URIEL''S STORY CONTINUES
The Children of the Gods Book 75
DARK ENCOUNTERS OF THE UNEXPECTED KIND

TURN THE PAGE TO READ THE PREVIEW—>

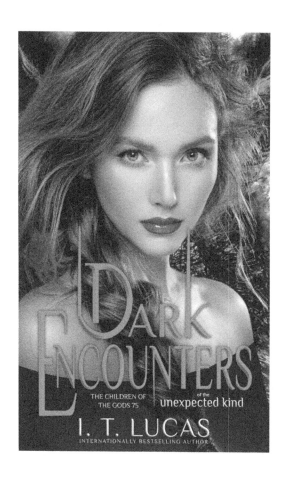

Who is Uriel?
Is he a lost descendant of the gods or just a gorgeous and charming human who has rocked Gabi's world?

ARU

"This wasn't one of your smarter ideas." Dagor's voice was tinged with barely veiled annoyance.

"Really?" Aru arched a brow. "I thought it was quite clever."

Dagor swiveled his laptop toward him. "Instead of showing up in person, they sent a drone to scout the area, and now they know it was a ruse and that we are not there."

It had seemed like a great idea to plant the trackers in the remote canyon, put a couple of surveillance bugs in place, and watch who showed up.

Aru shrugged. "How was I supposed to know that they would do that?"

The mysterious abductors or perhaps rescuers of the Kra-ell had outsmarted him, but that didn't mean that the move had been a waste of time and effort. Getting a drone instead of people was disappointing, and he still didn't know who they were, but at least they had shown up in some form, which meant that the trackers had done their job.

"I told you they wouldn't fall for that." Dagor let out a breath. "If you were in their position, would you have rushed to investigate the sudden emergence of new signals without taking every precaution you could think of?"

"I wouldn't." Aru had to admit that he had wagered on the abductors or rescuers taking the bait, but he'd known it was a long shot. "It was a gamble, and it was worth a try. The good news is that we know much more about these people now than we did before the drone showed up."

"Like what?" Dagor asked.

"We know that they have the ability to decipher the location of the trackers, and we also know that humans don't have the technology to decrypt the signals they are emitting. Also, they came to investigate, just not in person."

Dagor didn't look satisfied. "All we really know is that they are too sophisticated to fall into our trap. We still don't know who they are, and we won't know how to proceed without determining whether they are Kra-ell or human. The two require very different approaches."

"I agree with Aru," Negal said in his usual monotone voice. "What's important is that they showed their hand. It was a smart gambit that prompted the opponent to make a counter move, which, in turn, will inform our next one. The fact that they can decipher the location of the signals means that they captured Gor and tortured the information out of him. He never would have volunteered it. We should assume that he's dead."

Surprised that the old trooper was backing him up, Aru nodded his thanks.

Usually, Negal grumbled about the rookie getting promoted because of damn politics or nepotism, and every time Aru made a wrong move, Negal smirked in satisfaction.

Still, despite the trooper's attitude and occasional snarky comments, Aru appreciated having the guy on his team and wouldn't swap him for someone more accommodating even if he could. Negal had the experience that Aru lacked, kept him on his toes, and would never sabotage the mission just to try to prove that their commander had been wrong to nominate Aru as their team leader.

Dagor leaned back in his chair. "The fact that Gor's tracker stopped broadcasting doesn't mean that he is dead. It only means they took the tracker out of him—like they did to the other settlers before him."

When nearly all the trackers embedded in the Kra-ell settlers had simultaneously stopped broadcasting, Aru had assumed the cause was interference. Not many things could disrupt signals produced by the sophisticated trackers, though, so he and his teammates had to assume that the interference hadn't been caused by a natural phenomenon or an accident.

Regrettably, they had been too far away to get to the compound in time to see what had gone wrong.

At the time, they had been investigating a possible pod landing in Tibet. The remote location was four days on foot from the nearest paved road and nowhere near any international or even local airport.

Getting to Karelia to investigate what had happened had taken a long time, and in the meantime, the signals had come back online from the Baltic Sea, not too far from the port of Helsinki.

When they had started winking out one after the other, Aru had feared for the lives of the Kra-ell.

Not that he would have been allowed to intervene even if he and his team could do anything about it. Their job was observing and reporting, which they had been doing since discovering the surviving Kra-ell in Gor's compound five years ago.

Nevertheless, they hadn't reported anything about the latest events in the compound yet, and if what Aru suspected was true, they wouldn't be submitting a report regarding the fate of the Kra-ell anytime soon.

Thankfully, they had one hundred and fifteen Earth years before anyone came to check on them. That left plenty of time to collect all the relevant information and come up with a compelling story to tell their commander about why they had failed to discover the others before they had taken over Gor's compound, or rather Igor's, which was the name he had chosen to be known by on Earth.

What they knew so far was that someone had blown huge holes in the wall surrounding the compound, taken out everyone who was still alive, and put them on a ship. Then, the invaders had either killed everyone or just taken out their trackers.

What gave Aru hope that the Kra-ell were still alive was that it didn't make sense for the invaders to storm the compound, kill only a small number of Kra-ell, capture the rest, put them on a ship, and then kill them all. The invaders had to be a formidable force to take the Kra-ell captive to begin with, and the prime suspects were other Kra-ell settlers who had also woken up from stasis. But unlike those in Gor's compound, the others must have figured out that they had tracking devices implanted in their bodies and had taken them out before Aru and his team arrived on Earth and started tracking all the settlers whose devices were active.

It was a perfectly reasonable hypothesis, but Aru knew it wouldn't be good enough to appease their commander, who would view it as a failure. Their team's next mission would undoubtedly be in an even more godforsaken sector of the universe.

Hopefully, the other person Aru was secretly reporting to would intervene on their behalf and prevent their exile.

After all, Negal's rumblings about nepotism weren't entirely unfounded. In fact, they were spot on. Aru had earned the promotion not because of anything he had done in the service but because of his unique talent and its usefulness to that person whose name should not be mentioned even in thought.

Still, their commander could find other ways to make their lives miserable. Just the loss of favor would devastate Dagor and Negal. An unfavorable evaluation from the commander would ruin any chances of promotion for them, and no one wanted to spend hundreds of years in some wretched corner of the universe doing work that was of little importance to anyone back home.

In all fairness, though, Aru and his team had been instructed to stay away from the Kra-ell and not let their presence be known, so if the Kra-ell had gotten themselves free somehow, even with outside help, the commander couldn't blame Aru's team for being ignorant of what had been brewing inside the compound. That being said, if the rescuers were other settlers who had woken up from stasis, the commander wouldn't forgive their ignorance of that.

At the time of the attack, Gor and two other purebloods had been away, which suggested that the invaders had been waiting for just such an opportunity and had been helped by rebels from the inside, either with just intel or with active participation.

When Gor and his two companions had subsequently been captured and taken to Los Angeles, it had been the lucky break Aru had needed. It had given him a clue as to the whereabouts of the other settlers. But then their signals had winked out as well, and his team had been left in the dark.

Desperate for any thread or clue, Aru had come up with the idea to go to China and locate the trackers of the first

Kra-ell who had arrived on Earth—the scouting team that the Kra-ell queen had sent ahead of the settler ship.

The location where the bodies of the dead scouts had been cremated was known, and since the trackers were impervious to fire, it was only a matter of finding them. It hadn't been easy, but they had found five, of which only three were still operational. They could have kept digging, but Aru had decided that three was just the right number to lure the invaders out of hiding and show their hand.

His gamble had paid off, and they had gotten a response from the invaders. The question was what to do next.

KIAN

Kian walked into the war room, pulled out a chair next to the conference table, and sat down. "Syssi had a vision earlier today," he said without bothering with a long preamble. "She saw three men in a canyon, which was sparsely covered in vegetation." He flicked his gaze to the screen mounted overhead, where footage from the canyon the signals were coming from was still playing on a loop.

Shifting his gaze to his war room team, Kian assessed their reactions. They all knew of Syssi's reputation, and he doubted any of them would be foolish enough to make light of her prophetic vision.

Turner nodded, but his expression remained impassive. It took a lot more than a foretelling to get the guy rattled.

William wasn't showing any reaction either. But since he was focused on scanning the footage from the drone and looking for anything he might have missed at the first pass-through, he might not have heard Kian.

Jade seemed nervous, which given the Kra-ell's esoteric beliefs was to be expected, and Kalugal looked curious and somewhat amused, which could've been perceived as him downplaying the importance of the vision or of Kian's regard for it, but Kian knew it wasn't so.

His cousin's mate also occasionally experienced visions, so he knew to give Syssi's foresight its due respect. Unlike Kian, though, Kalugal didn't mind Jacki having them, and he didn't fear their negative effect on her well-being.

Then again, Jacki probably wasn't as drained after having prophetic visions as Syssi. She was a resilient female and not nearly as sensitive as Syssi. Her visions were also mostly less intense in nature, but not always.

The one she'd had about Wonder's caravan had been quite shocking.

Jacki's gift worked by touch, and when she'd held an ancient figurine, she'd seen Wonder fighting to save the lives of her caravan companions. A powerful earthquake had opened a chasm in the desert floor, swallowing wagons, animals, and people alike, and eventually Wonder herself had fallen victim to it despite her heroic efforts.

The vision Jacki had been shown was of an event that had happened thousands of years in the past. If Syssi had seen something of such a catastrophic nature, she would have been shaken by it for weeks, or even months, but not Jacki.

Perhaps Kalugal's wife was tougher because her life had been less sheltered than Syssi's, or maybe she'd just been born different.

As a father, Kian often wondered whether nature or nurture had a more significant influence on his child's character, and he leaned toward nature. There was no doubt in his mind that Allegra had been born with a strong personality, which she'd most likely inherited from him. Hopefully, though, she'd also inherited her mother's empathy and emotional intelligence, which would make her a much better leader than he could ever be.

Onegus was the only one to actually respond to his proclamation. "I assume that the three men Syssi saw in her vision are the ones emitting the signals?"

The answer to that was complicated, and since there was no one in the canyon, Kian wasn't sure what exactly Syssi had seen, but he had a theory. "Since the drone footage from the canyon indicates that there is no one there, we have to assume that Syssi's vision was from the near future. On the next fly-by, we should switch to the high-altitude drone and hope they won't notice it."

"Why?" Jade asked. "They are not there, so they are not going to see it in either case. We can fly the smaller, low-altitude drone."

"They might have hidden cameras right next to the trackers," Kian said. "Since there is no one where the signals are coming from, we have to assume that they somehow managed to rig the trackers to transmit without the benefit of a live host. That means they could bury them in the ground or hide them in the bushes."

The alien trackers were the size of a grain of rice, so even if they weren't buried under the rocks, there was no way William could find them in the footage. Normally, the devices needed a live body to provide the energy for them to transmit the signal, so another possibility was that the men had implanted them in small animals. But to keep the critters from scurrying away, they would have needed to put them in cages, and that was probably what William was looking for as he scanned the zoomed-in footage in slow motion on his laptop.

"The vision could also be from the far future," Anandur said. "What were the men in the vision wearing?"

Kian lifted a hand. "Let me finish telling you about the vision first. When I'm done, you can ask your questions, and I'll answer them to the best of my ability."

Anandur nodded.

"When Syssi's consciousness flew over the men, they were arguing, and then something caught their attention, and they looked up. Naturally, Syssi's first thought was that they could see her floating overhead, but she quickly realized that it must have been something above or behind her. She couldn't see or hear what it was, but that's the dreamy nature of visions. Many of the details are missing, and others are unclear, and it's never obvious whether the vision is a window into the past or the future."

Kian took a sip from his bottle of water before continuing. "One of the men pointed a strange-looking weapon at what I assume was our drone, but then one of his companions stayed his hand, and their argument resumed." He put the bottle down. "Syssi didn't know that we were flying a drone or that the signals were coming from a canyon, so you can rest assured that her vision wasn't influenced by anything I told her."

"What exactly did you tell her?" Jade asked.

"All I told Syssi was that the signals were coming from a nearby location, and just like the rest of us, she assumed they were being emitted by the Kra-ell—either by members of the scouting team that had been sent ahead of the settler ship or some of the awakened settlers themselves. Most of the pods from the settler ship are still missing, so that's the most logical assumption, provided that they had learned of the trackers and how to manipulate them."

After more than seven thousand years, the Kra-ell scouts shouldn't be alive, but there was a small chance that they had gone back into their stasis pod to prolong their lives and stayed there for hundreds of years at a time.

It was the logical thing to do, and Kian still believed that at least some of the scouts had done that, but it no longer seemed like the signals were coming from them, and he had arrived at that conclusion even before Syssi had told him about what she'd seen in her vision.

His next suspicion had been that other settlers had come out of stasis before Igor had figured out how to track the signals, and since some of them were assassins who had been smuggled among the settlers to eliminate the Eternal King's direct descendants, they'd known about the trackers and had also known that they had to remove them from their bodies so they couldn't be found.

Those assassins must have been tracking Igor and had followed his signal to Los Angeles, which would explain the sudden appearance of the three signals in the clan's backyard.

But after Syssi's vision, he had to consider other options.

Perhaps the gods had left a sleeper cell on Earth?

Had members of that team been tracking Igor?

Had they been aware of what he had done to the members of each pod that had come online, and done nothing about it?

How could they have stood by while he'd murdered innocent males, adults and children alike, and subjugated the females?

Were they following a non-interference directive and were supposed to only observe?

If so, why were they interfering now?

Did they suspect the involvement of immortals? The hybrid descendants of the exiled gods they had been sent to eliminate?

Kian had so many questions and so few answers, and he hated relying on visions to form his strategy, but it seemed like he had no choice. Right now, Syssi's vision supplied the only clues they had.

KALUGAL

Before meeting Jacki, Kalugal would have been dismissive of Syssi's vision, in a polite manner of course, but he'd been shown the power of clairvoyance by his mate and was no longer a skeptic.

Regrettably, Jacki was not in the same league as Syssi. He wouldn't have traded his Jacki for anyone, but there was no denying that Syssi's abilities far surpassed hers.

What his mate typically saw was small-scale, localized, and individual, while Syssi got to foresee or past-view epic events—like the Odus's decommissioning, or rather attempted eradication, and the Kra-ell who had been put in charge of it.

Kalugal didn't know all the details, but he imagined the vision had been cryptic, as all postcognition and precognition tended to be. Nevertheless, Jade had confirmed what Syssi had seen happening to the Odus.

In fact, he'd been told that Syssi had envisioned the Kra-ell years before the clan had learned of their existence. At the time, she hadn't realized that the fictional people she'd created for one of the Perfect Match Virtual Studios environments were not the product of her imagination but a glimpse into the future or maybe the past. She hadn't gotten all the details right, though, so despite her visions being legendary, they couldn't be taken verbatim.

There was another problem with the story Kalugal had been told about Syssi and her Krall version of the Kra-ell. The one detail everyone seemed to overlook was that the original Krall adventure had been created by the Perfect Match programmers before Syssi had come on board. She'd elaborated on and changed it, but someone had thought of it before her.

Was one of the humans working for Perfect Match a seer?

It wasn't such a great leap of logic. Humans had been known to have prophetic visions, and some weren't even aware of their abilities. They didn't realize that their minds had not created what they envisioned.

It was also possible that Syssi had played around with designs for the different Perfect Match environments even before Kian had bought a majority stake in the company for her and made her a board member.

Kian's team had been involved with Perfect Match almost from its inception, which probably included Syssi. He'd been a silent investor and stock owner in the company during the development stage, and when the original founders had gotten stuck and couldn't finalize the product, Kian had asked William to help them overcome their difficulties.

William had been instrumental in debugging the software and giving it the edge the founders had envisioned but couldn't quite achieve.

"What else did Syssi see?" Onegus asked.

Kian leaned back. "Syssi said that the weapon one of the men aimed at the drone looked like a monocular, which is odd on two accounts. One is that it had no visible trigger, so it couldn't have been a projectile weapon, and so we have to assume that it was a laser-based weapon or something that operated in a similar way. The other is that one of the males aimed it at our drone." He looked at Turner. "Correct me if I'm wrong, but as far as I know, no manmade handheld weapons can shoot down a drone at the height we were flying it."

Turner nodded. "That's correct."

"I wish the alien-looking weapon was the most troubling part, but it's not." Kian leaned forward and put his hands on the table. "When the three looked up at the drone, Syssi got a good look at their faces, and she was positive that none were Kra-ell. She thinks that they were gods."

Jade gasped. "I'll be damned. How the hell did they get here so fast?"

"My thoughts exactly. They couldn't have. They had to be here already," Kian said. "Syssi's impression was that they were friendly, but as much as I trust her visions, I wouldn't base our strategy on them."

"We all know not to take Syssi's visions lightly," Onegus said. "But gods? We've been searching for other immortals for centuries and haven't found any. Do you want to tell me that gods were hiding among humans this whole time, and we didn't know? Wouldn't they have recognized the technology we were drip-feeding to the humans? All they had to do was follow the breadcrumbs to us."

"It depends on when they arrived on Earth," Turner said. "We know that they are not part of the original group."

"Why not?" Jade asked. "Maybe more have survived. Until recently, you didn't know about Toven, and he didn't know about you."

The cogs in Kalugal's mind started spinning.

If the three males were indeed gods, they couldn't be contemporaries of the original group of rebels. Annani might not have known about another group who had settled somewhere else on Earth, but Mortdh would have, and he wouldn't have bombed the assembly while knowing that other gods could find out about his crime.

These gods must have arrived long after the original ones had perished. In fact, they had likely arrived after the Kra-ell ship had exploded and the pods had landed on Earth, which had been thousands of years later. That meant they possessed more advanced technology and know-how, which were priceless.

If Syssi was right and they were friendly, they might have sought out the clan to get its help or cooperation, and if contact was established, he should seize the opportunity and become instrumental in the negotiations.

That would not only grant him access to what those gods would offer up as part of the negotiations, but it would also increase his influence in the clan and get him the second council seat that right now was looking even less likely than it had originally.

With Toven joining the council and possibly Jade as well, Kalugal would have no grounds to request another seat. Jade represented nearly half of the village population, so if he got two seats, she could ask for six, and Kian would never allow the majority of the council to be comprised of non-clan members.

Leaning back in his chair, Kalugal crossed his arms over his chest. "Syssi's vision reinforces my earlier assessment that the three activated the signals as a way to make contact with us and not to lure us into a trap and harm us. In fact, I'm so sure of their intentions that I volunteer to head to the canyon with a team of no more than two warriors to meet them on equal terms. I think that would be received better than showing up in force, which would signal that we are afraid of them." He smiled at Kian. "Not to toot my own horn, but I'm a much better negotiator than you are, so if you were thinking about heading to the canyon yourself, I would advise against it."

"I wasn't planning to." Kian regarded him with thinly veiled amusement. "Thank you for the offer, but let's not get ahead of ourselves." He braced his elbows on the table. "We must not forget who created Igor and the other assassins and who programmed them to dispose of all legitimate heirs to the Eternal King's throne. These three might be the assassins' handlers, or alternatively, they could be genetically modified gods who were sent to Earth to complete the mission that the original assassins had been tasked with but failed to complete because their ship exploded and their stasis pods were damaged."

Turner nodded. "I agree with Kian. For some, assuming the best in people is natural and safe, but it is not so for us." He scanned the faces of everyone present. "We don't have the luxury of being naive and trusting. We need to assume the worst and hope to be surprised for the better."

As much as Kalugal wished he could argue with that, he couldn't.

Too much was at stake, including the lives of his mate and son. He'd rather succumb to Kian's paranoia than make a rushed decision that might endanger everyone he loved and cared about.

After all, he was a descendant of the Eternal King as well. Ekin, his great-grandfather, had not been the official heir to the throne because he'd been born to a concubine and not the official wife, and the same was true for his mother, who Ahn had fathered with a concubine. Still, Ekin had been the Eternal King's son, and Areana was the Eternal King's granddaughter.

Kian regarded him with his intense eyes. "Even if we decide to send a small welcoming party with a massive backup in case things go wrong, you can't be a part of it. As a council member, you are privy to information we can't allow to fall into enemy hands."

Kalugal was immune to most compulsion, but not all, and if any of the three possessed Igor's ability, he wouldn't be able to resist the compulsion to reveal all of his secrets, and those included much more than the location of the village and how to get there.

"Unfortunately, you're right." Kalugal sighed. "As the saying goes, with great responsibility comes great sacrifice."

Kian chuckled. "Actually, the saying is 'With great power comes great responsibility, and with great responsibility comes great accountability,' but in your case, sacrifice and accountability are probably one and the same."

KIAN

It was apparent to Kian that Kalugal's motive for volunteering was the same one that had prompted him to offer assistance with the Kra-ell rescue mission.

His cousin wanted to be in the know.

Kian didn't mind, but what Kalugal had forgotten was that as a council member, he was already privy to nearly everything that was going on in the clan and that the price for that knowledge was certain restrictions.

"I should be the one to go," Jade said. "And my team should be comprised of only Kra-ell. If these gods are recent arrivals, they don't know about the exiled gods producing half-breed descendants with humans. If they did, they would have tried to make contact with you or the Doomers, either in a friendly or unfriendly manner. But we should assume they know about the Kra-ell or they wouldn't be here. They must have been tracking us, and once we got rid of the implanted trackers, they lost us and needed to find out what happened to us. That's why they are making contact."

Jade's reasoning was solid, but Kian still had trouble treating her like he would any other warrior and not trying to shield her because of her gender. His instincts rebelled against letting her walk into danger without Guardians to protect her.

Given how strong and well-trained Jade was, it was a ridiculous sentiment, but he couldn't just ignore two thousand years of conditioning.

"That might be so." He shifted in his chair. "But we don't know if their intentions toward you and your people are friendly or hostile."

Jade shrugged. "If they meant us harm, they would have already disposed of us. Since they didn't do that and kept their presence a secret, we have to assume their goal is not to eliminate us. They were probably sent to complete the mission the assassin on our ship failed to complete." She shifted her gaze to Kian. "After discovering that the gods were gone, their mission was probably to locate the other descendants of the Eternal King, meaning the twins."

Kian tilted his head. "Why would they think we can lead them to the twins?"

Jade took a deep breath. "Perhaps they need Igor back because he can find the other pods and the Eternal King's grandchildren. Regardless of their intentions, it is better to keep them ignorant of your existence until we know what they are after. That's why I should take a couple of purebloods with me when I meet them."

Kian wasn't convinced that Jade was right about the gods wanting Igor, but he agreed with her assessment that it was better to keep them in the dark about the clan. "I'd rather keep our existence from them as well."

"I'm glad we see eye to eye." Jade squared her shoulders. "There are additional benefits to sending a Kra-ell team. We are faster and stronger and stand a better chance in the event of a confrontation." She looked at William. "Naturally, we will need to be equipped with compulsion-filtering earpieces."

Compulsion was a rare ability even for the gods, but that was according to Annani, and her information was seven thousand years old. The gods had had a long time to improve their genetic know-how and breed more compellers.

"Of course." William waved a hand without lifting his eyes from the screen.

"I see two possibilities," Turner said. "And each requires a very different approach."

It was about time the guy voiced his opinion on the situation. "I've been waiting for you to come up with a new angle no one has considered yet." Kian cast him a smile. "Let's hear it."

"I'm not sure it's a new angle," Turner said. "I'm just clarifying things. The first possibility is that these gods—provided that we are indeed dealing with gods—were sent by the Eternal King to make sure no threat to his throne remains on Earth. The second one is that they were sent by his wife to protect her children and grandchildren from the Kra-ell assassins. If it's the former, walking up to them would be foolhardy because we do not know what capabilities were engineered into them and their weapons. If it's the second option, and these gods were sent by the queen, they might assume that the Kra-ell approaching them are the assassins, shoot first, and ask questions later."

"They left Igor alive and didn't touch the rest of us," Jade scoffed. "If they were sent by the queen, they would have taken him out long ago to prevent him from going after her son."

"Maybe they couldn't," Kian said. "We're assuming that the queen operates secretly and pretends to be loyal to the king. If Igor had a way to communicate with someone on Anumati and the queen was aware of that, she couldn't tell her people to launch a direct attack on him without showing her hand."

Turner nodded. "That's possible. Also, don't forget that if they were sent to eliminate Ahn and the other exiled gods or to find the twins, they had no reason to bother with Igor. But as soon as a new player appeared on the stage, they followed the trail in hopes of potentially finding the exiled gods. Who else could have liberated the Kra-ell? Humans? Not likely. And they should know it couldn't have been a different Kra-ell faction, because if it was, they could have tracked the signals they emitted."

"Not necessarily." Onegus crossed his arms over his chest. "Those other Kra-ell could have removed their trackers before the gods arrived. I'm sure that's a scenario they took into consideration."

"Why would they?" Jade asked. "We didn't know that we were implanted with trackers. Igor knew, and yet he didn't remove his. Knowing how the gods operate, I wouldn't be surprised if the assassins were programmed to keep their trackers."

Kian was losing patience. They could engage in what-ifs for hours and get nowhere.

He lifted his hand. "The way to address both possibilities is to send a mixed group. Two pureblooded females and two immortals. Igor claimed there were no female assassins because of the gods' attitudes toward females and their reluctance to involve them in military missions. Therefore, this new team would know that the female Kra-ell couldn't be assassins, and they would have no reason to shoot at them. The two immortals could pass for humans, so even if these gods were sent by the king, they would have no reason to shoot them either. Naturally, we will provide the team with an aerial defense of armed drones and a backup force nearby."

Jade nodded. "I wish Kagra was here. She's my best fighter, and she's good under pressure."

Kagra was currently in China with Yamanu and the rest of the team that had been sent to find the origin of the signals. But then the broadcast location had changed while they had been en route, and instead of it coming from China, it was coming from Mount Baldy.

Onegus swiveled his chair to face Kian. "Speaking of the China team, what do you want them to do? Do you want them to continue to Lugu Lake to assist the crew working on Kalugal's archeological dig?"

Kalugal suspected that a pod was buried on the site, but since the place was rigged with booby-traps, digging had been progressing at a snail's pace, and the assistance of several super-strong Kra-ell would be greatly beneficial to speeding it up.

The team was awaiting instructions in Chengdu, the capital of China's Sichuan province, but Kian hadn't decided yet whether he wanted to send them to Lugu Lake to help with the archaeological excavation of the suspected pod crash or to instruct them to return home.

"Not yet. Keep them on standby."

Nodding, Onegus turned to Jade. "Do you have anyone else you trust for a mission like that?"

"Borga is a good fighter, but she's not a diplomat, and I don't trust her. I prefer Morgada, but she hasn't kept up with her training. I'll have to give it some thought." Jade looked at Onegus. "I leave the selection of the immortals to you."

"Do you have a preference for anyone specific?" Kian asked.

She shrugged. "It makes no difference to me."

Kalugal regarded her with an arched brow. "Don't you want Phinas to go with you?"

She shook her head. "Phinas is an excellent fighter, but he's even better as a father figure for Drova. One of us needs to stay alive for her, and it's not a good plan to have us both face danger together. I wouldn't mind taking Rufsur, though, and if Dalhu is a choice, I wouldn't mind having him by my side either." She leaned back in her chair. "He claims that he can smell evil, and if that's true, I would like him to sniff those supposed gods to ascertain their intentions."

"Dalhu is not a Guardian," Onegus said. "He's also happily pursuing his art and prefers to stay out of conflicts. I don't think he would want to take part in this."

Onegus didn't know Dalhu as well as Kian did. His sister's mate would have enjoyed some action, but the problem was that Dalhu was mated to Amanda, who was a council member and therefore privy to too much information.

Rufsur couldn't be part of the team for the same reason.

"Neither Dalhu nor Rufsur can go because they are both mated to council members and know too much. I suspect that mates don't keep secrets from each other even when they are supposed to." He looked at Kalugal. "Do you have anyone else?"

Kalugal shook his head. "Perhaps Boleck. He's an excellent sniper, in case you need one. Greggory is also a good fighter, and he's coolheaded."

Greggory had been Eleanor's inducer, and the two hadn't parted on the best of terms, but that didn't mean he was not a good choice. Still, he wasn't the right man for the mission.

"Frankly, I prefer Guardians to accompany the Kra-ell females." Kian raked his fingers through his hair. "It's not that I have anything against your men, but other than Phinas and Rufsur, none of them is qualified to handle a delicate mission like this."

Jade let out a sigh. "Fine, I'll take Phinas with me."

Phinas had proven himself during the Kra-ell rescue, both as a fighter and diplomat, and Kian had no problem with him meeting the gods, but Jade had a point about both of them going on a risky mission together.

"What about Drova?" He looked into her eyes. "You were right to point out that one of you should stay behind to be with her."

"You just have to ensure that both Phinas and I return to her."

"I'll do everything I can to ensure your safety, but I can't guarantee it." He turned to Kalugal. "Are you okay with Phinas joining the team?"

Kalugal nodded. "Naturally. Phinas is an excellent choice. "

"He's also charming," Jade said. "And he can pass for a human. His godly genes are not as apparent as in some clan immortals. He's not as perfect."

ORDER DARK ENCOUNTERS OF THE UNEXPECTED KIND TODAY!

Join the *VIP Club*

To find out what's included in your free membership,
click HERE or flip to the last page.

Note

Dear reader,

I hope my stories have added a little joy to your day. If you have a moment to add some to mine, you can help spread the word about the Children Of The Gods series by telling your friends and penning a review. Your recommendations are the most powerful way to inspire new readers to explore the series.

Thank you,

Isabell

Also by I. T. Lucas

PERFECT MATCH

The Children of the Gods Series Sets

Books 1-3: Dark Stranger trilogy—Includes a bonus short story: **The Fates take a Vacation**

Books 4-6: Dark Enemy Trilogy —Includes a bonus short story—**The Fates' Post-Wedding Celebration**

Books 7-10: Dark Warrior Tetralogy

Books 11-13: Dark Guardian Trilogy

Books 14-16: Dark Angel Trilogy

Books 17-19: Dark Operative Trilogy

Books 20-22: Dark Survivor Trilogy

Books 23-25: Dark Widow Trilogy

Books 26-28: Dark Dream Trilogy

Books 29-31: Dark Prince Trilogy

Books 32-34: Dark Queen Trilogy

Books 35-37: Dark Spy Trilogy

Books 38-40: Dark Overlord Trilogy

Books 41-43: Dark Choices Trilogy

Books 44-46: Dark Secrets Trilogy

Books 47-49: Dark Haven Trilogy

Books 50-52: Dark Power Trilogy

Books 53-55: Dark Memories Trilogy

Books 56-58: Dark Hunter Trilogy

Books 59-61: Dark God Trilogy

Books 62-64: Dark Whispers Trilogy

Books 65-67: Dark Gambit Trilogy

Books 68-70: Dark Alliance Trilogy

Books 71-73: Dark healing Trilogy

MEGA SETS
INCLUDE CHARACTER LISTS
The Children of the Gods: Books 1-6
The Children of the Gods: Books 6.5-10

Perfect Match Bundle 1

CHECK OUT THE SPECIALS ON
ITLUCAS.COM
(https://itlucas.com/specials)

FOR EXCLUSIVE PEEKS AT UPCOMING RELEASES &
A FREE I. T. LUCAS COMPANION BOOK

Join my *VIP Club* and gain access to the VIP portal at itlucas.com

To Join, go to:
http://eepurl.com/blMTpD

Find out more details about what's included with your free membership on the book's last page.

TRY THE CHILDREN OF THE GODS SERIES ON
<u>AUDIBLE</u>
2 FREE audiobooks with your new Audible subscription!

FOR EXCLUSIVE PEEKS AT UPCOMING RELEASES & A FREE COMPANION BOOK

JOIN MY *VIP CLUB* AND GAIN ACCESS TO THE VIP PORTAL AT ITLUCAS.COM
TO JOIN, GO TO:
http://eepurl.com/blMTpD

INCLUDED IN YOUR FREE MEMBERSHIP:

YOUR VIP PORTAL

- READ PREVIEW CHAPTERS OF UPCOMING RELEASES.
- LISTEN TO GODDESS'S CHOICE NARRATION BY CHARLES LAWRENCE
- EXCLUSIVE CONTENT OFFERED ONLY TO MY VIPs.

FREE I.T. LUCAS COMPANION INCLUDES:

- GODDESS'S CHOICE PART 1
- PERFECT MATCH: VAMPIRE'S CONSORT (A STANDALONE NOVELLA)
- INTERVIEW Q & A
- CHARACTER CHARTS

IF YOU'RE ALREADY A SUBSCRIBER, AND YOU ARE NOT GETTING MY EMAILS, YOUR PROVIDER IS

SENDING THEM TO YOUR JUNK FOLDER, AND YOU ARE MISSING OUT ON **IMPORTANT UPDATES, SIDE CHARACTERS' PORTRAITS, ADDITIONAL CONTENT, AND OTHER GOODIES.** TO FIX THAT, ADD isabell@itlucas.com TO YOUR EMAIL CONTACTS OR YOUR EMAIL VIP LIST.

Check out the specials at
https://www.itlucas.com/specials

Made in the USA
Las Vegas, NV
08 November 2023

80471297R00223